"Give me a call if you want to try services."

He hesitated for a brief instant, then cupped her hand in his while he flashed a careless grin. *"Your* services?"

Her throat tightened. Even as her brain told her that retreat would be wise, she allowed her hand to remain in his. Only one other time in her life had a man had such an immediate effect on her. Then she'd gone with emotion, listened to her heart instead of her head, and she'd wound up betrayed and hurt. Desperately hurt.

"My company's services, of course," she amended, keeping her voice light. "You might decide you want to meet your perfect match after all."

He kept his eyes locked with hers while his thumb stroked the inside of her wrist. Her pulse stuttered; then her stomach dropped to her toes.

"I won't."

She remained unmoving, her gaze tracking his movements as he walked toward the door while she waited for her pulse to settle. It didn't.

Dear Reader,

Have you noticed our new look? Starting this month, Intimate Moments has a bigger, more mainstream design—hope you like it! And I hope you like this month's books, too, starting with Maggie Shayne's *The Brands Who Came for Christmas.* This emotional powerhouse of a tale launches Maggie's new miniseries about the Brand sisters, THE OKLAHOMA ALL-GIRL BRANDS. I hope you love it as much as I do.

A YEAR OF LOVING DANGEROUSLY continues with *Hero at Large,* a suspenseful—and passionate—tale set on the mean streets of L.A. Robyn Amos brings a master's touch to the romance of Keshon Gray and Rennie Williams. Doreen Owens Malek returns with a tale of suspense and secrets, *Made for Each Other,* and believe me…these two are! RITA Award winner Marie Ferrarella continues her popular CHILDFINDERS, INC. miniseries with *Hero for Hire,* and in January look for her CHILDFINDERS, INC. single title, *An Uncommon Hero.*

Complete the month with Maggie Price's *Dangerous Liaisons,* told with her signature grittiness and sensuality, and *Dad in Blue* by Shelley Cooper, another of the newer authors we're so proud to publish.

Then rejoin us next month as the excitement continues—right here in Intimate Moments.

Enjoy!

Leslie J. Wainger

Leslie J. Wainger
Executive Senior Editor

Please address questions and book requests to:
Silhouette Reader Service
U.S.: 3010 Walden Ave., P.O. Box 1325, Buffalo, NY 14269
Canadian: P.O. Box 609, Fort Erie, Ont. L2A 5X3

Dangerous Liaisons
MAGGIE PRICE

Silhouette®

INTIMATE MOMENTS™

Published by Silhouette Books

America's Publisher of Contemporary Romance

To Major Richard Neaves:
Thanks, big brother! If it weren't for you, I never would
have found my way to the Oklahoma City Police
Department...where I found my *Perfect Match*.

 SILHOUETTE BOOKS

ISBN 0-373-27113-1

DANGEROUS LIAISONS

Copyright © 2000 by Margaret Price

Visit Silhouette at www.eHarlequin.com

Printed in U.S.A.

Books by Maggie Price

Silhouette Intimate Moments

Prime Suspect #816
The Man She Almost Married #838
Most Wanted #948
On Dangerous Ground #989
Dangerous Liaisons #1043

MAGGIE PRICE

turned to crime at the age of twenty-two. That's when she went to work at the Oklahoma City Police Department. As a civilian crime analyst, she evaluated suspects' methods of operation during the commission of robberies and sex crimes, and developed profiles on those suspects. During her tenure at OCPD, Maggie stood in lineups, snagged special assignments to homicide task forces, established procedures for evidence submittal, even posed as the wife of an undercover officer in the investigation of a fortune-teller.

While at OCPD, Maggie stored up enough tales of intrigue, murder and mayhem to keep her at the keyboard for years. The first of those tales won the Romance Writers of America's prestigious Golden Heart Award for Romantic Suspense.

Maggie invites her readers to contact her at 5208 W. Reno, Suite 350, Oklahoma City, OK 73127-6317.

IT'S OUR 20th ANNIVERSARY!
We'll be celebrating all year,
Continuing with these fabulous titles,
On sale in November 2000.

Desire

#1327 Marriage Prey
Annette Broadrick

#1328 Her Perfect Man
Mary Lynn Baxter

#1329 A Cowboy's Gift
Anne McAllister

#1330 Husband—or Enemy?
Caroline Cross

#1331 The Virgin and the Vengeful Groom
Dixie Browning

#1332 Night Wind's Woman
Sheri WhiteFeather

Romance

#1480 Her Honor-Bound Lawman
Karen Rose Smith

#1481 Raffling Ryan
Kasey Michaels

#1482 The Millionaire's Waitress Wife
Carolyn Zane

#1483 The Doctor's Medicine Woman
Donna Clayton

#1484 The Third Kiss
Leanna Wilson

#1485 The Wedding Lullaby
Melissa McClone

Special Edition

#1357 A Man Alone
Lindsay McKenna

#1358 The Rancher Next Door
Susan Mallery

#1359 Sophie's Scandal
Penny Richards

#1360 The Bridal Quest
Jennifer Mikels

#1361 Baby of Convenience
Diana Whitney

#1362 Just Eight Months Old...
Tori Carrington

Intimate Moments

#1039 The Brands Who Came for Christmas
Maggie Shayne

#1040 Hero at Large
Robyn Amos

#1041 Made for Each Other
Doreen Owens Malek

#1042 Hero for Hire
Marie Ferrarella

#1043 Dangerous Liaisons
Maggie Price

#1044 Dad in Blue
Shelley Cooper

Chapter 1

Jake Ford leaned against the bar, surveilling the blonde while she moved among the wedding guests with the skill of a seasoned pickpocket. Another time, another place, someone working a crowd with such adeptness would have spiked his inner radar to full alert. That wasn't the case this night. She wasn't covertly lifting valuables from the well-heeled guests and tonight he wasn't a cop, only a guest.

She was the groom's sister. He knew that because his partner, Whitney Shea—Whitney Taylor as of an hour and a half ago—had described her soon-to-be sister-in-law several times. *Stunning* was the term Whitney had used to sum up Nicole Taylor.

His partner had hit the mark.

Overhead, crystal chandeliers spilled light across the hotel's mirrored ballroom. Champagne flowed from a fountain that gurgled to a pool at the base of a swan sculptured in ice. A pianist caressed ivory and ebony keys, filling the air with a smoky love song. Jake was aware of the rustle of silk and the murmur of conversations as couples swayed on the dimly lit dance floor, but he kept his attention focused on Nicole Taylor. Smiling, sometimes laughing, she moved with abandon through the sea of some of Oklahoma City's most elite citizens. She tweaked a gray-haired judge on the chin, hobnobbed with the mayor, chatted up the district attorney. While she mingled, Jake caught more than a few appreciative male gazes aimed her way.

One of those was his own, he acknowledged. Her slinky blue dress had a scooped-out back and a side slit that offered flashes of leg he couldn't help admire. On occasion, she tucked what he figured was her business card into the breast pocket of a tailored suit coat or slid one into a manicured hand that clutched an evening bag.

He wondered what a woman who looked as if she'd stepped out of a man's darkest, most seductive dream did for a living.

He studied her profile, his gaze tracing one high, slanting cheekbone, the sweep of jaw that looked as if it had the potential to take on a stubborn slant. Her hair, a mix of blond and gold tones, was pulled back in an intricate braid coiled at the base of her long, elegant neck. Even from a distance he could tell that her eyes were a vivid blue to match her dress. His gaze slid downward to the glossy coral lips that curved into an intimate smile when she eased her card into the breast pocket of a tall, lanky Latino with smooth olive skin and an ebony mustache. From the smoldering look in the man's dark eyes, Jake figured he was contemplating devouring her in two bites.

Instinct told him she was a woman a man would beg for.

He clenched his jaw as he watched her polished nails skim tantalizingly down the Latino's lapel. It didn't please him that the sight of her curved, full lips stirred something dark and elemental inside him.

Something that hadn't stirred in a long time.

Pulling his gaze away, Jake stared into the glass he clutched. He wished fervently for Scotch instead of the tonic water he'd ordered. But, like a hell of a lot of other things he'd once savored and enjoyed, Scotch was in his past. So were cigarettes. And women.

Especially women.

He closed his eyes. He'd thought he had gotten past the bad dream. Had managed to go a few weeks without waking up in a cold sweat, then staring at the ceiling until dawn, thinking about his wife and daughters. Had actually thought that two months of meeting with the department's shrink had relegated the claw-infested demon to the murky depths of his subconscious. He'd been wrong. The dream had slammed into him again last night with a double-fisted punch, tormenting him with the haunting memories that had burned into his soul.

He'd lost so much. Too much.

It had been a hell of a lot easier to lock the racking pain deep inside him than it was to face it every day. But after more than a year and a half of drifting through a numb haze, reality had hit him square between the eyes when he'd been charged with the death of a woman he'd been seeing. And seven other murders. After that, he'd had no choice but to finally accept what his life now was.

Accept that his job was all he had left.

Things could be worse, he reminded himself. The insane hours that were a natural part of working Homicide suited him. As long as he was busy wading through blood, gore, paperwork and court appearances, he didn't have time to think. Time to regret. Time to want what he would never again allow himself to have.

He lifted the glass to his lips, grimaced at the tonic's sweet tang, then glanced back over his shoulder. He felt a tic of disappointment when he discovered that Nicole Taylor had faded into the crowd and was no longer in sight.

His gaze drifted past the dance floor to a maze of round tables covered in white cloths and topped with centerpieces of velvety red roses. Detectives from OCPD's Homicide detail had taken over a couple of the tables. Most had brought their spouses or significant others; from all the backslapping going on and the heads thrown back in laughter, it was evident that everyone was having a good time. On any other occasion, Jake would have joined his co-workers, but not tonight. Not at a wedding.

Tonight he preferred solitude.

A bark of nearby laughter caught his attention. The bride and groom, their respective parents, grandparents and siblings had moved a few feet from the bar and now formed a smiling group while a photographer snapped photos. Jake saw the joy that shone in Bill Taylor's eyes as the assistant D.A. leaned to kiss his bride. Dressed in a slide of pearl-dotted white silk, her auburn hair swept back, Whitney smiled up at her husband, her face a study in joy.

Jake's mouth curved. Theirs was a perfect match. A solid one. He'd had once-in-a-lifetime happiness like that. A long time ago.

That, he thought, was why he made it a point to avoid weddings. They reminded him of what he'd had...and lost. Still, it hadn't been a sense of duty that had brought him here tonight. He loved Whitney like a sister, and nothing could have kept him away. But he'd had enough and it was time to go.

Turning back to the bar, he drained his glass. The prospect of climbing on his Harley and running the engine wide open through the still September night eased the tenseness that had settled across his shoulders. Maybe by the time he got home his mind would be void of the memories the evening had stirred.

Maybe the dream would lay dormant tonight.

"Get you another?" the tuxedo-clad bartender asked when Jake sat his empty glass on the bar.

"I'll pass. One's my limit when there's no alcohol involved."

After stuffing a tip into the snifter on one side of the bar, Jake turned and nearly collided with a sea of white.

"Want to dance, handsome?"

He cocked his head. "Isn't the bride supposed to hang out with the groom at their wedding?"

"She's also supposed to dance with her partner," Whitney stated, her eyes glowing like rich emeralds. "It's the law."

"Look, Whit, I'm a little rusty at the social graces. I was about to head—"

"Later." She snared his hand, tugged him past linen-covered tables loaded with silver trays of sliced meats, breads, fruit and champagne by the bucket. "Dancing is like having sex," she stated over her shoulder. "You never forget how."

"Wanna bet?" he muttered, giving thought to the months of self-imposed celibacy he'd endured.

When they reached the dance floor, Whitney turned and gave him a level-eyed look. "Besides, it's bad luck to make the bride unhappy on her wedding day."

"Bad luck for whom?"

"You." She stepped forward, leaving him no choice but to shift into dance position. "If you don't cooperate, I'll shoot you in the kneecap."

He smirked as they moved to the slow beat. "You expect me to believe you're packing heat under that wedding dress?"

"Trust me, Ford, you don't want to find out."

"Guess not."

Whitney exchanged a few words with a couple who danced by, then stated, "Lieutenant Ryan looks happy."

Jake followed her gaze to the spot on the dance floor where their boss was locked in an embrace with his wife, A.J., head of the department's Crime Analysis Unit. "Yeah."

"Weddings have that effect," Whitney continued, then sighed. "They remind people of good times."

"I had that same thought."

Her gaze flew back to his, her eyes sobering. "Annie," she said softly. "You were thinking about your and Annie's wedding." Her hand tightened on his. "Jake, I'm sorry. I know how much you miss her and the girls."

He wasn't surprised Whitney had hit the mark. After all, they'd ridden the streets together, risen through the ranks with equal speed and then wound up partners in Homicide. At one time or another, they'd both been through their own private hell. His had begun two years ago when a bomb exploded on a plane over the Gulf of Mexico, killing his wife and infant twin daughters.

"Yeah, I miss them," he said quietly. "But I'm hanging in there."

"You're sure?"

"Positive."

The last thing he wanted was his partner worrying about him on her wedding night, so he opted for a change of subject. "You know, Whit, while you're lazing on some beach in Cancún, I'll be clearing the Quintero case," he said, referring to the drive-by shooting that had ended the life of a seven-year-old boy who'd been on the wrong street corner at the wrong time. "When I take down Cárdenas, the glory will all be mine."

She gave him a bland look. "Dream on. It'd be a stroke of luck to unearth Cárdenas's girlfriend. Even if you do, you'll never get her to testify she was in his car, much less that he was the shooter."

"Such little faith," Jake chided. "Maybe you ought to stay here and work the case, and I'll go to Cancún."

Whitney pretended to consider his suggestion, then shook her head. "I don't think Bill will go for that."

"I won't go for what?" the subject of conversation asked as he glided into view beside them, his sister in his arms.

Jake felt a jolt when Nicole Taylor's gaze met his. From across the room those sapphire eyes had seemed vibrant. Close up, they were mesmerizing.

Whitney gave her husband a coy smile. "You won't leave me here and take Jake to Cancún with you. Right?"

Arching a brow, the assistant D.A. glanced down at his sister. "I have no clue what's going on, but it sounds like I got here just in time. Mind if we switch partners so I can reclaim my wife?"

Nicole's gaze flicked back to Jake's face, then her lips curved. "Get lost, big brother."

He's not my type. Nicole sensed it the instant Whitney fluidly handed off her dance partner and Nicole found herself in the strong circle of the man's arms.

He was tall and lean, his straight, shaggy hair as black as the suit he wore. He had a handsome, rugged face with high cheekbones and a strong sweep of jaw. It was a combination that drew a woman's gaze. He had certainly drawn hers while he'd stood alone at the bar, nursing a drink. The sight of him had brought to mind a sleek, dark panther, coiled to spring. The closed look in his eyes had not encouraged company.

It was those eyes that now had an alarm clanging in her head. They were the color of rich, aged whiskey, and she could only think that she could blissfully get lost in them…the same way she had a long time ago when another dark gaze had turned her system just as jittery.

The memory of that disaster had her struggling to clear her thoughts.

"I'm Nicole Taylor," she said as he guided her over the floor with smooth steps. "Bill's sister."

"Jake Ford."

"Whitney's partner, right?"

"Right."

Nicole followed his lead, moving to the music's slow, sensuous beat. She told herself to relax, that their dance was just a casual social gesture that would last only a matter of minutes. Still, his body was so close, so firm.

She tilted her head. "I've heard about you."

"Then why are you still dancing with me?" he asked, his gaze locked with hers.

When she'd spied him from a distance, she had decided he was compelling. Up close, his dark looks and strong features had a devastating effect. As did the warm, musky scent of his aftershave that curled into her lungs.

"I'm still dancing with you because I love to dance," she answered. She knew the dim light and the piano's soft notes were meant to soothe, yet that hadn't stopped the nerves at the base of her neck from knotting. "Sebastian says dancing is good for the circulation. Helps your capillaries oxygenate."

Jake's forehead furrowed. "Whatever."

She let out a measured breath. The man was definitely not big on conversation. Good thing she was.

"Anyway," she continued lightly, "Whitney has only good things to say about you."

"I pay her well."

Inching her head back, Nicole stared up, studying his face. She found no glint of humor in those dark eyes. "If you didn't pay her to say good things," she began slowly, "what would Whitney have told me about you?"

"To stay away."

Against all reason, his gruff words quickened Nicole's pulse. She was suddenly aware of the firm presence of his hand against her waist. Cognizant that only a thin barrier of silk lay between his palm and her flesh.

"Why would your partner tell me to stay away from you?"

His gaze remained steady on hers. "Long story."

Without conscious thought, Nicole splayed her fingers over his shoulder, then tightened them. She felt something beyond the ripcord of hard muscle. Stress. Strain. Jake Ford was as tense as wire.

"Are you on duty, Sergeant Ford?"

"Jake. No. Why?"

"You're in cop mode."

He blinked. "Cop mode?"

"Expression hard. Noncommittal." Her fingers kneaded his shoulder. "Unyielding."

"What do you know about cop mode?"

She smiled. "Oh, I've matched a few police officers."

His eyes narrowed. "Matched?"

"Making matches is my business—"

"Matches, as in 'close cover before striking'?"

God, he was so intense...and handsome. "Matches, as in relationships. I have a high success rate. I can just sense when two people belong together—it's a gift." Having found her opening, she plucked a business card from the evening bag that dangled on a slim chain from her shoulder. "Here you go."

Jake moved his hand from her waist to accept the card. "'Meet Your Match,'" he read, then moved his gaze back to hers. "You work there?"

"Yes. I also own the company."

He looked back at the card, arched a dark brow. "You're a romance engineer?"

"That's right." She was proud of the title, of her company's success and the knowledge that she offered people the potential for a lifetime of happiness. "I engineer relationships. Quite successfully, if I say so myself. I'm working on franchising."

As if mulling that over, he remained silent. Around them, muted conversations hung in the air as couples drifted past, swaying to the soft music.

"In other words, people pay you to fix them up on blind dates," he finally commented.

"Not 'blind dates.' When we sign on a client, we conduct background checks and do an intense interview. The person actually knows a lot about their date, including what they look like, before they even meet."

She gave a subtle glance at the firm left hand that cupped her right. Interest—a purely business one, she told herself—stirred when she saw he wasn't wearing a wedding band. "So, Sergeant Jake Ford, is there a special woman in your life?"

The slow song ended, another began. Without missing a step, he continued moving in the same smooth rhythm.

"No."

"Maybe you'd like to check out our services?"

He handed her card back. "No."

This time, his hand settled against her back where silk gave way to bare skin. His touch was light, but potent enough to widen her eyes as an unexpected flash of need took her by surprise. Air clogged her lungs. She stiffened her spine beneath his palm and willed her feet to keep moving while she kept her gaze on his.

He was watching her with seeming ease, but she could see the shimmering intensity in his dark eyes.

"You okay?" he asked.

"Fine." *She needed oxygen.* She wasn't into self-deception. Just like another man in her past, Jake Ford's looks, his demeanor...his touch were tempting. Too tempting. Already, her hormones were surging in a direction where the fine edge of reason began to blur.

Now that she'd felt the heat of his flesh against hers, she wanted his touch to continue. Deepen.

Not going to happen, she told herself, putting mental skids on her thoughts. She would never again approach a relationship with her emotions calling the shots. She'd been down that road with her ex, and found it was full of potholes. Now she was smarter. Wiser. And she had learned how to face a problem head-on. The thing to do in this instance was to take control and go on the defensive.

She would feel a whole lot better—*safer*—if Jake Ford were off-limits. And she was the perfect person to make that happen.

"I have a client who might be perfect for you," she said as she began tucking the card into the breast pocket of his suit coat. "She's a doctor. A *medical* doctor, intelligent and gorgeous. Let me know if you change your—"

Her words slid back down her throat when he snagged her wrist. His hand was steady, his fingers unyielding as steel.

His dark eyes narrowed. "Not interested. And I won't change my mind."

The image of those firm, controlled hands exploring every inch of her body clicked into her brain, sending heat surging into her cheeks.

A shadow flickered across his eyes, then disappeared. He released her wrist. "No offense."

"None taken." Pursing her lips, Nicole dropped the rejected card back in her purse while regarding him. "Has anyone ever mentioned that your biorhythms might be in the negative range?"

He missed a step, picked the beat back up again. "My what?"

"Biorhythms. You strike me as being overly tense, so

yours might be in a negative cycle. Sebastian says if a person's biorhythms are negative, it's hard to do well in certain areas.''

"Who the hell is Sebastian?"

"Sebastian Peck, my personal trainer at Sebastian's."

Jake's mouth curved into a sardonic arch. "The prissy gym on the northwest side of town," he commented.

"Actually, it's a health club."

"Bet it's got piped-in music and a juice bar."

"That's right."

"Not my kind of place. I work out at the police gym."

Nicole's left hand slid down to settle on his biceps. The well-formed muscle evidenced a strenuous workout regime.

"Sebastian isn't taking new clients now, but he owes me a favor," she said, undaunted. "I can set up an appointment to get your biorhythms charted. It doesn't take long." By then, she might have figured out how to convince Jake to agree to a date with the gorgeous doctor.

"My biorhythms are fine."

"Just think about it. I'm in the book—call me if you change your mind."

His eyes narrowed at the same instant the music faded. From the opposite side of the dance floor, an uncle of the bride's announced that the wedding couple was getting ready to leave the reception.

"We should wish them well," Nicole said.

"You give Whit and Bill my best," Jake stated evenly. "I've stayed too long as it is." His hand was a light presence on her elbow as they walked to the edge of the dance floor.

Squaring her shoulders, Nicole turned to face him, offered her hand. "It was nice to meet you, Jake. Give me a call if you decide you want to try out my services."

He hesitated for a brief instant, then cupped her hand in his while he flashed a careless grin. "*Your* services?"

Her throat tightened. Even as her brain told her that retreat would be wise, she allowed her hand to remain in his. Only one other time in her life had a man had such an immediate, stunning effect on her. Then, she'd gone with emotion, listened to her heart instead of her head, and she'd wound up betrayed and hurt. Desperately hurt.

Now all of her senses screamed at her to do an about-face and run for the hills. For some incomprehensible reason, she stayed put.

"My *company's* services, of course," she amended, keeping her voice light. "You might wake up some morning and decide you want to meet the doctor after all."

He kept his eyes locked with hers while his thumb stroked the inside of her wrist. Her pulse stuttered, then her stomach dropped to her toes.

"I won't."

Even as he turned and walked away she took a step backward. Then another.

Feeling the aftershock of his touch in every pore, she curled her fingers over her palms. She remained unmoving, her gaze tracking his progress toward the door while she waited for her pulse to settle. It didn't.

Hours later, her nerves still thrumming, Nicole lay in her bed, thinking about Jake Ford. About his dark eyes and ruthless good looks. About the way the attraction she'd felt for him had hit her like a freight train and hadn't abated.

Even for a woman who knew he wasn't the type of man she wanted, those thoughts made him dangerous.

Too dangerous.

Stifling a groan, she dragged a pillow over her head and breathed deeply of the soft scent of vanilla that drifted from the linen pillowcase. At least Jake wasn't part of her brother's new family, she reasoned. He was Whitney's *partner;* there was no reason she and the cop with the whiskey-colored eyes would ever cross paths again.

And that, all of her instincts told her, was a very good thing.

Chapter 2

He shouldn't have danced with her. Shouldn't have touched her, shouldn't have stroked his thumb across her wrist.

Jake scrubbed a hand across his face. Over a week had dragged by since Bill and Whitney's wedding. *Over a week.* He had lost track of how many times he'd berated himself on the subject of Nicole Taylor. Even now, his mind kept wandering out of the parked detective cruiser in which he sat and back to the hotel's glittering ballroom. To the heady feel of her in his arms. To her tempting scent.

To her.

"Dammit!" Setting his jaw, he pushed away the maddening thoughts and focused his mind. He stared out the windshield at the decrepit brick apartment building that looked like a hulking mammoth on the dark, weed-infested lawn. A bare bulb glowed above the building's crumbling cement porch, sending weak rays into the moonless night. His most reliable snitch had sworn that the girlfriend of Ramon Cárdenas, primary suspect in the drive-by homicide of seven-year-old Enrique Quintero, planned to show up at the apartment building sometime tonight.

Jake had been on the stakeout since sundown. So far, no girlfriend.

He had the cruiser's windows open; the heat of late September hung heavy in the still night air. In the distance, traffic rumbled along the interstate that cut a swath through downtown. Several houses away, a dog broke into a flurry of barks, ending when a gruff male shout splintered the air. The police radio in the cruiser's dash crackled softly, the dispatcher sounding as if he were speaking a foreign language.

As if on automatic pilot, Jake's brain processed the garbled information, which included a female patrol officer notifying dispatch of a Signal 7 at Stonebridge, a swanky gated housing community in the far northwest part of the city. A Signal 7 meant a dead body. One of the Holy Grails of police work was that an unexplained death got treated as a murder right from the start. If his name had headed Homicide's list to take the next call, Jake would have responded. He glanced at the luminous dial of his watch, knowing that the team of detectives pulling night shift this month would head to the scene in a matter of minutes.

Settling down in his seat, he swallowed the last dregs of his convenience-store coffee, then tossed the foam cup over his shoulder. He gave an unconcerned glance at the back seat, littered with the wadded sacks and empty cups from that week's take-out meals. He had a few days before Whitney got back from her honeymoon—he would shovel out the cruiser before then.

With the bitter taste of coffee still on his tongue, his hand automatically went to the pocket of his chambray shirt, found it empty. He scowled. Dammit, he hadn't smoked in two months, five days and seven hours. When the hell was he going to stop reaching for the pack of cigarettes that wasn't there?

Smoking was the least of the things he missed, Jake reminded himself, his mood turning as dark as the night around him. He couldn't quite forget the bite of aged Scotch. Or the heady feel of a woman. A soft woman with stunning blue eyes. A woman who smelled good enough to make a man wonder how it would feel to have her move beneath him in the dark.

A woman like Nicole Taylor.

He exhaled a slow breath. He could still feel the way her pulse had spiked beneath his thumb. After that, it had taken all of his control not to press his mouth to that soft place on her wrist and find out if she tasted as good as she looked.

Doing that would have only compounded the already idiotic move he'd made when he'd slicked his thumb across her flesh. He didn't want to start something he knew didn't have a chance in hell of going anywhere. Didn't want to sample what he couldn't allow himself to have.

Yet, because he'd given in to the impulse to hold on to her longer than he should have, he couldn't forget the gratifying stutter his touch had put in her pulse.

That memory wasn't the only thing giving him trouble.

Until that night, all he'd wanted was to rid himself of the clawing dream that dragged him to that second in time when a bomb ignited and ripped apart his world. The dream had faded the past several nights, just as the police psychologist had assured him it would. Problem was, his subconscious had replaced that dream with one of Nicole. A dream that, in one way, was far more disconcerting because there was no therapy for it. No way to talk the woman out of his head, no logical way of ridding his system of her.

She was there. Inside him. All of his instincts told him he was going to have one hell of a time shaking her presence. But shake her, he would.

He had learned the hard way that what fate tossed out was not always kind. Learned in the most horrific way how fast a person's life could change. How, in a slash of time, happiness could transform into grief. Numbing, ceaseless grief.

Before he could switch off his thoughts, he saw again the memorial service crowded with relatives, friends and cops, where music drifted and the cloying scent of roses hung in the air. There had been no caskets—there couldn't be, not when jagged shards of the plane's fuselage were all that had been left floating in the Gulf of Mexico. He'd bought one cemetery plot, stood alone in grim silence while a granite headstone with the names of his wife and twin daughters was positioned at the head of the empty grave. He hadn't gone back to the cemetery since that day.

With the memories closing in on him, Jake rubbed the heel of his hand over his heart. Never again. Never again would he leave himself wide open for fate to deliver another staggering blow. For that reason, there was no room in his life for Nicole Taylor, or any other woman.

The sudden ring of his cell phone cut through the still night air, jolting him from his thoughts. Jake clicked the unit on, said his name.

"It's Ryan."

"What's up, boss?"

"Any luck on the surveillance?"

Lifting a brow, Jake propped his elbow in the door's open window. Lieutenant Michael Ryan didn't usually call to check on the status of a stakeout. "Negative. I plan on giving it another couple of hours for Cárdenas's girlfriend to show. Unless you've got something else you need me on."

"That's why I called. I want you to take the Signal 7 that dispatch put out about ten minutes ago," Ryan stated, then gave the location that had been broadcast on the radio.

"I heard the uniform call it in."

With a habit he'd picked up from a veteran street cop

when he was a fresh-out-of-the-academy rookie, Jake grabbed a pen off the dash, angled his hand to catch the pale wash of a streetlight, then jotted the address on his left palm. "Any reason you don't want Gianos and Smith on it?" he asked, referring to the detectives pulling night shift that month.

"It's not that I don't want them on it," Ryan commented. "In fact, Gianos gave me a call from the scene—he and Smith were wrapping up an interview a couple of miles from there when the call came out. After Gianos got ID on the woman who found the guy's body, he figured he'd better give me a heads-up. He was right. Taking that into consideration, I think it'd be best to put you on this one. Since you're without a partner while Whitney's on her honeymoon, Gianos and Smith can give you a hand with follow-up interviews and paperwork if you need help."

"Okay." Jake glanced across the street at the apartment building that seemed to breathe neglect. He wouldn't get a lead on Cárdenas tonight, but he would get the bastard. He'd made that promise to himself and to little Enrique Quintero's grieving mother. Jake knew too well what it felt like to lose a child.

"So, Lieutenant, who's the woman who found the body?" he asked as he switched on the cruiser's ignition.

"Your partner's new sister-in-law, Nicole Taylor."

Jake began to swear, slowly, steadily, as he stomped the accelerator and the cruiser shot from the curb.

Fifteen minutes after he'd hung up from talking to his boss, Jake pulled to a stop in a pool of light at the wrought-iron gate that blocked the entrance to the exclusive housing community. To his left sat a tidy security building; to his right, small spotlights hidden in manicured shrubs illuminated a brick wall with *Stonebridge* in flowing brass script.

He tugged his gold badge off the waistband of his faded

jeans. "Sergeant Jake Ford," he said, flashing the badge at the guard on duty inside the building. While the guard logged him in, Jake noted the nearby panel of buttons where visitors could contact one of the residents to get buzzed through the gate if the guard wasn't around.

Inching the cruiser forward, Jake waited while the gate drifted open on silent gears. On the far side of the gate sat several sprawling houses, outlined in the glow of gas lamps that lined the street like rows of tiny moons. Even at night, the houses all looked massive. About one hundred times too massive for a cop's salary, Jake decided as he steered the cruiser through the entrance and along the well-lit street.

After checking the address he'd inked on his palm, he turned a corner. The pulse of a blue-and-red strobe from the scout car parked in a circular driveway had him bearing down on the accelerator.

The house beyond the driveway was brick, and as immense as the others in the neighborhood. Jake figured if the stiff owned the house where his body had wound up, he was a *very rich* stiff.

Seconds later, Jake inched the cruiser past the medical examiner's black station wagon. He parked behind the lab's crime scene van, then climbed out. As he reclipped his badge onto his waistband beside his holstered Glock, the night air settled around him, still and gauzy, full of humidity.

Yellow tape had been strung from the house's columned front porch to manicured shrubbery, then fanned out to loop around two of the matching gas street lamps. From the back seat of the scout car that sat idling in the driveway, Jake caught the glint of light off golden-blond hair.

Nicole.

While he ducked beneath a stretch of crime scene tape, it registered in his brain that the last thing he expected to feel when he saw her was pleasure. As if sensing his presence, she turned her head, her gaze meeting his through the scout car's back window. The stress in her eyes tightened Jake's throat, had him hesitating with an inexplicable need to go to her, to comfort. He set his jaw. She had found a dead body—whether it was a homicide or a natural death, proper procedure was for him to get the facts from those already working on-site, then view the body himself *before* he talked to any witness. Doing that gave the investigator a better idea of what questions to ask. And an edge on knowing if a witness was lying, which happened a lot during homicide investigations.

"Evening, Sergeant."

Jake turned, relieved to have his attention pulled from Nicole to the female officer who approached him. She looked on the official side with her blond hair pulled back from her earnest face and a silver clipboard in one hand.

"Evening." The first time he'd worked with the patrol officer was at a scene a couple of weeks ago, and her name had slipped his mind. He checked the brass tag above the right pocket of her gray uniform shirt: C. O. Jones.

"Jones," he added. With more than a little effort, he kept his gaze off the scout car where Nicole sat. "You responded to the initial call, right?" he asked, remembering that it had been a female officer who'd called in the Signal 7.

"Affirmative." The red-blue lights from the scout car winked in rhythm as she jotted his name on the crime scene log.

"Who's the victim?"

"Man by the name of Phillip Ormiston."

Jake arched a brow. "Of Ormiston Funeral Home fame?"

"The same. He owns the entire chain."

"Any idea yet on cause of death?"

"The M.E.'s assistant is inside checking the body, but I haven't heard anything for sure. To me, it looked like Ormiston just dropped dead in his entry hall. No blood, no sign of trauma that I could see. According to one of the neighbors, Ormiston was into fitness. He jogged around the neighborhood and played racquetball a couple nights a week at a gym called Sebastian's.''

''Maybe Ormiston's biorhythms took a dive into a negative zone,'' Jake muttered.

''Excuse me?''

''Nothing.'' He moved his gaze to the scout car. Nicole's back was to him now, her gaze glued to the house's open front door. While he watched her, she raised her left hand and slowly curled her fingers through the metal security screen that kept the person in the back seat separated from the officer in front. For some reason he could not fathom, Jake's chest tightened at the thought of her being caged inside the black-and-white.

''That's who found Ormiston's body,'' Jones said, her gaze following his. ''Her name's Taylor. Nicole Taylor.''

''Yeah.'' He remet the officer's gaze. Jones had done things by the book—she'd checked the scene, secured it, then put the person who discovered the body in her scout car while she advised dispatch to contact Homicide.

He also had procedure to follow, Jake reminded himself when he again felt the pull to walk over and open the car's back door. Right now, it was his job to find out what Nicole had already told the officer on the scene.

He nodded in the direction of a sleek red Jaguar parked in the circular drive. ''Is that Miss Taylor's?''

''Yes. The registration checks to her.''

''What did she tell you?''

''That Ormiston is a widower and a client of the dating service she owns.'' As she spoke, Jones pulled a business card off her clipboard and handed it to Jake. He glanced down, saw it was identical to the card Nicole had tried to slide into his pocket while they danced. The remembered feel of her warm flesh beneath his palm rose in his brain like a seductive phantom.

"Can you imagine a man with Ormiston's money needing to hire somebody to find him a date?" Jones asked.

Frowning, Jake jabbed the card into his shirt pocket while picturing again the way Nicole had worked the crowd at the wedding. It wouldn't surprise him to find out that some of the men who signed with her company hoped to get a date with *her*.

"What does she say about her relationship with Ormiston?"

"She claims their association was purely business."

When Jake realized he felt stupidly pleased, he scowled. Any other woman, he thought, shoving his fingers through his hair. Why the hell couldn't it have been anyone else on earth sitting in the back of that scout car instead of the woman who'd crowded his thoughts for days? And nights. At this point, the best he could hope for was that Phillip Ormiston had dropped dead from a nice, tidy aneurism.

"What reason did Miss Taylor give for being here?" he asked.

"She said Ormiston didn't phone her with a report on the last date he'd had through her service. That's apparently a standard thing for clients to do. He also hadn't shown up tonight at the gym for his scheduled racquetball game. When he didn't answer his phone, Taylor says she got worried and decided to stop on her way home to check on him. She referred to it as an extension of the customer service she offers her clients."

Jake looped his thumbs in the front pockets of his jeans. "How did she get in the house?"

"She said she didn't realize the front door was only partially closed until she knocked. When she did, it swung open. She walked in, saw Ormiston lying on the far side of the entry." Jones paused. "She touched the body."

Jake expelled a muffled curse. "Why?"

"She said she thought he'd maybe fallen and hit his head,

that he was unconscious." Jones glanced toward the house. "The way he's lying there, I can see how she'd think that."

"If Ormiston was dead, he couldn't have buzzed her through the security gate. Did she say how she got in?"

"No. If you need me to, I can check with the guard to see if he let her in. And if so, why he did without authorization from the person she was visiting."

"Do that. Also find out if Ormiston had any other visitors tonight. Any idea who the victim's next of kin is?"

"Ormiston's a widower, with one son who lives a couple of miles from here. The neighbor I talked to is getting his address so we can make the death notification." Jones angled her chin. "You want me to do that, or will you?"

"I'll do it after I'm through here." Jake looked back at the scout car. Nicole's gaze had not moved from the house's front door; her fingers were still threaded through the security screen. His stomach tightened. Dammit, she wasn't under arrest, he *knew* that. She wasn't a suspect. She was a witness, waiting to be interviewed. Maybe, he thought ruthlessly, his reaction to seeing her caged was because it hadn't been that long since he'd been locked in a cell, charged with eight counts of murder.

"I need to have a look at the body," he grated. Turning, he stalked across the pristine lawn toward the house while Jones took two strides to his one to keep up. "While I'm inside, Jones, I want you to do something."

"What's that, Sergeant?"

Jake paused at the brick steps that led up to a porch lined by tall, fluted columns. "Move Miss Taylor to my cruiser."

"To your cruiser?"

He wanted Nicole out of that cage; he wasn't going to waste breath trying to explain why when he didn't understand it himself. "That's right, Jones, to my cruiser. Think you can handle that?"

"Sure thing, Sergeant."

"Tell her I'll talk to her as soon as I get done inside."

Jake took the steps two at a time. As he strode across the porch, he toyed with the seeds of suspicion that, when it came to Nicole Taylor, he was destined to act like an idiot.

When he walked through the wide front door, he saw the usual contingent of forensic people milling in the foyer. Opposite the door, a curving staircase of gleaming oak swept up to the second floor. The sight of Phillip Ormiston's body lying facedown at the base of the staircase centered Jake's thoughts on business.

He recognized the man crouched beside the body as Zack Upchurch, the M.E.'s assistant.

"Evening, Zack. What can you tell me?"

"Evening, Sarge." The man used his tongue to nudge a toothpick from one corner of his mouth to the other. "Not a whole lot at this point."

Jake nodded. No matter what time of the day or night he ran into Upchurch, the man's brown hair was always standing in spikes, as if he'd come to whatever scene he'd been called to directly from bed.

"Any idea of time of death?" Jake persisted.

"Twelve hours, give or take." The surgeon's gloves Upchurch wore gave his hands a grayish hue that matched the dead man's face. "Have to wait until we get him on the table to give you a better idea."

A flash of light to his left had Jake turning his head. Beyond an arched doorway, a lab tech wearing a blue jumpsuit snapped pictures in a living room with paneled walls, acres of matching upholstered furniture and a shiny hardwood floor.

Detective Wes Gianos, a tall, swarthy man, stood near the room's green marble fireplace, talking into a cell phone. When he saw Jake, he raised a hand.

"Ford just got here," Gianos said into the phone as he

walked across the expansive tapestry rug toward the entry-way. "Smith and I will head there in a few minutes."

"Got another call?" Jake asked as Gianos clicked off his phone and slid it into the pocket of his suit coat.

"This one's on the east side. Got two DRTs," he said, using cop shorthand for victims who were *dead right there.* "One shot, one stabbed. Sounds like the Gun and Knife Club is hard at work." Gianos nodded toward the staircase. "Meet Phillip Ormiston. Did the uniform outside bring you up to speed?"

"Yes. Any sign of a struggle in the house?"

"No. Smith and I also checked for signs of forced entry on the doors and windows. Didn't find anything."

"Any drugs around?"

"Negative."

Jake stepped forward. Leaning in, he examined the body, making sure not to touch anything that would get the forensic types all bent out of shape.

Dressed in a tan linen shirt, dark slacks and leather loafers, Ormiston looked as though he'd lain down on the marble floor to take a nap. His dark hair, fading to gray at the temples, lay sleek against his head. Beneath the spill of light from a crystal chandelier, a diamond winked from the ring on his left pinkie finger; a thick gold bracelet circled his wrist.

Jake figured he could mark robbery off the list of motives if it turned out someone had killed the man.

He met Upchurch's gaze. "Any sign of trauma?"

"None that I've seen so far. Nothing visible on his neck. No defense wounds on either hand. This guy's big and has the look of someone who works out, so it's not like he couldn't have fought back." The M.E.'s assistant rose. "I'll get a sheet from my station wagon, then turn him over. Maybe we'll find something on the front of him, but I'm not wagering money on that."

Gianos waited until Upchurch went out the front door, then looked at Jake. "Since Ryan wants you on this case, I didn't question Nicole Taylor. Figured you ought to handle that."

"Not a problem."

"There's something you need to check in the kitchen before you talk to her." As he spoke, Gianos aimed his thumb across one shoulder in the direction of a brightly lit hallway that led toward the rear of the house.

"What's that?"

"There's a basket from a bakery on the counter, partially filled with muffins. A couple of empty wrappers are inside, so you've got to figure Ormiston sampled a few."

Jake furrowed his brow while his mind fell into sync with Gianos's thoughts. They had a healthy-looking man with no sign of trauma who seemed to have dropped dead while walking across his entry hall. "You saying you think he was poisoned?"

"I think I don't know what to think." Gianos shrugged. "Look, I know Nicole Taylor is Whitney's new sister-in-law and her brother Bill is the number two man in the D.A.'s office."

Mentally, Jake missed a step. "What's that got to do with Ormiston maybe getting poisoned?"

"Could mean nothing…or something. All I know is there's a card with Nicole Taylor's name on it tied to the muffin basket."

Jake felt his spine stiffen. "What does the card say?"

"'Phillip, we've only just begun. Yours, Nicole.'" Gianos shook his head. "The patrol cop mentioned that when she questioned Taylor, she claimed her association with Ormiston was purely business."

"Yeah, that's what Jones told me."

"Maybe that's true," Gianos observed. "All I know is if a woman sent me a basket of goodies with a note like that,

I'd get the idea her interest in me went beyond business. If the woman looked as good as Nicole Taylor, I'd welcome that interest.''

"Holy hell," Jake muttered.

Gianos and Smith headed out the door just as Upchurch returned with a sheet. The M.E.'s assistant and one of the lab techs rolled Ormiston's body onto the sheet.

The toothpick in the side of Upchurch's mouth seesawed as he inspected the front of the dead man. "No sign of trauma on his neck, no blood visible." Upchurch raised a shoulder. "Too early to tell, Sarge, but this death might be a natural."

"And it might not be," Jake countered.

"Might not."

Jake knew that Gianos had been on target to turn a suspicious eye toward the muffins. At a death scene, you looked at everything that way.

Staring down at Ormiston's body, Jake expelled a slow breath while his mind worked. Muffins were mostly carbohydrates, which the body digested faster than fats and proteins.

"Upchurch, I need a quick autopsy," he began. "The M.E. needs to pay close attention to the stomach contents, the degree of digestion. Make sure he knows I want a tox screen on body fluids for poisons, both for time of death and cause of death."

Upchurch cocked an eyebrow. "Poison, huh?"

"It's possible," Jake said, then headed for the kitchen.

She'd had to keep busy, or go crazy.

Gnawing her bottom lip, Nicole stared down at the folded sacks, empty foam containers and cups she'd aligned beside her on the back seat of Jake's car. Now that she'd finished the task and had nothing to occupy her mind, she was again conscious of the clutching nervousness in the pit of her stomach.

At least she felt a little more calm in the back of Jake's car with its windows rolled down than she had in the police car with its cagelike effect.

In an unconscious gesture, she flipped her thick blond braid behind her shoulder, then twisted her fingers together while she gazed out the open window at the massive brick house. She had found Phillip's body nearly two hours ago, and her hands had yet to stop trembling. Except for attendance at an occasional funeral, she had never gotten close to a dead body. Certainly had never discovered one. Or touched one.

She'd done all three tonight.

Closing her eyes, she fought back a wave of unsteadiness. She concentrated on taking deep, controlled breaths, tried to remember the breathing exercises Sebastian had taught her to battle stress. The only thing closing her eyes did was bring a clear picture of Jake into her awareness.

He had looked grim, rugged and all-business when he'd climbed out of his car, *this car,* and headed across the lawn toward Phillip's house.

She had thought constantly about him since her brother's wedding. Crazy thoughts, she acknowledged. Thoughts she should have easily discarded because she knew the type of man she wanted to spend the rest of her life with, and she was certain Jake Ford wasn't even close. Still, she hadn't managed to rid her mind of him. Not since they'd danced…

The next instant the door beside her swung open, snapping her eyes open.

"What do you think you're doing?"

In the wash of light from the street lamps, Jake's eyes looked almost black as he leaned through the open door. "Uh…waiting for you. The female officer told me to stay—"

"The trash, Nicole," he stated through his teeth. "What the hell did you do to my trash?"

"Oh." Her gaze dropped to the sacks and empty containers sitting in rows beside her. "When I get nervous, I have to have something to keep me busy. To keep my mind focused."

His gaze stayed on her face, frank and assessing, as he propped a forearm along the top of the car's open door. "Sorting trash gets your mind focused?"

"It helps." No way was she going to admit that all she'd gotten from sitting in his car and organizing fast-food sacks were thoughts that had focused on *him*.

He swung the door open wider. "I need to talk to you. It'd be easier if we both sit in the front seat."

"Okay." She had answered what seemed like a million of the uniformed officer's questions, and she doubted she could give Jake any more information. On a sigh, she slid out of the car into the warm night air. When she turned to face him, she discovered that, without the strappy heels she'd worn while they danced, she was a full head shorter than he.

His eyes were cool, very cool, as they inched down her body, taking in her white, oversize dress shirt, navy leggings, thick socks and workout shoes. His slow, measured assessment filled her with unease. She wasn't sure if it was the man or the cop—or both—who made her feel as if she were not being looked at, but into.

The sound of muted conversation pulled her attention toward the sprawling brick house. The wheels of a stretcher holding a black body bag clattered as two men rolled it over the doorstep and onto the porch.

Her throat tightened. "He must have had a heart attack."

Jake closed the car's back door with a quiet snap, then turned. His handsome face held no expression. "What makes you think that?"

"Phillip confided in me that he'd had a heart attack a few years ago. It was a mild one, but enough to have him start working out and eating right."

"Phillip," Jake echoed. A muscle in his cheek jerked, but his eyes stayed level on hers. "Right now his death is unexplained. That's how I'm investigating it."

He leaned around her and pulled open the front passenger door. The movement brought him close enough for her to catch his warm, musky scent. For a mindless moment, they were back on that dance floor, their bodies swaying in slow, seductive unison. As if feeling again the heady sensation of his thumb against her wrist, she curled her fingers over her palms.

He pointed toward the front seat. "Climb in."

He said the words with such quiet authority that she instantly complied. She watched as he skirted the hood, pulled open the door, then settled behind the wheel.

"Tell me about Ormiston." As he spoke, Jake propped his wide shoulders against the car door and dangled one hand over the steering wheel.

Dressed in a rumpled chambray shirt and worn jeans, black hair on the shaggy side, Jake might come across as relaxed. Not to her. Nicole considered herself an expert when it came to reading people, and she saw the leashed intensity in the alert tilt of his head, the sharpness in his dark gaze.

"Phillip was a client of Meet Your Match."

"For how long?"

"Maybe six months. I'd have to check his file for the exact date he signed his contract."

"Did you know him before he became a client?"

"No."

"He just walk in off the street and sign on?"

"Well, I *did* meet him at a charity fund-raiser and gave

him one of my cards," she amended. "He showed up in my office the next day and signed a contract."

"Did you and Ormiston go out?"

She blinked. "I don't date my clients."

"Why were you at his house tonight?"

She told him the same thing she'd told the female officer, ending with "It wasn't like Phillip not to call the office when he was scheduled to. Wasn't like him to miss a racquetball game. I was concerned."

"Was he scheduled to play racquetball with you?"

"No, Sebastian. They played a couple times a week."

"Is it standard operating procedure for you to drop by each of your client's houses to check on their welfare?"

"Of course not. Phillip had been having...problems and I felt he needed special attention."

"What sort of...problems?"

"He was unhappy that I had yet to connect him with a woman whom he felt would make a suitable mate." She lifted a shoulder. "I understood his impatience. His wife passed away two years ago. He was lonely, and at a point where the loneliness was turning into depression. I'm a firm believer some people aren't meant to live their lives alone. Phillip is...was one of them."

When Jake didn't shoot back another question, Nicole realized he'd turned his head to stare out the windshield into the dark night. He seemed lost in thought, his profile hard and unyielding. As she studied him, the weak light from the street lamps seemed to shift, and for a brief instant, she saw what she thought was utter desolation in his eyes.

A quick, surprising tremor around her heart had her leaning to touch his arm. "Is something wrong?"

He jerked his head around so fast that she snatched her hand back. His eyes were hooded, his face as expressionless as carved stone. "So, Ormiston was unhappy you hadn't managed to find him 'Miss Right.'"

She took a deep breath. Whatever brief emotion she'd seen in his eyes had been replaced by a chilling remoteness.

"Yes, Phillip was unhappy. Some clients have a hard time at first understanding how long it can take to find their perfect match."

Jake flicked a look over his shoulder toward the house. "Ormiston was loaded. Seems to me he'd have no problem getting a date."

"He knew quite a few single women, but no one he wanted to get serious about. He ran a huge, thriving funeral business with locations all over the state. At the minimum, he put in sixty-hour work weeks. That limited the time he had to make connections. Phillip wasn't a twenty-year-old man who wanted to hang out in singles' bars, hoping to meet someone."

"How many women did you fix him up with?"

"Quite a few over the past couple of months." Frowning, Nicole shoved her braid over one shoulder. "Phillip claimed nothing clicked with any of his dates, which surprised me."

"So, you had a dissatisfied customer on your hands. Was he planning on ending your association?"

She linked her fingers, twisted them. "Yes. The last time I saw him he said he wouldn't renew his contract."

"When was this?"

"A few days ago."

"Where?"

"At Sebastian's." She looked out the windshield just as the black station wagon into which the men had loaded the body bag crept slowly along the street. Sadness for the man she had known settled inside her. "I guess none of that matters now," she added quietly.

"Since Ormiston thought he got a raw deal, he might have planned to bad-mouth your company. I doubt that would have made you happy."

In the next heartbeat, Nicole vividly understood that the

man with whom she shared the car's close, intimate confines was not conducting an interview, but an interrogation. It wasn't fear that stiffened her spine, but temper.

"Of course that didn't thrill me. I'm in business to make my clients happy. I feel a lot better when I succeed at my job. Don't you?"

"There's a lot of people behind bars who can swear to that."

"Are they all guilty?" she asked coolly.

He gave a short laugh. "Most claim they aren't."

For a slow, languorous moment he studied her, his dark eyes on hers. Watchful. Nicole tried to ignore the knots that tightened in her stomach.

Finally he asked, "Do you think Ormiston would have been happier if you had agreed to go out with him?"

His question caught her like a slap in the face. "What makes you think he wanted me to go out with him?"

"You slide your business card into his pocket at a charity to-do. The next morning he shows up at your office. Not hard to figure out what was going on."

"*Nothing* was going on, Sergeant. I don't date my clients."

"But he did ask you out, right?"

"Once, after he signed his contract." The lethal sureness in Jake's eyes brought all of her nerves swimming to the surface. "I refused, and Phillip didn't ask again. I told him to be patient, that we'd only just begun looking for his perfect mate."

Jake reached into his shirt pocket, pulled out a small plastic bag. "'We've only just begun,'" he murmured, angling the card inside the bag until it caught light from the nearby street lamp. "Sounds familiar."

As she read the message with her name below, a shiver skittered like a bony finger down the back of Nicole's neck. She lifted her gaze. "Why do you have the card in a bag?"

"It's evidence."

"Of what?"

"That you sent Ormiston a basket of muffins."

"Of course I sent them." She forced her voice to remain even while anxiety shredded her insides. "I don't understand—"

"Did you bake the muffins?"

"No, I bought them."

"Where?"

She gave him the name of the bakery a few blocks from her office. "I have an account there."

"Why did you send them? If Ormiston was going to cancel his contract, why bother with muffins?"

"He called my office yesterday, said he'd decided to renew his contract. I had my assistant order the basket, with directions to deliver it to Phillip's office."

"Why muffins? Why not a bottle of wine? A couple of cigars?"

"Like I said, Phillip was into healthy living. The muffins were low fat."

Jake held up the plastic bag. "Is this your handwriting?"

"No, I told my assistant the message I wanted on the card. He dictated it when he placed the order."

"So you didn't go to the bakery? You didn't pick out the muffins? Didn't deliver them yourself?"

Her hands and her jaw constricted with equal force. "I've never seen them. My assistant, Melvin Hall, ordered the muffins over the phone. *He's* never seen them. Are we done, Sergeant? It's been a hell of a day and I want to go home."

"Almost." Jake slid the bag back into his shirt pocket. "How did you get in here tonight?"

"The guard on the gate let me in."

"So, you've visited Ormiston's house so many times that the guard recognized you?"

"I've never been here before tonight." She raised her

chin. "I guess the guard thinks I have an honest face. When Phillip didn't answer the guard's call, the guard buzzed me in so I could leave a note on Phillip's front door."

"Did you leave a note?"

"No, I found Phillip's body instead. Are we done?"

"For now."

She shouldered open the door, was out of the car like a shot.

"Hold on."

She'd taken two steps when he caught up with her.

"I said hold on."

She wheeled on him just as he snagged her elbow. Momentum had her stumbling forward, her body colliding with his. For a split second, she had the impression of slamming into rock-hard muscle.

"You said we were done."

He reached out his other hand when she teetered. "You're upset. I want to make sure you're okay to drive."

"Of course I'm okay!" she flung back, jerking from his hold. "I'm used to finding dead bodies. *Touching* them. Accustomed to getting grilled by a cop. A cop who accuses me of...of..."

"I haven't accused you of anything, Nicole."

"Sending bakery muffins!" she shot back.

His mouth quirked. "So far, I've restrained myself from hauling you in on that charge."

She closed her eyes for an instant. "Was Phillip poisoned? Was there something in the muffins?"

"I have no idea."

"Then why were you asking—"

"It's my job to ask," he said quietly, his face awash in light and shadow as he gazed down at her. "I told you upfront I'm investigating this as an unexplained death. That means I work it as a murder until I can prove it wasn't."

"What if it was?"

"Then I'll find out who did it."

She shook her head. "Do you think Phillip was murdered?"

"Nobody knows until the M.E. knows." He shrugged. "Until then, I have to ask a lot of people questions. I may have to ask you more. That's because I can't exactly ask Ormiston."

She dragged in a shaky breath. "You may be used to dealing with death on a daily basis, but I'm not. I can't believe this happened to someone I know."

Eyes narrowing, Jake studied her face. "If you don't feel up to driving home, I'll take you." The concern in his voice tugged at something deep inside her. "I have to go see Ormiston's son," he said quietly. "It'll be no problem to take you home first."

They were standing close, their bodies more casual than intimate, and she knew full well what was between them was business. Yet, the thought of again sitting beside him in the close confines of his car sent a pool of heat spreading through her belly that made her legs go weak.

That heated weakness had her remembering how she'd succumbed so easily to another man's touch. How a twin flood of need and desire had swept her away until she'd nearly drowned. How she'd hurt when she discovered the truth about the man she'd known next to nothing about when they'd rushed into marriage. How easily he'd betrayed her trust.

Never again, she reminded herself. She'd resolved a long time ago that logic—not emotion—would guide her on her search for her soul mate.

Right now, logic told her to run as far away from Jake Ford as possible.

"Thanks," she said, taking a step backward toward her Jaguar. Then another. "I can drive myself."

Chapter 3

"Yeah, yeah," Jake said into the phone the following morning as he rocked back in his city-issue desk chair. "Cárdenas's girlfriend didn't show last night at that apartment building like you told me she would. You know what that means, Julio?"

"What?"

"You gave me bad information."

"Look, man—"

"No, you look. Cárdenas shot a seven-year-old boy just for standing on a street corner. His girlfriend can make him for the homicide. I *want* her."

"She got wind you're looking for her, so she's lying low."

"Not low enough so you can't sniff her out," Jake countered. "I told you, you want my help with that warrant hanging over your head, you'll get me a line on where I can find her. *Tonight*."

Jake slammed down the receiver on a curse. Almost immediately, the phone rang. He snagged it up, checking the clock above the assignment board where grease-penciled letters displayed each homicide team's working cases. Nine-o-five. He needed to be at Ormiston's office when it opened at ten, and he hoped this was the call from the M.E. he'd been waiting on.

It was.

"I just finished the autopsy on Phillip Ormiston." The deep timbre of Dr. John McClandess's voice boomed across the line. Jake pictured the man eternally garbed in a white lab coat, his gaunt face sharpened to the bone, black eyes vibrant, gray hair combed back from the temples. "My assistant left a note saying you wanted me to call with my preliminary findings."

"That's right." With his desk in its usual state of avalanche, Jake had to dig to unearth a pad and pen. "So, Doc, do we have a healthy man who dropped dead of natural causes?"

"We do not. As you said, the victim was healthy. He didn't have a heart attack. Didn't suffer an aneurism or a stroke. I have ruled out natural death as the cause."

Jake tensed. "Was it something he ate?"

"You're referring to the muffins, which my assistant mentioned in his report."

"Right." Jake pictured again the stunned disbelief that had settled in Nicole's blue eyes when she realized where his line of questioning about the muffins she'd sent Ormiston was headed. That look had haunted him throughout the night.

"I see in the report that you've sent the muffins to Sky Milano in your forensics lab. A chemical analysis needs to be run just to be sure, but I doubt Sky will find anything suspect."

"Good." Jake didn't realize he'd been holding his breath

until the word came out in a hiss. "So, what *did* kill Ormiston?"

"I found a minute puncture on the right side of his neck," McClandess answered. "He was given an injection, Sergeant. Of what, we won't know until the toxicology results come back. Whatever substance he was injected with caused the muscles necessary for respiration to shut down. Official cause of death is respiratory paralysis."

Jake's eyes narrowed. "So, the guy suffocated?"

"Basically, yes."

"You got any idea what it was someone pumped into Ormiston?"

"It's conjecture at this point. Certain drugs could bring on that kind of paralysis. A few poisons come to mind, too, all undetectable except by chemical analysis."

"How fast can you get the tox test results to me?"

"A week."

"That's too long, Doc."

McClandess sighed. "I'll put a rush on the tests, but I can't promise anything. Our lab is as backlogged as OCPD's."

"Yeah." While his mind cataloged the steps he needed to take to get the Ormiston investigation rolling, Jake rubbed his gritty eyes, then glanced at the tidy desk that butted against the front of his. Whitney had a few days to go on her honeymoon. He hoped to hell she was enjoying herself.

"Okay, Doc, what's your best guess on time of death?"

"The air-conditioning in the house was on a low setting. The victim was lying on a marble floor, which cooled his body at a faster rate than normal. I estimate Ormiston had been dead about five hours before he was found, give or take an hour."

Jake slashed notes across the pad. He knew that establishing time of death was more elusive than most people thought. It couldn't be pinned down exactly unless the death was witnessed or the victim's Timex stopped ticking during the crime.

"So, you're saying the killer showed up at Ormiston's house between four and six yesterday afternoon."

"Yes."

Jake tapped the end of his pen against the notepad. They hadn't found an appointment book at Ormiston's house to indicate he had anything scheduled yesterday afternoon. Jake hoped his luck would change when he got to Ormiston's office.

After checking a few more facts with the M.E., Jake hung up, eased back in his chair and gave an idle glance around the office.

At this time of the morning, most of his co-workers were out on calls, doing follow-ups or cooling their heels in court. Only two other cops—Grant Pierce and his partner, Elizabeth Scott, were at their desks. Scott, an expert on statement analysis, had replaced Pierce's mentor, Sam Rogers, who'd died of a heart attack. Jake made a mental note to ask Pierce how Scott was working out before he shifted his mind back to his case.

"Respiratory paralysis," Jake muttered, his gaze settling on the notepad. "By injection."

Nothing at the crime scene indicated the killer had gained entry other than by knocking on the front door. There had been no sign of a struggle. No defensive wounds on Ormiston's hands to indicate he'd tried to protect himself. It was logical, then, to go with the assumption that the two knew each other, that Ormiston felt no immediate threat, even trusted his killer to some extent. Could be a family member, Jake mused. A friend. Maybe someone Ormiston knew on a more casual basis. Someone he'd dated?

Last night, the guard at Stonebridge had copied the log of every person and vehicle who'd gained access to the gated community in the past twenty-four hours. The only person logged in to see Ormiston was Nicole Taylor. That didn't mean a lot, Jake acknowledged. The list didn't cover people who Ormiston might have buzzed through the gate while the guard wasn't around. It also didn't list everyone who lived there, or the yard crews, housekeepers and other service workers who knew that month's security code. And Jake knew that the killer could have parked his car outside of Stonebridge, scaled the seven-foot brick wall that surrounded the complex, then walked to Ormiston's house. If that were the case, the killer had to be in good shape.

Maybe someone who owned a gym and played racquetball on a regular basis?

He opened his desk's bottom drawer, hefted out the yellow pages and checked the address for Sebastian's. Lifting a brow, he realized the gym shared space in the same building with Meet Your Match, Nicole's dating service.

When Jake caught himself wondering just how chummy Nicole and Sebastian-of-biorhythm-fame were, he scowled. He ought to be entertaining that thought solely because they both had links to a homicide victim, but Jake knew that wasn't the case. Dammit, he couldn't get Nicole out of his head. He'd spent most of the night picturing how she'd looked at the crime scene when he first saw her sitting in his cruiser. Her spine had been board-stiff, her face bathed in a mix of thready light and shadow that made her skin look pale. Too pale. Her eyes had been closed, and he could have sworn she'd been doing some sort of deep-breathing exercise. The vulnerability that had seemed to wrap around her had touched off twin urges inside him to take and protect.

He expelled an oath that had both Pierce and Scott swiveling their heads in his direction. Holding up a palm, Jake muttered, "Forget it." The partners exchanged a look, then shifted their attention back to their own work.

Jake shoved the yellow pages back into the desk and

slammed the drawer shut. Where Nicole Taylor was concerned, he wasn't going to take *or* protect. She was a material witness in what only minutes ago had turned into an active homicide investigation. Nothing more, nothing less.

During their initial interview he'd gone by the book, treated Nicole like any other witness. He had given her every opportunity to lie to him, yet his sixth sense continued to send the message that she'd told him the truth. Plus, there were logical points in her favor. She'd discovered and immediately reported finding Ormiston's body. Admitted her connection to the victim. Had no compelling, obvious motive to kill.

When murder was involved, all those things added up.

What didn't add up was that he couldn't seem to wipe the woman from his mind. That alone was dangerous. She was a temptation, and he was a man who didn't want to be tempted.

Right now, what he wanted didn't matter, Jake reminded himself. The job mattered. Now that he knew for sure her client had been murdered, he had no choice but to pay Nicole a visit.

With the late-morning sun beaming behind him, Jake shoved through a revolving door and stepped into the cool, sumptuous foyer of the sleek office building that lanced upward from a forest of blue and purple hydrangeas. Raking his fingers through his hair, he crossed the wide lobby with its pink marble columns and glossy ornamental trees. He paused near a bank of elevators to check the building's directory. Names of high-priced boutiques, specialty shops and several cosmetic surgeons were listed. As were a beauty salon and skin-care clinic with French-sounding names. Seconds ticked by while he continued scanning the list of trendy businesses that occupied the building's ten floors. His gaze paused on the name Sebastian's. He slid a hand into the pocket of his navy sport coat, fingered the key ring he'd found in Ormiston's desk drawer when he'd searched the victim's office. The instant he'd seen Sebastian's and the number seventy engraved on the key, Jake realized Ormiston had a locker at the gym. He'd called dispatch and had them send a patrol cop to the gym to make sure no one opened the locker. Jake then called Gianos and Smith. Right now, the two detectives were getting a search warrant. While he waited for the paperwork to arrive, Jake figured it would be a good time to see Nicole.

He needed to get a lead on something soon, he thought, punching the elevator's call button. Except for the key, the office from which Ormiston had operated his funeral home empire had been devoid of clues. There had been nothing on the man's calendar to show he planned to meet anyone yesterday afternoon. Neither his secretary nor his assistant— or anyone else—knew of anyone who wished Ormiston ill.

Someone did, Jake thought as he stepped into an elevator. Someone thought ill enough of the man to stab a needle into his neck and inject him with something that paralyzed his lungs.

Seconds later, the elevator chimed its arrival at the building's top floor. The doors glided open; a tall man stalked on, his shoulder ramming into Jake's.

"Sorry."

Though the man uttered only one word, Jake registered his thick accent.

"No problem." As he stepped into the hall Jake's gaze swept the man's face. His eyes narrowed while the cop in him cataloged the familiar sharp cheekbones, olive complexion and black mustache over the mouth set in a hard line. Jake made the connection just as the elevator doors slid closed. *The Latino.*

His thoughts scrolled back to Bill and Whitney's wedding reception. He'd watched Nicole tuck her business card into the man's breast pocket while he gazed down at her with simmering desire. Today, it had been anger in the man's eyes. Jake wondered if Nicole had another unsatisfied customer on her hands. If so, why?

He strode down the quiet, carpeted corridor that led to a waiting area furnished with coral-colored sofas and glass tables. As he approached the desk that rose from a pool·of shell-pink carpet, he was aware of the low strains of classical music drifting on the air.

"Welcome to Meet Your Match." The woman behind the desk was a good-looking brunette with big, wide-set eyes. She wore a trim, midnight-black suit and candy-red lipstick. "Are you interested in speaking with one of our relationship counselors?"

"If your boss is one of the counselors."

"Do you have an appointment with Miss Taylor, sir?"

"I don't need one."

The woman's perfect mouth thinned a fraction. "I'm sorry, sir, Miss Taylor is unavailable. I'll be happy to arrange a consultation with one of our other counselors."

Jake shoved back one flap of his sport coat to reveal the badge hooked to the waistband of his jeans. He was aware that only a few months ago he would have grinned, slid a hip onto the brunette's desk and charmed his way into her boss's office. Maybe even invited the receptionist to meet him for a drink after work. If the chemistry was right, finessed her into his bed. Those days were over, he acknowledged with grim acceptance. The I-don't-give-a-damn lifestyle he'd embarked on after Annie and the twins died had led to the murder of a woman he'd dated and resulted in his being set up to take the fall for eight homicides. If it hadn't been for Whitney's dogged belief in his innocence, he'd probably be locked in a cell right now.

Those sobering experiences had opened his eyes, made him realize he had to face the pain of losing his family and live with the hand fate had dealt him. Fine, he was working on that. What he didn't have to do was leave himself open to having his heart ripped apart again.

"Sergeant Jake Ford," he said while the brunette's gaze scanned his badge. "Please ring Miss Taylor's office. *Now.*"

"Of course." Nerves had the woman's hand shaking as she snatched up the phone.

Seconds later, she shook her head, replaced the receiver and rose. "Mel—Miss Taylor's assistant—isn't at his desk. I'll need to escort..." Her voice drifted off when the phone trilled.

"Better answer that." Jake pointed toward a softly lit hallway behind the reception desk. "Her office that way?"

Lifting the receiver, the woman moistened her red-glossed lips. "Yes, but you can't—"

"I can." Letting the flap of his jacket fall back into place, he stepped around the desk and headed down the hallway.

The next waiting area was cozier, its pale upholstered chairs, polished tables and soft watercolors lending a more personal atmosphere. An oak desk with a computer and empty swivel chair sat to one side of a door marked Private. A nameplate at the desk's front edge read Mel Hall.

Because his natural inquisitiveness had paid off more times than he could count during past homicide investigations, Jake strolled to the desk where a single file folder lay. Using a fingertip, he turned the file his way, read the label. DeSoto Villanova. Jake lifted the file's cover. The Latino's smiling face stared back at him in vivid color, which emphasized the man's swarthy good looks. Clipped on the opposite side of the file was a form titled Confidential Questionnaire with all the blanks neatly filled in. Pursing his lips, Jake closed the file, wondering again what had riled Villanova.

Turning from the desk, Jake neared the closed door. What he now recognized as Nicole's just-under-the-smoldering-point scent settled around him. Without any effort, he again felt her soft flesh beneath his palm as their bodies swayed to the pianist's love song. He clenched his teeth. Never before had he known a woman who could haunt and inflame.

Annie, his first love, his only love, had been comfortable, solid, a part of his soul. Nicole made him feel as if a flare had ignited inside him.

The knowledge of how just her scent affected him hitched his irritation level up a notch. He rapped once on the door; without waiting for an answer, he shoved it open, then froze. All of his senses zeroed in on the compelling sight of a barefoot Nicole bent nearly double in front of her desk, her trim, skirt-clad bottom tilted upward. Her hands were clamped onto the desk's front edge, and for a split second Jake wondered if she was trying to shove the solid piece of mahogany toward the far wall where a floor-to-ceiling window gave an impressive view of the Oklahoma City skyline.

He might have sworn off women, but the hot ball of lust that lodged in his gut sent the message he was far from dead. Slanting one shoulder against the doorjamb, he crossed his arms over his chest and enjoyed the enticing view of woman. Seconds later, Nicole's hips did a quick, enthusiastic twitch and he swallowed back a whistle. After it appeared she might wiggle indefinitely, he figured he'd better make his presence known.

"Waiting on a date, Taylor, or will you take pot luck?"

At the sound of his voice, she bolted upright and whirled to face him. "What are…?" Color flared across her cheeks as she raised a hand to smooth her sleek French twist. "Sergeant Ford, usually visitors don't just barge into my office."

Last night, she'd turned an oversize shirt, leggings, white socks and workout shoes into a fashion statement. Now she looked incredibly polished in a trim, traffic-stopping red suit. It occurred to Jake the woman could wear a gunnysack and look good.

"I knocked," he said, angling his head toward the reception area. "Your secretary's not around."

"My *assistant,* Melvin...Mel, is in the kitchen making tea. I always have tea after my daily yoga session."

"Yoga? Is that what that was?" Pushing away from the door, Jake roamed into the office, cataloging the chairs and sofas upholstered in peach, gleaming wood tables and glowing brass lamps, all arranged against a background of soft tan walls. "I thought yoga was where you sit on the floor with your legs crossed and your palms up."

"That's a different discipline. I study under Sebastian."

"Under?"

Her chin lifted. "He's my *instructor.* Sebastian says the best positions are those that put you into the moment."

Jake paused inches from her. The smoldering scent that had settled around him in the outer room now snaked into his lungs. He felt the quick, helpless pull of need, and damned both himself and her for it. "Sebastian has a point," he agreed. "That position certainly put me into the moment."

Nicole could feel the hammer of her heart against her ribs as she gazed up into Jake's dark eyes. His black hair skimmed the collar of the white dress shirt he wore beneath a blue sport coat. A bright paisley tie hung down the front of the shirt; his faded jeans accentuated his lean, muscular thighs and rangy build. He looked, she thought as her stomach muscles knotted, irresistibly handsome.

The spicy male tang of his cologne drifted around her, conjuring up the heady moments she'd spent dancing in his arms.

He's not what you want, she reminded herself, and took a step backward.

"Can I help you with something?" As she spoke, she slid her feet into the pair of spiky red heels she'd toed off earlier.

"Yeah—" Obviously aware of movement behind him, Jake turned.

Nicole watched his sharp cop's eyes narrow as they took in the man who'd stepped through the door carrying a small tray. Her assistant was tall with dark blond hair, blue eyes and a square jaw. Today, Mel was dressed in neat slacks and a white shirt that emphasized his broad shoulders. In the four months he'd worked for her, Mel's efficient, friendly demeanor had won her undying gratitude. Her decision to help pay for his college tuition had garnered her assistant's total devotion.

"Oh, sorry, boss," he said with an easy smile. "Didn't realize you were with a client."

"It's all right." Glad for an excuse to distance herself from Jake, Nicole moved to the seating area in one corner of the office. "Sergeant Ford isn't a client."

A thought had her hesitating when she reached the coffee table around which a love seat and two wing chairs were grouped. She gave Jake a look across her shoulder. "Unless you're here because you've decided to go out with the gorgeous doctor?"

"I'm here about Ormiston."

The tightness she'd felt in her chest since she found Phillip's body intensified. She'd lain awake all night, haunted by images of her client collapsed on the marble floor at the base of the staircase, of his glassy, sightless eyes....

"I need to look at his file," Jake said.

"Of course." She nudged a few magazines to one side of the table. When a gold pen rolled across the table's polished surface and onto the toe of her shoe, she frowned.

"Something wrong, boss?" Mel asked.

"No." Realizing who the pen belonged to, she slid it into her suit pocket, then swept a hand at the table. "Just put the tray here, Mel. And please bring in Mr. Ormiston's file."

"Sure."

She met Jake's gaze. Because she wanted to maintain as much distance from him as possible, she gestured toward one of the wing chairs. "Would you like something to drink?" she asked, settling onto the love seat.

"No, thanks."

"The tea's Siberian ginseng," Mel pointed out.

Despite the tenseness that gripped her, Nicole fought a smile at her assistant's expectant look. Not in any circumstance could she picture Jake Ford sipping tea out of a china cup.

"I'll pass."

With a shrug, Mel settled the tray holding her favorite china teapot and matching cup and saucer on the table.

"How about some coffee instead?" Mel asked. "We have several blends. Or maybe you'd prefer an espresso or latte?"

"Just the file."

"Sparkling water?" Mel persisted.

Jake raised a dark eyebrow. "The file."

"I'll bring it right in."

While Mel headed toward the door, Nicole picked up the teapot. She felt the intensity of Jake's gaze on her while she filled her cup.

"Siberian ginseng?" he asked. "That one of Sebastian's brews?"

"No, Mel blends all of our teas. He gets the ingredients from his uncle Zebulon, who cultivates fresh herbs as a hobby."

Jake leaned forward, propping his elbows on his thighs. "Tell me something. Do you know any normal people?"

She blinked. "Normal?"

"Somebody who doesn't know what the hell a biorhythm or yoga discipline is? One person who doesn't give a damn if their capillaries breathe because they're too busy loading their system with fried food and black coffee? Someone who can find a date on their own without paying to get fixed up?''

Raising the china cup to her mouth, Nicole forced herself to project an outward calm. She took pride in her work and her lifestyle, and she did not appreciate the man's cynical attitude. However much she'd like to smash her teacup over his head, she wouldn't do it.

"You, Sergeant," she said coolly. "From seeing the fast-food sacks in the back of your car, I'd say you're overly normal. Probably veering toward average. Perhaps even on the dull side."

The instant narrowing of his eyes gave her some small sense of satisfaction. It also reminded her of how irresistibly drawn she was to his intense, dark looks...and how intrigued she was by the man.

He sat back in the chair, raised a hand. "Look, I didn't mean—"

Whether he was about to apologize she would never know because Mel chose that moment to whisk back through the door.

"Need anything else, boss?" He gave her his usual warm smile while handing her Phillip Ormiston's file.

"Not right now. Thank you."

A faint beep sounded. Mel angled his left wrist, pushed a button on his watch. "I'll need to leave in fifteen minutes." He slid Jake a look before his gaze resettled on Nicole. "I could reschedule the appointment if you need me here."

"Nonsense," she stated. "Edna needs to see her doctor. In fact, why don't you leave now so you won't be rushed?"

"If you're sure."

"I'm sure."

"Leave the tray. I'll deal with it in the morning."

Jake waited until Mel closed the door behind him, then said, "My bet is your eager-as-a-puppy assistant is on the sunny side of twenty."

"He turns twenty-one next month," Nicole replied. "Mel's two semesters from getting a degree in marketing. He works here full-time and takes care of his mother—she has severe diabetes and arthritis. Her prognosis isn't good," Nicole added, feeling a tug of worry over the increasingly frail woman. "Mel has a lot of responsibility, but he never complains. He does a wonderful job and he isn't afraid of long hours. I consider the day he answered my ad for help one of the luckiest in my life."

"Well, there's a glowing recommendation."

"Trust me, Sergeant, Mel has earned every word."

Jake's gaze dropped to the file she'd placed on her lap. "The M.E. called this morning with a cause of death on Ormiston."

With the change of subject, her hands became so unsteady that she replaced the china cup on its saucer. "It wasn't a heart attack, was it?"

"No. Someone gave your client an injection that paralyzed his lungs. He basically suffocated to death."

"Poor Phillip." She spoke quietly, feeling the blood drain from her face when a dizzying realization set in. "It wasn't something in the muffins, then?"

Jake angled his head. "They're at our lab for analysis. But, no, the M.E. doesn't think the muffins had anything to do with Ormiston's death. Even if they did, the bakery verifies your story. Mel called and placed the order, had the muffins delivered to Ormiston's office."

She nodded slowly. "That doesn't mean I didn't inject Phillip with whatever it was that killed him."

One corner of Jake's mouth lifted. "Here's a tip. Don't point out things like that to a homicide cop."

She gave him a thin smile. "I'm sure you've already thought of that."

"Everyone's a potential suspect, until I can prove them

innocent. In fact, why don't you tell me where you were yesterday afternoon so we can get that out of the way?"

Nicole shifted on the love seat's cushions. Logically, she understood why Jake had to ask the question. Still, that didn't stop a little ball of discomfort from wedging in her stomach.

"I attended a benefit luncheon at the Overholser Mansion," she began. "After that, I drove downtown and met with my attorney about the prospect of franchising my company."

"Met with him until when?"

"About four. I drove to my decorator's shop where I spent an hour or so selecting fabric for drapes I'm having done."

"Then?"

"I came back here, worked out at Sebastian's and drove to Phillip's house. You know the rest."

Jake's gaze returned to the file in her lap. "I need the names of the women you fixed Ormiston up with."

When she hesitated, he added, "I can have a subpoena here within the hour if you have a problem giving me the information."

"No." She slicked her tongue over her lips. "It's just that I promise my clients privacy. Confidentiality."

"You promised that to Ormiston, too. If someone he met through this dating service killed him, they gave up all right to privacy."

"Yes." She stared at the fingers she'd linked together. "It's my company's responsibility to make matchmaking a safe process. We do an intensive screen on all of our clients. Conduct background checks. Credit history. Psychological and personality tests. What if we missed something?"

"They run checks on potential cops, too," Jake pointed out. "Bad ones sometimes still make it into the academy.

When they do, we go after them and toss them out. That's all you can do.''

For some inexplicable reason, she found it comforting he'd put that aspect of their careers on the same level. ''I'll have copies of everything run for you,'' she said, handing the file across the table. ''Mel's leaving and I have a meeting in an hour. Can I deliver the copies to you this evening?''

''I'll be tied up.''

She tried to ignore an instant flare of disappointment. ''You have a date?''

''Yeah, with a low-life snitch who swears he'll deliver the witness to a drive-by shooting.'' Jake paused, then sent a sideways look at her closed door. ''Speaking of Mel, I need the name and address of all your employees who had anything to do with Ormiston.''

Restless, Nicole rose, wrapped her arms around her waist and began to pace. ''I hate to think one of my employees might have had something to do with Phillip's murder.''

''I have to look at everyone.''

Although she kept her gaze ahead of her, she sensed it when Jake stood, felt him tracking her progress from one wall to the other as he spoke.

''Did Ormiston's contract with Meet Your Match cover services from any other business in this building?''

''No. All the companies have different owners. We make referrals to one another. And give one another's clients a discount.''

''You referred Ormiston to Sebastian's?''

''Yes. The referral will be noted in his file.''

She heard the ruffle of paper when Jake opened the file. ''Is this list of ten women everyone you matched him up with?''

''It should be.'' Turning, she walked across the office to stand by Jake. ''Yes,'' she said after scanning the list. ''Phillip went out with all ten on his match list. The checks beside each name are the number of times he went out with each.''

"Three being the highest number.''

"As I told you, Phillip was hard to please.''

Jake closed the file. "I have to talk to all these women. I need a rundown on their backgrounds, along with addresses, phone numbers.''

"Do you want copies of their videos, too?''

"Videos?''

"We make videos of our clients where they talk about their interests—what they like to do, where they like to go. Other clients can watch the tape, find out what that person likes up front, get an idea of their personality. If they still want to meet, we arrange it.''

"Then chemistry comes into play,'' Jake observed, his gaze settling on her mouth. "That's what this business is about, isn't it? Chemistry.''

"No,'' she countered, while her stomach jittered. "The most important thing is not to let oneself get carried away by emotion.'' *Like I did,* she thought. "That's why we do the background checks, credit investigations, personality profiles. This business isn't just about dating. It's also about finding your perfect match. To do that, it's vital to know as much as possible about a person you might become involved with.''

"Doesn't all that put a damper on finding out pleasant surprises along the way?''

"It also prevents *unpleasant* ones.'' If she'd known the truth about Cole Champion, she'd never have married him and saved herself a lot of heartache.

Jake raised a shoulder. "I want copies of the videos, too.''

Nicole walked to her desk, jotted a note. When she turned, she discovered he'd moved and was standing inches behind her. Knots of unease bunched across her shoulders. For the second time in her life she felt off balance with a man. She knew full well the dangers of the whirlwind of sensation that erupted inside her whenever Jake Ford got close.

"Here's my card," he said. "Call me when the copies are ready."

"All right."

"If you think of anything else about Ormiston, or the women he went out with, call me. Day or night."

When his fingertip brushed hers, she felt a thudding in the pit of her stomach. She knew it was useless to try to deny the pull that existed between her and Jake. She also knew firsthand that, over time, the sharp edge of attraction would dull, the need that swirled inside her would fade, then disappear.

She'd been young and foolish when she'd met Cole, but she was older now and wiser. Far wiser. She would never again allow herself to be seduced by desire that erased all logic. She had convinced herself long ago that when she found the as-yet-faceless man she thought of as her soul mate, she would feel the steadiness, the slow, sweet beginning that promised a forever. She would not let her emotions detour her from that goal. She would find him. Eventually, she would find him.

In the meantime, she wasn't going to repeat her same mistakes with another man who was all wrong for her.

"Before you leave, we should talk about the lady doctor," she said, forcing a smile as she looked up into Jake's eyes.

"Did she go out with Ormiston, too?"

"No. She should go out with you. I can have a copy of her video made for you."

Still holding the file folder, he stared down at her, his mouth thinning. "You don't give up easily, do you?"

"I don't give up. Period."

"You need to ease up where I'm concerned, Taylor. I've got no interest in hooking up with *any* woman. Not now. Not ever. No interest at all."

"No interest in women..." Her forehead furrowed as she slid his business card into her pocket. "Are you trying to tell me you're gay?"

"Hell no!"

Her eyes widened when his words bounced off the ceiling. "I understand now." She gave his forearm an encouraging squeeze. "It's nothing to be ashamed of, Jake. Your condition is probably treatable."

He angled his chin. "My *condition?*"

"Several products are known to improve the sex drive. Some are all-natural. There are also practices you can engage in that..." Her voice drifted off as incredulity blanked his face.

His eyes sparked. Swearing a crude oath, he tossed the file on her desk, clamped his hands on her shoulders and backed her against the nearest wall.

"Jake, I—" The rest of her thought was forgotten when he layered his body against hers, molding her spine against the wall, trapping her. With her heels on, they were eye-to-eye, chest-to-chest, pelvis-to-pelvis.

"*Improve* my sex drive," he muttered, his mouth hovering over hers.

"You said...you're not interested..." The feel of his body against hers had her stunned mind going hazy at the edges.

"Forget the biorhythm check," he said, his breath sliding like silk against her lips. "Herbal teas. Beaming me into a parallel universe. I'll just get back on track with *this.*"

"This?" she asked weakly when she saw something akin to the light of battle glinting in his eyes.

"This."

His lips grazed hers while heat pulsed between them. Slowly, gently, the tip of his tongue traced her mouth, outlining her lips with exquisite, excruciating care.

Her eyes fluttered shut; her heart pounded in her ears, her

egs trembled. Already she could feel need building inside her, was aware of the solid ridge of male flesh that pressed against her belly.

When his mouth claimed hers, desire shot like a bullet through her, stirring the pulse deep inside her to life. Her lips yielded beneath his, parted, then matched the urgent demand in his kiss.

One of his hands settled at her waist, the other cupped the side of her throat. His thumb slid beneath the neckline of her jacket to stroke the hollow beneath her collarbone. On a soft moan, she plunged into the mindless whirl of her senses and allowed herself to feel. Just feel. He was far from the first man to kiss her, but for the first time in her life, she understood that one kiss could helplessly seduce.

Her breasts rose and fell against his chest as her lungs strained for air that had become too thick to breathe. Her taut nipples strained against her silk bra, aching for his touch. She had forgotten what it was like when a man's taste invaded her system, when she thirsted for only him.

Just him.

Jake made her remember. The world narrowed and all that existed was the hot press of his mouth against hers, the weight of his body molding against every inch of hers. Nothing. Nothing else mattered; she wanted no other man, only him.

Some dim spark of sanity flickered in her brain, sending the alarm that she teetered on the edge of a treacherous cliff.

When he murmured her name, angled his head and deepened the kiss, the alarm faded beneath a rushing tidal wave of need.

She breathed his name on a ragged sigh. Her hands slid up, feeling the hardness of muscle and tension in his shoulders before her fingers linked around the back of his neck. She would jump off a cliff with this man anytime.

When he shoved himself back, her skin was damp from

the heat that burned between them. Lungs heaving, she leaned against the wall, keeping her eyes closed, as if she could somehow hold what they'd shared inside her.

"Look at me." His voice was gruff, as were the hands that cupped her face. "Nicole, look at me."

She forced her eyes open, saw the heated flush in his skin, the raw emotion in the dark eyes that lasered into hers.

"I don't want to go out with your damn doctor. I sure as hell don't need help with my sex drive. Have you got that?"

She could barely make sense of his husky words over the thunder of her heart. "Uh... No. I... Yes."

"Good. Now, stay the hell out of my way."

On that, he turned and stalked out the door just as his pager started beeping.

Chapter 4

Fifteen minutes later, Jake's blood was still churning.

With the warrant in his pocket for Phillip Ormiston's gym locker that had just been delivered by a patrol cop, Jake retraced his steps back across the building's pink-marbled lobby. He'd done a hell of a lot of stupid things in his life, but kissing Nicole Taylor topped the list.

"Idiot," he muttered as he stalked into an empty elevator.

Never before—not even with Annie—had he been so aware of a woman from the moment he met her. In truth, he'd been aware of Nicole Taylor the instant he *saw* her at Bill and Whitney's wedding.

Dammit, he'd spent more than a week trying to banish the woman from his thoughts. She was still there, clinging like a silk-covered burr. Always in the past he'd been able to shift his work to the forefront, concentrate on the job. Even the intricacies of a homicide investigation couldn't keep thoughts of Nicole at bay.

Now, to make matters worse, he had the rich, hot, potent taste of her whipping through his system.

He stepped off the elevator onto the third floor, his brisk footsteps ricocheting like gunfire off the hallway's granite tiles. *Help with his sex drive!* The thought had him biting back a curse. Hell, yes, he needed help! He had done what he'd sworn he wouldn't do—he'd lost his grip on control. It had taken all of his willpower not to drag her onto the plush office carpet, rip off her clothes and take her there. *Right there.*

He had wanted her with a savageness that stunned him.

"Last thing I need," he muttered as he jerked open one of the double doors with Sebastian's artfully etched into the glass. He stopped short when a redhead sauntered out, wearing tiny bands of spandex that strategically crisscrossed impressive curves. Hiking the strap of a leather tote higher on her shoulder, she cast him a look, then her glossed mouth curved. "Looking for someone, handsome?"

"Yeah."

"Will I do?"

An image shot into his head of Nicole, dressed in a similar eye-popping outfit that would give every man in the gym a preview of the lush curves that minutes ago had been pressed against his own body. The thought darkened his already black mood.

The glower he sent the redhead had her scooting down the hallway.

His teeth grinding hard enough to crack fillings, Jake walked into an airy reception area where the sweet scent of fresh flowers mingled with that of earthy workouts.

A trim, twentyish blonde dressed in a pink leotard sat behind a desk fashioned from illuminated glass blocks. Her eye shadow and lipstick matched her leotard. She brought to mind a cloud of billowing pink cotton candy. "Help you?" she said.

Shoving back his coat flap to reveal his badge, Jake identified himself. "I need to see your boss."

"We already have a cop here. He's waiting in the men's locker room."

"I know, I sent him. I need to see Sebastian Peck."

She swiveled toward a keyboard; fingers with nails painted to match her frothy pink leotard skimmed the keys. "Sebastian is engaged right now, Sergeant Ford," she said, eyeing the computer's monitor. "Can one of his associates help you?"

"No. I need to see Peck."

"I'm sorry, he doesn't like us to disturb—"

"I've got a warrant to serve," Jake stated. "We can do this the easy way, or the hard way, it's up to you. If you don't want to get hauled in for interfering with official process, you'll get this show on the road. *Now.*"

"Interfering?" Her mouth trembled, and her eyes welled with tears. "I...I can page a trainer...to...to take you to Sebastian."

Jake took a deep breath. It wasn't the blonde's fault that he was so churned up he wanted to rip her desk apart, one glass block at a time. "Just tell me where Peck is. I'll find him."

"He's...playing racquetball." As she spoke, a man wearing a dark suit and carrying a gym bag strode through the door.

Jake watched while the man jotted his name and the time on the clipboard positioned on one corner of the desk. That done, he turned and disappeared through a set of doors behind the desk.

Jake looked back at the blonde. "Are the racquetball courts through there?"

"Yes. I can have a trainer—"

"Forget it." He skirted the desk, shouldered open the doors and was immediately hit with a torrent of light, bouncy music.

He couldn't exactly call Sebastian's a gym, Jake acknowledged, thinking of the room at the police training center where cops pumped weights and pummeled punching bags amid the acrid stench of sweat. *Health palace,* maybe, he mused, studying the impressive array of exercise equipment that stretched around the spacious, brightly lit room.

Judging by the look and age of the clientele using that equipment, Jake deduced that a number were harried executives who'd abandoned their offices to come here and sweat out their stress. Not all looked like executives, though. On his left, a spandex-clad woman with a body as well-toned as a model's jogged on a treadmill. Beside her, a silver-haired woman with chunky thighs and diamond studs the size of gumdrops in her ears pedaled an exercise bike. Across the room, a Schwarzenegger look-alike reclined on a slant board before a mirrored wall. Using free weights, Mr. Muscle did a set of arm curls that made his biceps bulge like a balloon taking on a shot of helium.

"Holy…"

Shaking his head, Jake flagged down a trainer wearing a T-shirt with the gym's logo. The trainer escorted Jake past a blue-tiled swimming pool where a water aerobics session was in full swing. After stepping through another set of doors, the trainer pointed to one of the enclosed, glass-fronted racquetball courts. "'Bastian's the big dude," the trainer said before stepping back through the doors.

More like huge, Jake decided, watching Sebastian Peck slice the air with a racket that sent a ball careering toward a concrete wall. The guy had to be at least six foot five—a hulk in a tight white muscle shirt and shorts that contrasted with bronzed shoulders and thighs that looked a little harder than cinder blocks. The mountainous build, along with the long blond mane held back with a black sweatband, had the term *Nordic warrior* popping into Jake's brain. He fervently hoped he wouldn't someday be faced with the prospect of physically taking down *this* mountain.

Peck's opponent, a tall, lean man with dark hair graying at the temples and sweat pouring down his face, managed to avoid the ball whizzing toward his nose. He swung his racket; when it connected with the target, Jake could hear his strangled grunt coming through the glass. With the smash and echo of the ball, the smell of heated sweat and the sound of labored breathing around him, Jake spent the next few minutes observing Sebastian Peck.

Despite his bulk, the man's movements were smooth, precise and exact. Jake figured it would take little effort for Peck to scale the seven-foot brick wall that surrounded the gated community where Ormiston lived. And if Peck didn't feel like climbing the wall, he could tear it apart with his bare hands.

Game ended, the players pounded each other on the shoulder, shook hands. The dark-haired man grabbed a gym bag, opened the door to the court and passed by Jake while chugging water from a plastic bottle in deep, greedy gulps.

Jake pursed his lips, thinking again of the minute puncture the M.E. had found on Phillip Ormiston's neck. The man had been scheduled to play racquetball with Sebastian Peck the night someone had plunged a needle into him. That in itself didn't make Peck a suspect, but it did put his name on the list of people Ormiston would let get close.

Jake stepped to the door of the court where the gym owner was swilling an orange liquid out of a plastic bottle. "Nice backhand."

Lowering the bottle, Peck sent a winner's grin across the court. "Thanks. Are you my next game?"

Jake raised a brow at the trace of a Swedish accent that would doubtless reduce some females to bubbling pools of wanting. "No, but you and I have business."

As he crossed toward Jake, Peck pulled the black sweatband away from his blond mane. "What sort of business?"

Jake took in the chiseled face, sharp cheekbones and gray

eyes that looked almost silver and contained a coldness that put his cop's radar on alert.

"I'm Sergeant Jake Ford." When he swept back the flap of his coat, Peck's grin dimmed. "I have a warrant to search Phillip Ormiston's locker."

"It's about time you got here," Peck said as he accepted the warrant from Jake. "That cop you've got milling around the men's locker room is making some of my clients nervous."

"Really?" Jake asked pleasantly. "Might be interesting to find out why."

"I'll tell you why," Peck said, holding up a hand with fingers that looked like rods of iron. "People come here to get away from stress. Most cops emanate an aura of stress and cynicism that transfers to those around them."

"I'll try to hold my emanations to a minimum while I'm here."

When the hunk angled his head, blond hair skimmed his muscled shoulders. "Nicole mentioned she met a cop who had negative biorhythms. That would be you, right?"

Jake's thoughts skimmed to Nicole, to the kiss that had been all steam heat and exploding passion. He tightened his jaw. "This visit isn't about me, Peck. It's official."

Peck glanced at the warrant, then remet Jake's gaze. "Technically, you don't need this to look in Ormiston's locker."

Jake propped a hand beside his holstered Glock. "Is that so?"

"Only Ormiston's name is on the locker. No one else has legal access to it. Dead people have no reasonable expectation of privacy."

Jake narrowed his eyes. "You a lawyer?"

"No, I used to date one." Peck's mouth curved. "Monique is a master of the Eastern philosophy, *feng shui*. I always listened to what she had to say."

"I'll bet you did."

Jake had to admit that Peck had made a valid point about the warrant. And it told him there was more than just empty space beneath all that blond hair. Technically, Jake didn't need a warrant to open Ormiston's locker. But technicalities sometimes blurred when defense attorneys got hold of them. For all Jake knew, someone—maybe even the killer—could have given Ormiston something to stash in the locker that could be used as evidence. If that was the case, and the police didn't have a warrant before opening the locker, a defense attorney could argue that his client *did* have a reasonable expectation to privacy, so the cops violated his client's rights because they didn't have the proper piece of paper. If a judge agreed, the prosecution could find itself up to its neck in alligators.

"Having a warrant just ties everything up into a nice, neat package," Jake commented.

"I assume the reason you've got a cop watching that locker, and the fact that you went to the trouble to get a warrant, is because Ormiston was murdered."

"You don't need to assume anything. It's a fact."

"I *knew* he didn't die of a heart attack."

"Why's that?"

"Too healthy. Ormiston worked out on a regular basis, watched what he ate. Mostly, he was in alignment."

Jake resisted the urge to roll his eyes. "Yeah, well, not in alignment enough to keep himself from getting murdered. I understand he was scheduled to play racquetball with you yesterday evening."

"That's right." Peck raised his plastic bottle, chugged more of the orange liquid. "He didn't show."

"Did you try to track him down and find out why?"

"No."

"Why not?"

"It's common for a client to miss an appointment. Things

come up. Sometimes an evening spent lying on the couch sounds better than a hard workout.'' He shrugged. ''I prefer it when a client calls to cancel so I can shift my schedule. But I don't dwell on it if they don't.''

Jake dug the key ring he'd found in Ormiston's office out of his suit coat. ''Let's have a look at what's inside locker number seventy.''

''Sure. This way.''

Jake followed the Norse god out the door and past the swimming pool where the water aerobics class was breaking up.

''You play racquetball?'' Peck asked over his shoulder as he and Jake skirted the workout gallery's perimeter.

''When I get time.'' Over the sound of clanking weights and huffing lungs, Jake heard a giggle. Shifting his gaze, he saw a slinky brunette clad in a turquoise leotard and matching headband, white socks slouched artfully around her ankles, while she clutched what looked to be a five-pound weight in each manicured hand. The giggle was for the benefit of the tall, muscled trainer who rested his palms low on her belly and back to correct her posture for a lift.

''We should schedule a game.'' Peck paused at the entrance to a brightly lit hallway. ''That could be the problem with your biorhythms. I sense you don't balance relaxation and work well.''

The earnestness in Peck's expression told Jake he was absolutely serious. ''It's hard to work Homicide and keep things balanced. People don't exactly make a point to get killed weekdays between eight and five.''

''Even more reason for you to strive for harmony.'' Peck stepped into the hallway, then turned into a locker room with rows of polished wood lockers, benches and dove-gray wall-to-wall carpet.

Jake had never before been in a men's locker room that smelled like roses.

A uniformed cop with a flat stare sat on one of the wood benches in front of a row of lockers. His grizzly-bear girth was a sharp contrast to the two towel-draped men with washboard-flat stomachs who stood in front of open lockers several feet away.

"How's it going, Andrews?"

"Fine, Sarge," the cop said, rising off the bench.

Jake nodded toward the locker with the number seventy engraved on a small brass disk. "Anything going on?"

"Not a thing."

Jake reached into his coat's inside pocket, pulled out a pair of latex gloves and eased them on. "Let's see what we can find." Stepping forward, he slid the key into the lock and swung open the door.

"One pair of shoes," Peck said, peering across Jake's shoulder.

"And an envelope." Jake's gloved fingers plucked the envelope from beneath one of the shoes. He lifted the unsealed flap, pulled out what was obviously a newspaper clipping. "An obituary," he added, scanning the column. He looked up at Peck. "Did you know Eddie Denson?"

Something flashed in Peck's eyes. "He was a college kid who worked out here. He died in a car wreck a couple weeks ago."

Jake cocked his head. "How does a college kid afford a membership to this place?"

"His parents belong. They have a family membership."

Jake shifted his gaze to the end of the obituary, saw that Denson's service had been handled by one of Ormiston's funeral homes. Why, Jake wondered as he slid the envelope and clipping into his coat pocket, had Ormiston hung on to *this* obituary?

Jake turned back toward the locker. He picked up a shoe, shook it, slid his gloved fingers into the toe, making sure nothing was hidden inside. He repeated the process with the second shoe, then looked back at Andrews. "Bag these and log them into the property room."

"You got it, Sarge."

"Looks like your visit was a waste of time," Peck observed.

Jake peeled off his gloves. "Not so. I have to interview every suspect."

Peck's gray eyes narrowed. "Am I a suspect?"

"Ormiston trusted his killer enough to let him or her get close. Everybody who falls into that category is a suspect, until I can prove they didn't do it. You're on the list."

While Andrews loaded Ormiston's shoes into a paper bag, Jake leaned a shoulder against a locker door. "How long had Ormiston been a member here?"

"About six months. I'd have to check his file to get an exact date."

"Do that. Did he miss other racquetball games he had scheduled with you?"

"No." Peck crossed his arms over his massive chest. "We play…played once or twice a week. He'd always shown, until last night."

"Which didn't concern you."

"I have to admit I was relieved."

"Why's that?"

"Lately, Ormiston had a lot of complaints."

Jake sent him a thin smile. "I thought he was in alignment."

"I said *mostly* in alignment. His mind and spirit had moved out of synch. His aura had become muddy."

Out of the corner of his eye, Jake saw Andrews's brows shoot up his forehead. Jake held back a sigh. How much better could this get? "What did Ormiston complain about?"

"Two things. Nicole, and an investment that went sour."

Jake kept his expression neutral. ''What about Miss Taylor?''

''He had yet to find a suitable mate through her agency. He said several times that Nicole wasn't trying hard enough. I know the opposite is true. I told Ormiston that. No one is more dedicated to making her clients happy than Nicole.''

''Did you tell Miss Taylor about Ormiston's complaint?''

''Yes. She had a right to know he was bad-mouthing her and her company. He could have caused her to lose clients and damaged her professional reputation.''

''What was her reaction when you told her?''

''She was naturally upset.''

Jake had worked Homicide long enough to know that killing someone because they'd bad-mouthed your livelihood was not that far-fetched a reason. After some of the bizarre and petty motives he'd seen, he was willing to accept almost anything within some very wide bounds.

Still, according to Nicole, Ormiston had second thoughts and phoned her office the day before he died to tell her he was renewing his contract. Because of that call, she'd had Mel Hall order the basket of muffins. Something had obviously changed Ormiston's mind about the service she offered. Jake needed to find out what that something was.

''What do you know about Ormiston's investment that went sour?'' Jake asked.

''Just that he'd made one. He complained he'd lost a lot of money, but he didn't say how.''

''And you didn't ask?''

''None of my business.''

Jake made a mental note to call Ormiston's son to see if he knew anything about the investment.

''Ever overhear Ormiston argue with anyone?'' Jake asked. ''Ever *hear* about him arguing with anyone?''

''Nothing comes to mind.'' Instantly, Peck slid his gaze

down the length of the locker room to the two men who had abandoned their towels in favor of street clothes.

He knows something, Jake thought. "If you think of anything, call me." He pulled a business card out of his pocket and handed it to the Swede.

Jake gave a nod to Andrews when the uniformed cop walked away, carrying the brown paper bag. Jake looked back at Peck. "I noticed when I got here that one of your clients logged himself in at the front desk. That standard procedure?"

"Yes."

"Do people sign out before they leave, too?"

"Yes. The receptionist enters the data into the computer. We can go to each client's file and see how often they're here, and how long they work out during each visit."

"How about your employees?"

"They punch a time clock when they arrive and leave."

"I need a copy of all your logs for the past week, through closing time last night." Part of Nicole's alibi was that she had worked out at Sebastian's the previous evening. Jake acknowledged he wasn't questioning that alibi—his cop's sixth sense told him she had nothing to do with Ormiston's murder. It was the man who wanted to make sure the alibi was airtight. The why of that was something he didn't care to examine too closely.

"Anything else, Sergeant?"

Jake got the feeling Peck was itching to get the interview over with. "Is there a back door to this place? A way to get out where you don't have to pass by the receptionist?"

"There's an emergency exit at the back of the gym. An alarm goes off when it opens."

"Any other door?"

"One in my office," Peck said after a slight hesitation. "It opens onto the hallway."

"So you can come and go without anybody keeping tabs on you."

Peck's mouth tightened. "That's right. This is my place. I come and go as I please."

"Where were you yesterday between noon and closing time?"

"Here."

"Did you use the door off your office at any time yesterday to come and go as you please?"

"I went out that way at closing time."

"Anybody see you leave?"

"Not that I remember."

Jake pursed his lips. "You got any problem with me hanging around here awhile to talk to the trainers on duty, some of the customers?"

One of Peck's massive hands fisted against his thigh. "As long as you're discreet. I don't want my staff or my clients upset."

"They won't be, unless they upset me first."

Peck's eyes narrowed on Jake's face, measured. "You should take Nicole's advice and let me chart your biorhythms," he said finally. "She's good at body language."

Jake thought about how good her body had felt crushed against his. About how her mouth had opened beneath his, inviting him in. The lady was good at body language, all right.

And a definite threat to his peace of mind.

Ten hours, Nicole thought as the Jaguar's headlights licked the curb along the dark, unfamiliar street while Mozart played from the CD. Ten hours since Jake pressed his body against hers and kissed her senseless. Ten hours and she still had to make a conscious effort to pump air in and out of her lungs whenever she thought about that kiss.

Which had been about every five minutes since he'd stalked out of her office.

The woman in her had wanted to curl up on the love seat and savor the liquefying pleasure of that kiss. The business owner had patted the loose tendrils back into her French twist, smoothed the jacket of her red suit, then left to attend the first of a series of meetings.

When she returned late in the afternoon, one of the clerks had finished copying the files and videotapes Jake needed for his investigation. After checking the number on the business card he'd given her, Nicole had left a message on his voice mail. An hour later, a uniformed officer arrived and picked up the copies.

Nicole knew it was best Jake hadn't run that errand himself. She was realistic enough to admit that if he had walked into her office again, she would want to repeat that kiss.

Just the thought was dangerous. As was the knowledge that her attraction to Jake Ford was not something she could fight for long, not even something she could manage, but rather an elemental force that could easily overwhelm her.

"Not going to happen," she murmured as the Jaguar crept along the street that ran straight as a ruler past well-tended homes illuminated by generous spills from porch lanterns and yard lights. Passion alone was not to be trusted. She knew that better than most. When Cole Champion walked into her life, emotion had engulfed her, overwhelmed her, swept her away. It had been the first time she had offered her heart to a man.

And the last.

She was far more savvy than she'd been at twenty—a woman tended to fortify her defenses when she came home and found her husband buck naked on the dining room table with some floozy. Devastated, Nicole had turned a deaf ear to Cole's pleas for forgiveness, erected a barrier around her scarred heart and resolved that no man would ever cost her so dearly again.

No man, she reminded herself when the image of Jake's handsome face flashed through her mind. Just because he was gorgeous…and his kisses left her dizzy and dazed, she wasn't going to let him rock her boat. In truth, she wanted the same thing for herself that her clients wanted—to find her perfect match, her soul mate. She intended to do that by listening to her head, not her heart.

She would *know* when she found the right man. Her soul mate. Until then, she intended to put all her energies, all her emotions into making her business a success.

That was why she had just sat through a dull, sedate dinner with a potential male client. That was why, instead of going home, she was driving down this dark street, searching for the address she'd gotten from DeSoto Villanova's file. DeSoto, a client, had dropped by her office earlier that day and left his solid gold pen on her coffee table. She'd noticed the pen while Jake was there, slipped it into her suit pocket where she'd forgotten about it until hours later.

Keeping one eye on the street, Nicole flipped on the interior map light, angling the card on which she'd jotted DeSoto's address…1804. Her lips curved when she spotted the number on a two-story brownstone, its lower floor bulging into large bay windows.

The driveway was empty; no lights glowed from inside. Nicole hadn't expected DeSoto to be at home since he had a date for the evening with one of the women on his match list. Nicole fervently hoped tonight's encounter went well. DeSoto was a lot like Phillip Ormiston in that he had yet to find a compatible partner in the months he'd been a client. Yet, DeSoto wasn't in the least bit dissatisfied. In fact, he'd signed a renewal contract just that morning, using his gold pen.

Pulling into the driveway, Nicole shut off the Jaguar's

purring engine, then retrieved the envelope from her purse in which she'd sealed the pen with a note. She planned to leave the envelope in the mailbox, then phone a message to DeSoto's answering machine to tell him where she'd left the pen.

Sliding out of the car, she skirted its hood, her high heels clicking smartly up the driveway. The full moon that skimmed in and out of fat gray clouds rendered the front walk and flower bed in subdued shades of gray, with occasional patches of white. Those patches gave a ghostly tint to the sea of pale pansies that lapped the edges of large ornamental rocks.

Nicole climbed the stairs to the porch. On one side of the front door a carriage light illuminated the brass mailbox. The lid on the box squeaked a thready protest when she lifted it and dropped the envelope inside. Her fingers were still grasping the lid when the porch light snapped off. Her heart made a beeline for her throat and she stood frozen in pitch dark, listening to the sound of her own racing heart.

The lid of the mailbox closed with an eerie groan when she released it, adding to the jangling in her nerves.

"Get a grip," she whispered. Her hand crept to her throat while she stood in the oozing shadows, waiting for her eyes to adjust to the dark. It did little good to remind herself that lightbulbs burned out all the time.

The next instant, the front door swung inward and her breath sucked in on a gasp. A tall, black-clad figure rushed from the house, slamming into her. She stumbled backward, her high heels nearly sliding out from under her while slippery fingers of fear prickled her skin.

Before she'd regained her balance, a fist slammed into her temple. Jagged lights shot behind her eyes. A scream tore up her throat as she staggered sideways, then toppled off the porch.

The air *whooshed* out of her lungs; pain exploded as her

head smashed against one of the ornamental rocks she'd admired moments earlier. Stomach roiling, she tried to push up, got as far as her hands and knees. Her vision doubled, tripled, then blacked out completely as she crumpled onto the pansies.

Jake stood in the velvet-draped parlor of the Ormiston Funeral Home amid sedate upholstered sofas, soft lighting and quiet classical music. The heavy scent of roses perfumed the air, reminding him of the men's locker room at Sebastian's.

Across the parlor near the front entrance, Bradley Zucksworth, a short, roly-poly man wearing a black suit and a grim expression, talked softly with a woman dabbing at her eyes with a wad of tissues. After searching Ormiston's office that morning, Jake had verified Zucksworth's alibi that he was present at an all-day seminar when someone deep-sixed his boss.

Jake scrubbed a hand over his face. After he left Sebastian's, he'd spent the rest of the afternoon and evening running background checks, then poring over the files and watching the videos on the women whose names he'd gotten from Meet Your Match. Nothing hinky about any of the ten women Ormiston met through the dating service had jumped out at him. Still, he knew that didn't mean anything—he'd booked people for murder who, on the surface, appeared to be saintlike. He figured it was safe to assume that all the women on Ormiston's match list would have been able to get close enough to slide a needle into his neck. All of them were suspects and he'd set up appointments to interview them, starting first thing in the morning.

Jake glanced at his watch, saw it was nearly nine. His snitch, Julio Lira, had called earlier and assured him that the drive-by shooter's girlfriend would be at a bar called Angel's tonight around ten o'clock. Jake planned to be there, too.

He blew out a breath. Whitney still had two days to go on her honeymoon, he had too much work and not enough time to do it in. Still, he had a chance tonight to get closer to nailing Ramon Cárdenas for the murder of a seven-year-old boy, and Jake intended to take that step.

Across the parlor, Bradley Zucksworth escorted the weeping woman to the towering wood front door. After locking the door behind her, he turned and headed across the cushy maroon carpet.

"Sorry to keep you waiting, Sergeant. Some of the bereaved need more care than others."

"No problem." Reaching into the inside pocket of his suit coat, Jake pulled out the obituary on Eddie Denson and handed it to the man. "I found that in your boss's locker at his health club. Can you tell me anything about Denson?"

"Denson, Denson." Zucksworth lifted the reading glasses that dangled from a gold chain around his neck and jabbed them on. "Ah, yes," he said, peering at the obituary. "The car wreck on I-40. His parents were both quite aggrieved."

"Any idea why your boss had the kid's obit in his locker?"

"I remember Phillip saying something…" Zucksworth tapped a fingertip against his pursed lips. "Phillip met with the family when they arranged the service. I don't know what was said during that meeting, but immediately after, Phillip went to the embalming room and viewed the body. That was something he rarely did." Zucksworth peered over his glasses at Jake. "It's not the most enjoyable experience, but I imagine you know that."

"Yeah. Go on."

"Phillip told me that Denson, who was barely twenty, had extraordinary bulk—Phillip called it the 'Mr. Universe' syndrome. His jaw muscles also had a somewhat bloated appearance. Both physical traits are a sign of steroid usage."

"Steroids," Jake said thoughtfully when Zucksworth returned the obituary.

"Which are legal if one has a prescription."

"And illegal without one."

"Certainly."

"Did Ormiston say anything else about the Denson kid?"

"No, that was all."

Jake nodded. "Did your boss mention he'd made an investment that went sour? One that cost him a lot of money?"

"I don't believe so...."

Zucksworth's voice trailed off when Jake's cell phone rang. Unclipping the phone off his belt, he flipped it open. "Ford."

"Jake... I..."

Nicole. His scalp prickled at the fear in her voice. "Nicole, what's wrong?"

"He...hit me," she began, panic welling in her every word. "I couldn't..."

"Are you hurt?"

"I...fell...my head."

Jake shoved back the fear for her that shot through him. Not until that instant had he known that some small part of her had managed to slip under his skin.

"Are you at home?" As he spoke, Jake clamped a hand on Zucksworth's arm and dragged the man toward the door.

"No, at...DeSoto's. In my...car."

"DeSoto Villanova?" Jake pictured the anger he'd seen in the Latino's eyes that morning when the man stalked onto the elevator after leaving Nicole's office.

"Yes."

Jake tightened his jaw when Zucksworth fumbled his key ring. When he finally twisted a key in the lock, Jake shoved open the door. His gait ate up the sidewalk as he rushed toward his cruiser, which he'd parked at the curb. "Is Villanova there?"

"Don't…know. Door's open. The house…is dark. I…don't want to go in."

"Don't go in." Jake pulled open the cruiser's door, slid behind the wheel and started the engine. "Stay in your car. Are the doors locked?"

"Yes."

"What's the address?"

"I…can't…remember…." She responded slowly, as if she were testing each word as she spoke it. "I see two of…everything. My…head…hurts."

Concussion, he thought. "Sit tight. I'll find you."

He grabbed the microphone off the dash, radioed dispatch for an address on Villanova. The dispatcher came back with the information in less than forty-five seconds.

"Send a patrol unit to that address to check the welfare of an injured woman in a red Jaguar," he said. "Dispatch an ambulance there, too. I'm en route."

Jake jammed the cruiser into gear, then laid rubber while he gripped the phone. "Nicole, I'm on my way. A scout car may get there before me. Keep the doors locked until one of us shows."

"Can you…hurry?"

The thought of her being hurt, just the thought of it, iced his blood. "Like I've never hurried before."

A scout car and ambulance had reached Villanova's house by the time Jake pulled beside the curb. The fact that a uniformed officer was in the process of wrapping yellow crime scene tape from tree to tree gave Jake his first inkling that more than Nicole's assault was involved.

"What have we got?" he asked a second cop with a clipboard.

"One female assault victim," the cop replied as he jotted Jake's name and rank on the crime scene log. "And one stiff."

Jake jolted. "Who the hell's dead?"

"Probably the homeowner. When my partner and I got here, we found a woman—Nicole Taylor—locked in her car. She took a blow to the head so she's disoriented. From what we could get out of her, she claims she was putting a gold pen in the mailbox when the porch light went out. The pen's there, by the way. Next thing she knows, the front door flies open, someone rushes out and smacks her upside the head. She falls off the porch, slams her head on a rock." The cop glanced over his shoulder at the ambulance. "Messed up the side of her face some."

Jake's heart stopped. "Define *some*."

"Cuts, bruises. Nothing permanent." The cop nodded toward the house. "The front door was standing open, so I checked inside while my partner saw to the woman. Found the dead guy lying in the living room. I backed out of the scene, notified dispatch. They advised you were en route."

Jake stared at the house, illuminated by patches of silver moonlight. "Any sign of a struggle? Forced entry?"

"None that I could see."

Just like Ormiston. Out of the corner of his eye, Jake saw the lab's van pull up. "Get more uniforms here, have them start a door-to-door. Maybe one of the neighbors saw something."

"You got it, Sarge."

Jake turned, headed toward the ambulance, its light bar flashing red and blue against the dark landscape.

His insides tightened when he got his first glimpse of Nicole. She lay still as death on a gurney, her eyes closed, the deep purple bruise on her right cheek a stark contrast to the white sheet on which she lay. She wore the same red suit she'd had on when he visited her office. Now the suit was streaked with dirt, the left sleeve ripped at the elbow.

"What's her condition?" he asked the EMT who was strapping a blood pressure cuff around her upper arm.

''Possible concussion,'' the EMT stated at the same time Nicole's eyes fluttered open.

Pain flickered across her face. ''Jake.''

Crouching beside the gurney, he forced a smile, fighting back the rage that was a hot ball in his throat. Someone had hurt her. He wanted to hurt that person. ''How you doing?''

''I...my head hurts.''

''I'll bet.'' Her speech wasn't slurred the way it had been on the phone. As far as he could tell, her pupils looked normal.

''I...shouldn't have...called you. After I...woke up and got to my car...I couldn't see good. I hit the redial on my cellular.'' She closed her eyes, as if just the effort of speaking hurt. ''I'd called you earlier about picking up...the copies you wanted—''

''So you got me when you hit redial.''

''Yes.''

''I'm a cop, Nicole. You're supposed to call me when something happens.'' He settled his palm over her hand. The trembling he felt in her fingers tightened his chest.

''You said...to stay...out of...your way. You said that...after...''

We kissed. ''Yeah.'' Without conscious thought, he linked his fingers with hers.

''I was...''

His heart constricted when a sob bubbled up her throat. ''You were what?''

''So scared.''

''You're safe now,'' he said softly.

She had stumbled on to the bodies of two of her clients in as many nights. In no way did Jake think coincidence had anything to do with that. If the dead man turned out to be Villanova, Jake would bet the title to his Harley that the M.E. would find a pinprick somewhere on the Latino.

The fact that both men had solid connections to Nicole

had Jake frowning. He suspected that if he analyzed his feelings for her, he would discover they went deeper than he cared to admit. So, he wouldn't analyze. He was a cop, investigating the deaths of two of her clients, one of whom had been murdered. He needed to keep his perspective.

He looked down at their joined hands, forced himself to let hers go. "Did you see who hit you?"

"It was…so dark. Too dark." She swallowed hard. "Maybe DeSoto knows who it was."

Problem was, DeSoto was probably dead.

The EMT gave Jake the sign they were ready to roll.

He looked at Nicole, resisted the urge to nudge back a wayward blond tendril from her cheek. "I need to get out of here so these guys can take you to get checked."

She touched a tentative hand to her cheek and winced. "I hate…hospitals. Not staying."

"You may run into a doctor who thinks different."

"I'm tougher. Don't like them…poking at me."

"You don't have to like it, just let them do it."

"Okay. Maybe." The smile she gave him was weak and didn't last. "Thanks."

Despite the ambulance's medicinal odor, Jake could smell her sexy scent. How the hell was he supposed to keep his perspective when all he wanted was to gather her close and ease her head onto his shoulder?

He wasn't going to do that, he told himself, even as he felt something move inside him, struggling against the lock he'd clamped on his feelings. He knew what it was like to find one special woman. He also knew what it was like to lose her. Never to be free from the dragging grief. To have pain boil through you like acid, eating at you on the inside.

He wouldn't let that happen again. *Couldn't* let it happen.

"Don't thank me. I'm just doing my job," he said, then climbed out of the ambulance and headed for the crime scene.

Chapter 5

Nicole lay in the hospital's emergency room, her entire body achy and sore. Although the painkiller the nurse had given her half an hour ago had eased the hammering behind her eyes, she now felt as if she had thick, sticky cobwebs in her brain. The drug had done nothing for the nausea rolling in her stomach. Nausea that swelled every time she thought about the dark, faceless man who'd rushed like a demon out of DeSoto Villanova's house.

She *thought* it was a man, anyway. When the body collided with hers, she'd had the instant impression of smashing into solid muscle. Felt the corded power behind the fist that slammed into her cheek. Yes, it must have been a man.

Still, she wasn't positive because the shadows that had oozed across the porch had concealed her attacker's features.

Her stomach churned with memories of the fear that had washed over her. Of the jagged pain that had exploded behind her eyes when her head smashed against the rock. Of the sick panic that her attacker might grab her and do God-knew-what.

In those terrifying seconds before she'd lost consciousness, she had wanted only one person: Jake.

I'm just doing my job.

His expression had been as remote and cool as his voice when he'd spoken those words before he climbed out of the ambulance. Yet, before that, while he'd crouched beside her, she had seen more than just the cop with a flat stare. She had glimpsed a man with intense concern swirling in his eyes. A concern that had filled her with a dangerously heady sensation. And when he'd twined his fingers with hers, she had felt the link between them deepen—she was sure about that. Just as she was sure something had stirred inside her, something she hadn't felt—hadn't *chosen* to feel—in a long time.

Something she didn't want to feel, not for a man she knew was so wrong for her.

Still, she couldn't deny it was Jake whom she had wanted during those terrifying seconds. Couldn't deny she was lying there this very instant, longing for a man whom logic told her she didn't really want. Not for the long run, anyway.

Not for *any* run, Nicole corrected herself when an alarm screeched in her brain.

Frowning, she assured herself the blow she'd suffered had done more than just make her head pound. It had addled her thinking, made her momentarily forget what had happened when she'd jumped into a relationship based on scalding heat and clawing lust. She'd rushed headlong into marriage with Cole Champion, and when the fire between them banked, she'd gotten her heart handed back to her, battered and scarred. She'd resolved then that she would never jump into *that* kind of fire again.

She wasn't in danger of doing that with Jake, she told herself. The reason her thoughts had arrowed to him during the attack mirrored what he'd said in the ambulance—he was a cop. Who better to long for when one's head had been smashed in?

She touched an unsteady fingertip to her right cheek and whimpered when pain knifed through her temple. After the requisite X rays, poking and prodding, a doctor had determined that nothing was broken and she'd suffered a slight concussion. In Nicole's opinion, there was nothing slight about it, considering the way everything from her neck up throbbed. But she was keeping that to herself. Even without her letting on how obscene the pain was when she'd arrived at the ER, the doctor had wanted to keep her for observation. She'd forced a few thin smiles, finally cajoled him into agreeing to send her home if she had someone to wake her every hour throughout the night. After a quick call using her cell phone, she'd assured the doctor that Kathy Key, her close friend who lived in the apartment next to hers, was more than willing to do nursing duty. Trouble was, Kathy's car was in the shop and her husband was out of town, so she had no way of getting to the hospital. Undaunted, Nicole had asked Kathy to call Mel Hall.

Kathy had phoned back to assure Nicole that her dependable-as-the-sunrise assistant was on his way.

Anticipating Mel's arrival, Nicole shoved back the sheet that covered her and eased into a sitting position. She was immediately sorry when the small cubicle began to spin.

"It'll pass," she muttered, gripping the edge of the gurney while waiting for the sensation to fade. When it did, she pulled the sheet over her lap and bare legs to dispel a chill that had nothing to do with the thin gown she was wearing and everything to do with the events of the evening. She wanted to be in her own home, in her own bed, where she felt safe.

From somewhere outside her curtained cubicle came a jumble of voices, the squeak of crepe-soled shoes on tile, the beeping of some sort of instrument. The noise, the sense of nearby movement, reinforced the knowledge that anyone could wander in. Anyone, including the person who'd attacked her.

Paranoid, she told herself while dragging in a deep breath against a fresh surge of nausea. She had sensed the man had been as surprised as she when he'd rushed out the door and smashed into her. He couldn't identify her any more than she could him. Why, then, had he hit her? There had been no lights on in the house, so maybe she'd surprised a burglar whose first reflex had been to strike out? She simply didn't know. Maybe by now Jake had talked to DeSoto and had the answers that eluded her.

"Nicole! Oh, my sweet Lord, Nicole." Mel, dressed in khaki slacks and a loose-fitting shirt, stood in the opening between the curtains, his face ashen.

She forced a smile. "Mel, I'm okay—"

"I can see you're not."

He was beside her in a flash, his eyes filled with distress. His hands gripped hers, tightening until bone rubbed bone.

When she winced, he instantly loosened his hold. "I'm sorry," he said. "It's just...*your cheek.* Don't you think you should lie down?"

"I've been lying down for over two hours." She tipped her head. "The look on your face tells me I ought to avoid mirrors."

His blue eyes softened as he stared down at her. "I'm sorry. I...I'm so sorry."

"About what?"

His brows slid together, smoothed again. "That you're hurt."

"The doctor said I'll be as good as new in a few days."

"How do you feel now?"

She eased one of her hands from Mel's, patted at her French twist, which now sagged hopelessly onto her neck. "The same way I'm sure I look. Awful."

"You're so beautiful. So perfect. You could never look awful. Never."

She squeezed his hand. "Not only do you cut through paperwork like a lawnmower, you stroke my ego. Remind me to give you a raise."

"Okay." He flashed a grin. "I'll start earning that extra money by calling the insurance company about your Jaguar."

She blinked. Her car had been fine when the EMTs eased her out of it. As far as she knew, it was still parked in DeSoto's driveway. "What happened to the Jag?"

"Weren't you in a wreck?" Mel whisked a hand through his blond hair. "All Kathy said when she called was that you'd been hit, were hurt and you needed me. I didn't ask questions. I just assumed someone had hit you in the Jag. When I saw the cop outside, I figured he was here to take a report."

"There's a cop outside?" Nicole asked, struggling to think past both the pain and the drug.

"On the other side of the curtain. I had to give my name before he'd let me in."

"Jake didn't mention he was sending anyone."

"Jake?"

"Sergeant Ford. You met him in my office today."

"I remember. What's he got to do with this?"

"He came to DeSoto's house when I called."

"You were in a wreck at Villanova's house?" Mel asked, peering down at her with bewilderment.

"No."

Massaging her aching forehead, she gave Mel a rundown on how their client's leaving his pen in her office that morning had led to her getting assaulted on his porch that night.

Mel's lips thinned. "You should have asked me to return his pen. I'd have done it for you."

"There was no reason—"

"God, Nicole, don't you realize you could have been killed?"

"Yes." With her free hand, she clenched the edge of the gurney. "Mel, I don't feel up to a safety lecture."

"I'm sorry, it's just that you're *hurt*." He shook his head. "Are you sure you didn't get a good look at the man?"

"I didn't get any kind of look at him. It was too dark, things happened too fast. Whoever it was, he was big, muscular and packed a punch. That's why I'm guessing it was a man."

"Well, the first item of business is for me to take you home. I'll get you settled, then make a warm compress for your cheek." He angled his chin. "You having any nausea?"

"Some."

"I'll brew ginger tea. That always settles Mother's stomach."

Nicole sighed. Edna Hall was lucky to have a son like Mel.

"Keep this up and I'll double that raise." Nicole glanced down at her pink hospital gown. "Actually, the first order of business is finding a nurse to help me get dressed." She eased her hand from Mel's comforting grip. "Kathy will spend the night—"

"I'll stay with you."

"No, you have your mother to consider."

"On your couch," he continued, his handsome face set in stubborn lines of worry. "I've arranged for a neighbor to stay with Mother."

This was one time Nicole took little delight in Mel's eagerness to please. Her head hurt, she was groggy and her stomach was flip-flopping like a beached trout. She didn't have the strength to explain how inappropriate his spending the night on her couch would be. "I appreciate it, Mel, but—"

"I'm taking Miss Taylor home."

Nicole had no idea how long Jake had been standing just inside the cubicle. All she knew was that the instant she heard his voice, her heart did an unsteady cartwheel in her chest.

If she hadn't realized before that she had wandered into an emotional quagmire, she did now.

Mel turned. "No offense, Sergeant Ford, but wouldn't your time be better spent finding out who assaulted my boss?"

"No offense taken. This time."

When Jake crossed to her, Nicole noted that the dark stubble shadowing his jaw only made him more attractive, especially when combined with hair a week late for the barber. Despite her present groggy state, she recognized the deep desire to be his that curled inside her. When he placed a gentle finger beneath her chin and nudged upward, that desire deepened into an ache.

Her fingers gripped the sheet closer around her as if to form a barrier between them. She knew too well the heartbreak that could come from indulging that kind of ache.

"How you doing?" he asked, his whiskey-colored eyes filled with grim assessment as he examined her cheek.

"You tell me." She forced her eyes not to flutter shut when his thumb slid down her throat. "Does my cheek look better than it did two hours ago?"

"I wouldn't say better. I'd say more purple. And swollen."

"You've got a way with words, Jake Ford."

"So I've been told." He dropped his hand. "If you feel up to it, I've got some things to go over with you—"

"Can't that wait?" Mel asked, his voice carrying a thread of indignation. "Nicole is obviously in pain."

Jake turned his head, skewering Mel with a stare that

could cut through steel. "Some things can wait, Hall. Others can't."

"Not even until morning?" Mel persisted.

"No."

Jake looked back at her, his eyes softening. "Did I hear you say a nurse is going to help get you dressed?"

"If she ever shows up."

Jake glanced back at Mel. "How about you find that nurse?"

Mouth tight, Mel shifted his gaze to Nicole. "What do you want me to do, boss?"

Understanding that he felt as if he were being dismissed, she resisted the urge to pat his hand. "It would be a big help if you could find the nurse."

"Sure." He touched her, a brushing caress on her shoulder. "I don't like to see you hurt."

"I'm fine now."

"After you find the nurse," Jake began, "meet me in the waiting area. I need to check a few things before you head out."

"Fine." Hands crammed into his pockets, Mel disappeared through the curtains.

Jake dipped his head. "Where you're concerned, your puppy dog assistant has a streak of pit bull in him."

"Mel's very protective."

"Yeah." Jake used a fingertip to nudge a wisp of hair off her injured cheek. "I got that message, loud and clear."

Before, Nicole had been conscious of all the sounds around her, of the hospital's daunting size. Now, alone with Jake, she was suddenly aware of the stillness in the air. Of the cubicle's intimate size. Of the instinctive urge to lean into Jake's broad chest and rest her aching head against his shoulder.

Which would be a huge mistake, she reminded herself.

"You feel up to talking while we wait for the nurse?" he asked as he slid onto the gurney beside her.

"Yes."

"Okay, start by telling me what time you left your office."

"Around six." She paused, forcing her fuzzy brain to focus. "I met a potential client for dinner."

"Who and where?"

"Harold Young, at Logan's Bistro."

"Did this potential client sign a contract tonight?"

"No, Harold wants to think things over. I left Logan's a little after eight. I drove to DeSoto's to return the pen he'd left in my office this morning."

"Did Villanova know you were coming by?"

"No. I knew he had a date tonight with a client from his match list. I didn't expect him to be there."

"Did you see a car parked anywhere near his house?"

Frowning, Nicole thought back. "No," she said after a moment. "I was paying attention to the house numbers, so there could have been a car and I didn't notice."

"What happened after you got on the porch?"

"I put the envelope with the pen into the mailbox. That's when the porch light went off and...whoever it was—a man, I think—rushed out the door."

"Why do you think it was a man?"

"It was like smashing into a wall of muscle. And when he...hit me..." Her voice began to shake. "I stumbled sideways...fell. Hit my head. I tried to...get up. I thought... Oh, God, Jake, I thought he might..."

He took her hand, his fingers curving firmly, gently around hers. "You're safe now."

"I know." Swallowing hard, she clenched her fingers around his, as if holding on to a lifeline. "I just don't feel too steady."

"Understandable." Jake's eyes stayed on hers. "What could you tell about his size?"

"He seemed big. Huge. But that could have just been because of the dark."

"Around the size of your friend Sebastian?"

"It's poss..." Her chin jutted upward. "Are you asking me if it *was* Sebastian?"

"No," Jake said evenly. "I asked if the guy was around his size."

"He *seemed* that size. And, yes, Sebastian knows DeSoto. But DeSoto wasn't at home, so what reason would Sebastian have to be there?"

Jake studied their joined hands. "DeSoto was at home."

"But the house was dark...." Nicole's voice faltered when she saw the grimness in Jake's eyes. "What's happened to DeSoto?"

"Villanova's dead."

Nicole's spine stiffened against the shock that punched through her. "No, you're wrong." When she tried to tug her hand away, Jake tightened his grip. "*Phillip's* dead. Last night—"

"Villanova's dead, too. We found him inside his house. I won't know until the M.E. does an autopsy if he was murdered, but I'm betting he was. Just like Ormiston."

"The man who hit me..."

"Probably killed them both."

Tears welled in her eyes. "DeSoto is...was a friend of Bill's. He came to his and Whitney's wedding."

"I saw Villanova there. With you. Was he your date?"

"No, Mel escorted me to the wedding. Bill introduced me to DeSoto over a year ago. We went out a few times, but we were always just friends. Then a couple of months ago DeSoto signed a contract with Meet Your Match. He's been a client ever since."

"And you don't date your clients."

"That's right, I don't."

"If he was a client, how come you put one of your business cards into his coat pocket?"

Nicole furrowed her brow, trying to remember. "DeSoto was teasing me about how I'd given my card to everybody except him. So I slid one into his pocket."

"I ran into Villanova this morning on my way to your office. He was getting on the elevator and he was mad. Any idea why?"

Nicole shook her head, and instantly regretted it when a pain like an ice pick stabbed her right temple. Concentrating, she worked her way past the discomfort. "DeSoto was fine when he left." The breath she exhaled was as unsteady as her voice. "First Phillip and now DeSoto. Jake, why?"

"I don't know. Yet." His mouth tightened. "I heard you tell Mel you have a friend who'll stay with you tonight."

"Kathy Key. She and her husband live next door."

"What about your parents? Could you stay with them?"

"They left on a cruise two days after the wedding."

"I met a couple of your brothers at the reception. Surely one of them has a spare bedroom."

"Bill's the only brother who lives in town."

"Okay. When we get to your place, I'll drop by your friend's apartment and tell her you won't need her."

"But—"

"I'm bunking on your couch tonight, Nicole. We'll figure out other arrangements tomorrow."

"Other arrangements…" His meaning had the blood draining from her cheeks. Earlier, she'd toyed with the possibility of her attacker stepping into the cubicle, but that was all it had been—a possibility. Now it looked as if the man had killed twice in as many nights. If he thought she could identify him…

She stared into Jake's somber face while her insides knotted. "You think he knows who I am. That he'll come after

me. The porch was dark, but there were patches of moonlight through the clouds, so he can't be positive I didn't see
him.'' She fisted her free hand against her gowned thigh.
''That's why you stationed a cop outside.''

''I don't think your attacker can ID you from your encounter on the porch,'' Jake said quietly. ''But your car was
parked in the drive. Whether he saw it—and the tag—depends on which way he ran after he hit you.'' As he spoke,
Jake's thumb swept across her knuckles. ''I'm not taking
chances with your safety, Nicole.''

Fear caused acid to settle in the pit of her stomach. She
knew she should combat the sensation by doing the stress-
reducing breathing exercises Sebastian had taught her. Instead, all she wanted was to bury her face against Jake's
chest, burrow inside him. ''Thanks.''

''You don't have to thank me.''

''I know.'' The smile she sent him didn't gel. ''You're
just doing your job.''

''That's the way I want things to be,'' he said, his voice
soft on the still air. ''*Need* them to be.'' He lifted a hand,
traced a fingertip along her jaw. ''That's not the way things
are.''

Nicole sighed while undeniable longing for the man
peeled away another layer of resistance.

''No, it's not,'' she agreed.

He wished to hell the job was all that was involved, Jake
acknowledged moments later when the nurse shooed him out
of the cubicle. He knew that if it were any woman other
than Nicole needing protection, he would have arranged for
a female officer to catch the bunk-on-the-couch assignment.
But Nicole wasn't any other woman. She was his partner's
new sister-in-law. She was the sister of the number two man
in the D.A.'s office. She…

Dammit, she *mattered*. And that was one hell of a problem

because he didn't want her to. Didn't ever again want another human being to matter, not the way Annie and the twins had.

Still, in the short time he'd known her, he'd come to care about Nicole. He wasn't sure how much—didn't want to *know*—but he did care. That alone was a huge and frightening admission, and one he was certain he couldn't make out loud.

Frowning, he strode down a corridor, the hospital's sterile scent filling his lungs. He hadn't been able to push aside thoughts of her while he'd worked the Villanova crime scene. All he could think about was how she'd looked, chalk-white and trembling, in the back of that ambulance. He of all people knew it had been pure luck that the bastard who'd killed Villanova hadn't hung around to finish off a potential witness.

Nicole had come close to dying tonight. Damn close. Jake wondered if the eerie sensation creeping up his spine was the devil's own footsteps.

Nicole's business was relationships. With two of her clients lying in the morgue, it looked as if someone had decided to turn that business into murder. Jake clenched his hands. *His* business was also murder. Whoever had started this game would have to deal with *him*.

Turning a corner, he caught sight of Mel Hall leaning against one end of the ER's admission counter. From behind the counter, a blond nurse slicked her gaze down Mel's tall frame, appreciation glowing in her eyes.

Oblivious to the nurse's attention, Mel pushed off the counter when he spied Jake. "Is the nurse helping Nicole change?"

"Yes. I want to leave when she's ready, so let's get our business out of the way."

Mel crossed his arms over his chest. "What business?"

"Where you were tonight, starting around seven o'clock?"

"At home with Mother."

"If I contact her, will she verify that?"

"Well, no." Mel lifted a shoulder. "Mother's ill. Very. She went to sleep around six. She was still asleep when Nicole's friend Kathy called to tell me Nicole had been hurt and needed me."

"No one can verify your whereabouts tonight?"

"No." Mel's eyes narrowed. "How could you even think I hurt Nicole?"

"Everyone stays on my list until I know for sure who slammed his fist into her temple." Jake locked his gaze on Mel's. "And maybe killed Villanova."

"Look, I..." Color drained out of Mel's face. "Did you say *killed* Villanova?"

"Yeah." Jake decided Hall was either one hell of an actor, or the news had taken him by surprise. "Right now it looks like whoever murdered Ormiston also did Villanova. That's two of your clients in as many nights. Two people whom you knew."

"That doesn't mean I killed them."

"What kind of mood was Villanova in this morning when he left Miss Taylor's office?"

"Okay, I guess."

"Did you have words with him?"

"Words?"

"Yeah, *words.* A disagreement. Did you argue?"

"I said *goodbye,* and he left. Then I went to the kitchen to make Nicole's tea. That's where I was when you showed up."

"Where were you yesterday when Ormiston died?"

"I don't know what time that was."

"Start with the afternoon."

"I was at the office until six. Then I went to Sebastian's. I worked out a couple of hours, then went home."

"What time was that?"

"Eight. Maybe a little later."

Jake pursed his lips. Nicole had found Ormiston's body around nine-thirty. "Was your mother awake when you got there?"

"No." Mel closed his eyes. "She's sick. I'm not sure how much longer she has."

"Sorry to hear that."

Mel scraped a hand across the back of his neck. "Look, Sergeant, you can accuse me all you want, but I'm the last person you should suspect."

"Why's that?"

"I owe everything to Nicole. She hired me. She doesn't blink when I need time off to take Mother to the doctor. If Nicole wasn't helping to pay for my college, I would have to drop out. I would never hurt the company, much less Nicole. Part of my job is to watch out for her."

Out of the corner of his eye, Jake caught sight of a grizzled man with one forearm wrapped in a towel and blood seeping from a cut on his forehead shuffle to the counter. The blond nurse who'd given Mel the eye earlier streaked into action.

Jake looked back at Mel. "So you wouldn't hurt Nicole. Any idea who might?"

"I don't know anyone who would want to hurt *her*. I do know someone who wants to hurt any man who tries to get close to her."

"Who?"

"Sebastian Peck."

Jake's spine went rigid. "What about Peck?"

"He has it bad for Nicole. Real bad. She considers him a friend. He wants to be more. A lot more."

Jake ignored the twist of annoyance deep in his gut. "Did Peck tell you that?"

"He didn't have to. It's all over his face anytime some guy at the gym pays her attention."

If Nicole looked as good in spandex as Jake imagined she would, he figured she got a lot of attention.

"I know that Ormiston had a membership to Sebastian's," Jake stated. "What about Villanova?"

"Him, too. He's a tall, swarthy Latino—tons of women at the gym went crazy over him. Mostly, he hung around Nicole, which got him some go-to-hell looks from Sebastian."

Jake reached into his pocket, pulled out the obituary he'd found that morning in Ormiston's locker. "You know anything about a guy named Eddie Denson?"

Mel glanced at the column. "I met him at Sebastian's a couple of months before he died in that car wreck."

"Did Denson ever mention he used steroids?"

"No, but he looked like he took them." Mel's mouth settled into a grim line. "Ormiston must have thought that, too."

"Why do you say that?"

"Once, I walked past Sebastian's office while Ormiston was there. I heard him accuse Sebastian of turning Denson on to steroids."

"What did Peck say about that?"

"He told Ormiston he didn't appreciate being accused of something he hadn't done. Then he told him to get out of his office."

"Was anyone with you when you overheard that conversation?"

"No."

Jake nodded. He now knew the reason Peck had avoided his gaze when asked if he'd ever heard Ormiston arguing with anyone. Ormiston had argued with *him*.

Mel scrubbed his hands over his face. "I'm sorry I got short with you earlier. Now that I know about Villanova, I realize why your questioning Nicole couldn't wait. If he was murdered, whoever hit her could have killed her, too."

"That sums it up," Jake stated.

"When you take her home, you'll stay there?"

"Yeah, on her couch. Just in case."

Mel blew out a breath. "She needs arnica for her temple and cheek."

Jake scowled. "Arnica?"

"It's a herb that helps reduce swelling and bruising. I planned to make a compress, but I doubt you're up to that."

"Look, I—"

"There's an all-night pharmacy near Nicole's apartment." Mel grabbed an admission form and pen off the counter and began jotting a list. "Ask the pharmacist for lotion with arnica. Apply some to Nicole's temple and cheek as soon as you get her home. Then again in the morning."

Jake shifted his stance. Somehow, the interview had ended and Mel had switched into healer mode. "Right."

"She's nauseated, so brew her some ginger tea."

"*Brew* it…?"

Mel rolled his eyes. "Buy her ginger ale," he said, handing over the list. "You sure you don't need me to take her home?"

Jake crammed the list into his pocket. "I can handle the job."

That was the truth, he thought—he could handle the job. What he wasn't sure he could handle was knowing he was beginning to long for things he'd put behind him. Things he didn't dare take because he knew how easily fate could snatch them away, leaving vicious, gaping holes that could never be filled.

That was one nightmare he had no intention of reliving.

So, he would force everything else to some deep corner of his brain and concentrate solely on the job.

It was his bad luck that a killer had shoved Nicole right into the middle of that job.

Chapter 6

One hour later, Jake eased the cruiser into the parking lot outside Nicole's apartment building. The reflection of security lights splashed against roofs of well-polished cars. He pulled into a spot, killed the engine, then let his gaze drift. He watched for any sign of movement through windshields, a reflection in a side mirror, a glint off a piece of chrome.

Nothing.

He shifted his attention to the nearby high-rise where artfully lit planters spilled ivy and vibrant blooms over each apartment's balcony. As far as he could tell, nothing looked out of place. Nothing hinted that the bastard who'd assaulted Nicole earlier that night—and maybe murdered Villanova—lurked in the shadows, waiting to get a second chance at her.

Easing out a breath, Jake looked over at the passenger seat. Nicole had slipped into sleep while he was inside the drugstore buying ginger ale and whatever-the-hell kind of lotion Mel Hall had written in his precise, exact script on the list he'd made.

With her face angled toward him, enough illumination seeped into the cruiser so that he could make out the dark bruising that marred her right temple and cheek. Her hair had come uncoiled and now fell like golden rain off the shoulders of her dirt-smudged suit. Experimentally, he brushed a palm down that tangled mass of blond silk.

Her lips parted on a sigh.

Desire, hot and potent, slammed into his system.

He needed. He'd forgotten what it was like to really need. To thirst for a woman. For one woman.

This woman, he conceded.

He didn't want to want her, but he did. Wanted her with such fierceness that this very minute he could cover her mouth with his and take her in one greedy gulp.

"Dammit." He fought back the urge by reminding himself of how vulnerable she'd looked sitting on the hospital gurney, her cheek battered and pain swimming in her eyes. The wrinkled gown and sheet she'd clutched around her had made her seem small and defenseless.

For Nicole, the past twenty-four hours had been hell. She'd stumbled on to Ormiston's body last night. *He'd* nearly taken her like an animal that morning in her office. A couple of hours ago a probable murderer had slugged her hard enough to give her a concussion. Now she was in danger of getting mauled by the cop who was supposed to protect her. Mauled while she slept, for crying out loud.

"Smooth move, Ford," he muttered.

Knowing he'd better get out of the car before he lost his senses completely, he snagged the bag from the pharmacy, swung open the door, then snapped it closed behind him. Resting his palm against his holstered Glock, he scanned the still, quiet parking lot. The warm breeze drifted against his face; he could hear nothing but the faint swish of traffic several blocks away.

Satisfied that no threat hovered, he tucked the bag under

one arm, rounded the hood, then pulled open the passenger door.

"Nicole?" Leaning in, he pressed his palm to her shoulder. "You're home."

"Hmm..." Her head lolled toward him, her lashes fluttering upward. "Jake?" His name was a husky murmur on the night air as she snuggled deeper into the cruiser's upholstery.

"Stay with me," he said when her lashes fluttered again. He squeezed her shoulder. "All you have to do is stay awake long enough for me to get you into bed." He bit back a groan when he realized what he'd said. "Get you settled," he amended.

"Right. Okay." Her hand moved with the sluggishness of sleep when she nudged back one side of her hair. She blinked; her eyes went from slumberous to sharp as she pushed past the disorientation and peered through the windshield. "We're home."

"Yeah. After I put lotion on your cheek and fix you some ginger ale, you can go back to sleep. For a while, anyway. I have to wake you up every hour. Doctor's orders."

Her mouth curved as she pulled the strap of her purse onto her shoulder and slid her long, shapely legs out the open door. "If you ever want to stop being a cop, you can get work as a nurse."

"I'll hold on to my badge for now." Positioning one hand on her elbow for support, he eased her up and out of the cruiser.

"Thanks. Jake, I..." She nearly toppled into him. "I'm just..."

"Light-headed and dizzy?" he asked, scooping her off her feet and into his arms.

"A little."

"The doc said that's to be expected."

"Hmm." She nestled her head against his shoulder with an ease of familiarity that tightened his gut.

Her warm scent wrapped around his senses so that he drew her in with every breath. Jake closed his eyes. Standing there, holding her lush body against his while clouds scuttled across the star-infested sky, he felt like a man rushing headlong over the verge of safety into the unknown.

She dipped her fingers into her purse; a key ring dangled from the hand she pressed against his chest. "My apartment's on the top floor." She tilted her chin up, gave him a sleepy smile. "Right about now, I bet you're hoping the building has an elevator."

Cocking his head, he studied the play of light and shadow slanting across her face. "If it doesn't, I'll just toss you over my shoulder and carry you up the stairs."

"This must be what it feels like to be rescued," she murmured, nuzzling her nose into the curve between his shoulder and neck.

The gesture went straight to his head like hot whiskey.

Setting his jaw, he turned and headed toward a lighted sidewalk lined by ground-hugging plants and flowers.

What the hell was she doing to him? How could she make him feel so many different emotions in so short a time? He knew if he let himself go, let down his guard, she could take him to that teetering edge of reason and insanity.

Knew also, if he did, he would be the one who would need rescuing, not her.

Feeling groggy and stiff, Nicole woke the next morning with a small moan. Her stomach did one flip, then settled. While the remnants of sleep faded, she kept her head still on the linen-encased pillow and assessed the damage. The titanic headache that had held her brain in a vise had been replaced by a slight pulsing behind her eyes. Her right cheek—which she knew must be a mass of bruising—ached like a bad tooth.

With careful movements she banked pillows with delicate edgings of lace behind her then inched upward, pulling the linen sheet with her. When her head failed to commence the lazy spinning that had plagued her the previous night, she sighed with relief.

Across the room, the first rays of dawn suffused gossamer curtains, glowing faintly on the ornate grillwork of her big brass bed. The calming scent of chamomile wafted from a crystal potpourri dish on the bleached-pine bureau. Always before, her bedroom had seemed an oasis of serenity with its warm lighting and white linen and lace, but not today.

Not when two men she'd known were dead. A sudden rush of tears filled her eyes and she blinked them away.

Had her attacker murdered DeSoto? she wondered. If so, was it the same man who'd injected Phillip with some substance that had paralyzed his lungs and suffocated the life out of him? She shuddered at the thought. Two of her clients were dead. At least one of them had died horribly. A thread of dismay wound through her at the almost unimaginable possibility that their deaths might be somehow linked to Meet Your Match.

Hugging her elbows, she pushed away the thought and cautioned herself not to panic. Not yet, anyway. Jake had said he didn't know if DeSoto had been murdered. Wouldn't know until later this morning after an autopsy had been done.

With an effort, she drew herself in. She had learned long ago the best way to survive a crisis was to keep busy. So, she would, she resolved, making a mental list of to-dos. She needed to call Bill. Though he and Whitney were due home from their honeymoon the next day, she didn't want to take a chance her brother might find out about his friend's death by reading about it in the newspaper. She also wanted to call Phillip's son to ask again if the family needed anything and to find out if his father's funeral had been scheduled. If so, she would have Mel send flowers and clear her calendar to attend the service.

Feeling better now that she had a plan, Nicole glanced across the room at the love seat covered in ivory damask. Her tattered red suit sagged over one rolled arm like a wilted rose. Her brows slid together while she tried to remember getting undressed. Her mind formed the hazy image of Jake stirring her awake in his cruiser, of him lifting her into his arms. Of his warm, musky scent as they rode the elevator. Of being cradled against his hard, solid chest while he angled her key into the lock on her front door. She remembered him easing her down onto the edge of the bed, knew she'd barely kept from falling back to sleep while he stroked lotion on her cheek.

But, no, she had no memory of undressing herself.

Glancing down, she lifted the edge of the sheet. Relief swept through her when she saw she was still wearing the black bustier and matching bikini panties she'd had on under the suit. She no longer wore her thigh-high black hose. Her blood heated at the thought of Jake slipping off her suit. Of his hands skimming her flesh as he peeled wisps of nylon down her legs.

God, she *wanted* his hands on her. Wanted his mouth on hers again. Every instinct told her Jake was wrong for her. Yet, something about him made her want to tempt fate. What that something was, she had no idea. She just knew she wanted more of him.

A lot more.

She didn't want to accept that her emotions could spin out of control so quickly, or leave her such little choice. But they had.

Right now Jake was only a short flight of stairs away, down in her living room, probably still asleep on her couch.

Did he look as appealing in the mornings as she imagined he would with his dark hair rumpled and his eyes heavy from sleep?

Her fingers curled against the desire that thudded in the pit of her stomach. She would do well to remember that Jake was downstairs solely because he was a cop. He'd spent the night guarding her. And checking on her, she now recalled as the image of him waking her throughout the night floated back.

Yes, he was with her because he was a cop, but nursing care went well beyond his duties. At the hospital, Jake admitted she had become more than just a job to him. How much more, she didn't know. Wasn't sure she *wanted* to know.

Blowing out a sigh, she closed her eyes and wondered who she was trying to kid. She wanted to know everything about this man.

After a quick shower, Nicole dressed in a long turquoise blouse and black leggings, then bundled her hair on top of her head. The smell of bacon frying lured her downstairs. Barefoot, she padded into the living room she'd furnished with warmth and a sure touch. The sight of the holstered gun and gold badge lying on the coffee table in front of the sofa had her pausing. She supposed when one lived with a cop, one got used to the trappings of the profession. She raised an eyebrow at the image of her orderly brother Bill waking to the sight of Whitney's police gear strewn across their coffee table.

Smiling at the thought, Nicole veered past the cozy dining room with its polished table and armoire heavy with silver and crystal. The kitchen she'd had converted into an extension of the living room came into view.

Though she knew he was there, the sight of Jake standing at the stove, poking a long fork into a skillet of sizzling bacon, gave her heart a jolt. He was barefoot, dressed in jeans and his rumpled white shirt he'd yet to button. His dark hair was temptingly rumpled, his jaw stubbled.

Yes, she thought, biting off a sigh as she answered the question she'd asked herself earlier. Jake Ford looked as appealing in the morning as she'd imagined he would.

She swallowed against a flash of heated desire. She was afraid, very afraid she was close to losing all perspective where the man was concerned. "I didn't expect you to cook breakfast on top of everything else."

He looked over his shoulder. His gaze traveled from the top of her head down to her polished toenails, then back up to settle on her bruised cheek. A muscle in his jaw jerked, but his eyes stayed level. "How do you feel?"

"Better than last night." A sudden case of nerves had her hovering in the arched entrance when she realized he looked very much at home in her kitchen with its warm slate counters and creamy white appliances. *Too much at home.*

She nodded toward the stove. "I can finish that."

"I've got a handle on it," he said, using the fork to nudge the sizzling strips. "I came in here to fix coffee. I couldn't find any, so I decided to cook." He dipped his head toward the skillet. "The package said this stuff's *turkey* bacon."

"That's right. It's nitrate-free."

"That another way of saying it's pork-free?"

"Turkey's much healthier."

Jake slid her a sidelong look. "Did your pal Peck tell you that?"

"I read books on nutrition. But Sebastian does embrace the philosophy that a person will never be at his peak unless he eats right."

"Does Peck also embrace you?"

Nicole hesitated. "Are you asking if Sebastian and I are lovers?"

Jake lifted a dark brow. "The subject of your relationship

came up during an interview. Whether you have a thing going might play into the investigation."

"I see." She jutted her chin against a flare of disappointment, knowing Jake had asked solely because of the case. If she'd harbored hope that she still had some objectivity left when it came to Jake Ford, she knew now she'd totally lost it.

"The answer is no, I'm not having an affair with Sebastian." And because she felt so off balance, she added, "Some people can't understand that a platonic relationship between a man and a woman can exist."

When Jake grunted, she moved out of the doorway to one of the glass-fronted cabinets. "I don't have any coffee, but I can brew some tea."

"Tea?" He sounded as though he'd spoken through clenched teeth. "You got any with caffeine in it?"

The edgy growl in his voice had her lips curving. God, why did everything about the man lure her? "In your honor, Sergeant, I'll bypass the decaf and go with the high-test stuff. I've got a special blend that Mel made from one of his uncle Zebulon's recipes."

"That the uncle who grows fresh herbs as a hobby?"

"Yes. You've got a good memory, Sergeant."

"Comes in handy for a cop."

She filled a kettle with water, then moved to the stove and switched on a burner. Up close now, she saw the shadow of fatigue beneath Jake's eyes, the lines at the corners of his mouth. Guilt tugged at her, knowing he'd gotten up throughout the night to check on her.

The sudden urge to press a soft kiss against those lines of weariness had a knot of nerves tingling at the base of her neck.

"I, ah, I guess you're addicted to cop coffee?" The sight of his broad chest darkened by sleek black hair seemed to dull her talent for small talk.

"Cop coffee?"

"Every movie or TV show with cops has them swilling coffee, whether they're shoving paperwork around a desk or on a stakeout." She retrieved china cups and saucers from a cabinet, positioned them on floral place mats at the high counter that separated the kitchen from the living room. "If Hollywood is to be believed, all cops take their coffee strong and black."

"Guzzling the equivalent of battery acid helps protect our macho image." He transferred the bacon to a plate, put it in the oven to warm, then grabbed a bowl sitting on a nearby cutting board.

"An omelet, too?" she asked, watching him dump a mixture of eggs, cheese, chopped bell peppers and mushrooms into the skillet. "I'm impressed."

"Don't be. You're witnessing my total culinary skills." Looking up, he flashed her a reckless grin. "I usually know when a meal's done by the ringing of the smoke alarm."

She remembered another time in her life when the air clogged in her lungs simply because a man grinned at her. With a siren screeching in her head, Nicole reached for a colorful tea tin. It would be smarter—and much safer—to get her mind off the man and focus on the reason the cop was in her kitchen.

"When I woke up, I had an instant when I thought everything that happened last night had been a bad dream." While she spoke, she filled a teapot glazed to a buttery glow, set it aside to steep. "That I hadn't gotten hit by the equivalent of a speeding truck. That DeSoto was alive."

"He's not." Jake folded the omelet, nudged it around in the skillet. "I wish I could tell you different."

"You're almost certain he was murdered, aren't you?"

"Yes, but I've been wrong before. When you work Homicide, you learn fast not to make assumptions until you've got facts to back them up. Even after I get a confession, I do my best to make the suspect prove to me that he or she did it.'' He glanced at the green-marbled wall clock hanging amid a collection of framed restaurant menus. ''I called the M.E. last night from the scene. He agreed to go in early this morning and do the autopsy. I'll probably know something within the hour.''

Keeping one eye on the stove, Jake leaned a hip against the counter. ''I need to ask you more questions about Villanova.''

Nicole plucked up a carafe of herbal vinegar, set it back down. ''Okay.''

''You said Bill introduced you.''

''Yes.'' She frowned. ''I think they met through a case Bill tried. I guess you already know DeSoto owns...*owned* the Cadillac dealership on May Avenue.''

Jake nodded. ''I talked to his sister last night. She said he was divorced several years ago. Has no kids.''

''That's right. DeSoto was like Phillip—he spent most of his time working and didn't get out much. Plus, DeSoto didn't drink, didn't like to party, so that left him with few ways of meeting women with common interests and goals.''

''When you and I talked in the emergency room, you said Villanova was fine when he left your office yesterday morning.''

''Yes.''

''Did a message come through on his pager while he was with you? Maybe he got a call on his cell phone?''

''No, he didn't get a page or a call.'' She blew out a breath. ''I remember you saying he looked upset.''

''Not just *looked*. When he stepped on the elevator, he rammed into me hard enough to dislocate a shoulder. He was steamed about something.'' Jake divided the omelet onto two plates, then pulled the bacon out of the oven. ''Did he and Ormiston go out with any of the same women?''

Nicole rubbed at the dull ache in her right temple. ''Several, I think. I can access both their match lists on the computer in my study. If you like, I'll check now.''

"When we're finished eating is soon enough," Jake said, handing her the plate of bacon.

"You still think one of the women on Phillip's match list and now DeSoto's could be the killer?''

"It's possible.''

"Even though I'm ninety-nine percent positive the person who raced out of the house and plowed over me was a man?''

"That leaves one percent odds it was a woman. I don't discount any possibility. If it winds up Villanova died the same way Ormiston did, then it's a sure bet they were murdered because of something they had in common. So far, you and your company head the list. Number three is the fact that both men belonged to Sebastian's.'' Jake paused. "Whoever offed Ormiston didn't do it on impulse. The killer took the time to get whatever substance it was that paralyzed Ormiston's lungs. Then he or she came up with a good enough reason for Ormiston to let him or her get close enough to inject him without him putting up a struggle. All that takes planning.''

"I just…'' Nicole's voice hitched with emotion. "I just wish we knew who…and *why*.''

"When I know why, I'll know who.'' Jake's eyes narrowed. "Did you know a college kid named Eddie Denson?''

"Yes, he worked out at Sebastian's. In fact, he was driving home from there the night he was killed.''

"You ever hear anything about him using steroids?''

Nicole blinked. "No, nothing.''

"Did Ormiston mention he'd lost money in a bad investment?''

"No. Do you think Phillip got murdered because of something that had to do with Eddie and a bad investment?''

"At this point, anything's possible." Jake's eyes gentled. "Look, unless you're a cop, talking motives for murder doesn't make for soothing breakfast conversation. Let's eat, then pick this back up."

Seconds later, they were sitting side by side on high-backed stools at the counter.

Nicole took a bite of omelet, savored the flavor. "This is awesome."

"Do I detect a note of surprise in your voice?" Jake asked, forking strips of bacon onto her plate, then his.

"Considering your reference to a smoke alarm, I was half expecting a somewhat hickory flavor."

"You'd be choking down something akin to rubber if I'd cooked anything else," he said while Nicole poured tea into the china cups.

"I'll count my thanks that you stuck with breakfast."

He sliced off a bite of omelet while giving her a considering look. "So, why matchmaking?"

"Why?"

"I know why I'm a cop. Why are you a romance engineer?"

"I was born with a soft spot for matters of the heart." Her mouth curved. "My four brothers claim I got my start in the business by sticking my nose into their respective love lives."

"Did you?"

"Of course. Who better to experiment on than four single, good-looking males who lived under the same roof with me? I had a captive audience." She scooped up another bite. "When I was in junior high, I sent a questionnaire to all the girls in each of their classes, then analyzed the results. I sneaked into the principal's office, got on the PA system and announced who each brother's perfect date to the spring dance would be."

Jake chuckled. "I bet that was a special moment for everyone involved."

"Bill, especially, got his nose out of joint." She raised a shoulder. "After that, my friends started coming to me, asking who I thought they'd go good with. I arranged quite a few dates during my school days."

"Did those matches work?"

"Almost all of them." She gave him a bright smile. "It's like a gift. I just *know* what people are right for each other."

Jake sipped his tea, grimaced, then went back to his omelet.

"So how come the consummate matchmaker-with-a-gift is single?" he asked after a moment.

"I wasn't always." Angling her fork, she nudged a bite of omelet around her plate. "Six years ago, I worked for a PR firm. One night I went to a client's party and met a man who swept me off my feet. I didn't think, didn't *want* to think, I just went with the chemistry. I fell in love—at least at the time I thought it was love. Before a month was up, we got married. Six months later, I came home to pick up a file I'd forgotten and found my darling spouse and some skinny waitress, naked on top of my dining room table." Nicole glanced across her shoulder toward her dining room. "The scene of the crime," she murmured. "I got rid of my husband and the table the same day."

Jake's gaze followed hers as he let out a long whistle. "Kind of hard to put a positive spin on that kind of evidence."

"You can bet Cole tried," she said, her index finger playing along the teacup's handle. "After the divorce was final, several people told me they'd seen him out on the town with one woman or another. I had no idea."

"How'd he keep that from you?"

"Two ways. Cole Champion's the kind of guy people like instantly. He's charming, fun to be around and talks a good game. There's just not a lot of depth behind the facade, but it takes time to find that out.'' Her mouth lifted into a wry curve. ''Once I accepted that he was incapable of being faithful, I forgave him. We've settled into a comfortable friendship. I even got him his present job in a roundabout way.'' Her eyes widened. ''Oh, my gosh, I completely forgot!''

''What?''

''DeSoto was in my office one day when Cole dropped by. I introduced them. A few days later, Cole called to tell me DeSoto had hired him. Cole still works at the dealership.''

''Now, there's a connection.'' Jake angled his head. ''How long has Champion worked there?''

''About half a year.''

''He and Villanova have any problems?''

''On the contrary. DeSoto mentioned several times what a stroke of luck it was that he'd been in my office that day when Cole showed up.''

''Why's that?''

''Cole could sell manure to a cattle rancher. You can imagine how well he does when someone who is already in the market for a car shows up. He's DeSoto's top salesman.''

''Did your ex also know Phillip Ormiston?''

''I don't think so. Neither of them ever mentioned meeting the other.''

''Okay.'' Jake gave her a long, steady look. ''You said Champion kept you in the dark two ways. What's the second?''

''Actually, that was more my doing than his. I was so crazy about Cole I didn't bother getting to know him or learn much about him before I jumped off the cliff.''

''If you had, would that have made a difference?''

''I'd like to think so.'' She looped a wispy strand of hair

behind one ear. "Anyway, after our marriage failed, I decided to make some changes in my life. I had a knack for matchmaking. My experience with Cole taught me the value of finding out up-front as much as you can about a person you might consider becoming involved with. I formed Meet Your Match five years ago next month."

"And the rest, as they say, is history."

"Right." Because her stomach still held an edge of unsteadiness, Nicole pushed her plate aside and sipped her tea.

"So, Jake Ford, you now know all about me. What about you? Why did you become a cop?"

"My reasons are pretty black and white. I believe in rules. In right and wrong. When somebody goes against those things, they should pay the consequences."

"You could be any kind of cop and still do that. Why Homicide?"

"For me, murder is the ultimate crime. Which is ironic when you consider that not too long ago I was sitting in a cell, charged with eight counts."

"You, you…" He might as well have smacked her over the head with his plate. "That was *you?*"

"That was me."

Nicole swallowed hard. "I heard about it on the news, that a cop had been arrested for all those murders. I didn't realize it was you."

"The bastard who committed the murders killed a woman I knew and set me up to take the fall for everything. He was smart, I was careless. If it hadn't been for Whitney believing in my innocence and your brother giving me the benefit of the doubt, I'd probably still be locked up."

"That…must have been terrible for you."

"Not as terrible as for the victims."

"No, of course not." Her eyes met his over the rim of her cup. "How do you deal with it? How do you handle a job that puts you close to murder day in and day out?"

''I don't look at things the same way a civilian does. I can't.'' He nudged his empty plate next to hers. Leaning back, he reached into his shirt pocket, then swore under his breath.

''Problem?''

''I stopped smoking nearly three months ago. Sometimes I forget that.'' He shoved a hand through his hair, leaving it even more appealingly rumpled. ''Back to homicide. It probably sounds callous, but at this point there's little that surprises, sickens or shocks me.''

''It doesn't sound callous. It sounds like a survival technique.'' She replaced her cup on the saucer, thinking of the care he'd taken with her last night. Of the gentleness she'd seen in his eyes. Behind all that macho cop lurked a kind heart. ''It's a technique I doubt would help a lot if someone you knew got hurt.''

She saw the instant barrier come up in his eyes. The hand he'd rested on the counter curled into a fist. He was sitting only inches away, yet she felt him distance himself from her. He had lost someone, she realized. Suddenly. Perhaps violently.

''Jake, I'm sorry, I—''

''Yeah, it makes a difference when it's someone you care about.'' His eyes had gone as flat as his voice. ''And kids.'' He looked away. ''Kids make a difference. A big one. I'm working a drive-by shooting right now. A seven-year-old boy died just because he was standing on a street corner the shooter considered *his*. That's one bastard you can bet I'll nail.''

Nicole curved her hand around his fist, bringing his gaze back to hers. ''I wouldn't want your job. But I'm glad there are people like you willing to do it.''

When he swiveled his stool toward hers, their knees bumped. He adjusted by sliding his thighs on either side of hers. ''That makes us even. I wouldn't want your job, either.''

The intimate contact made her nerves simmer. She dropped her gaze to his still-full cup. ''You...don't like the tea.''

''No offense to Mel's uncle, but his tea tastes like a flower garden.''

''I can brew a different—''

Jake's hand tightened on hers. ''Forget it.'' He dipped his head toward her plate. ''Something wrong with the omelet?''

''No, it's wonderful. My stomach's still a little iffy from last night.''

''There's more ginger ale in the fridge. Mel the Magnificent insisted it does the trick for iffy stomachs.''

''Mel is right. I'll have some after I call Bill. I need to tell him about DeSoto.''

''He knows. I called him and Whitney last night and brought them up to speed on what's happened. They're cutting their honeymoon short a day and flying home this morning.''

''Because you need Whitney's help on the case?''

''I can use it. Mainly they're coming home because we all agree you need a safe place to stay until this case gets solved.''

Nicole glanced across the length of the living room at the bolted front door. ''You really think I'm not safe here?''

''Not when there's even a remote chance a killer thinks you're a witness. The fact no one showed up here last night is a good sign, but I'm not taking chances.''

She looked down at their joined hands. At some point, Jake's long, bronzed fingers had twined with hers. ''I...haven't thanked you for taking care of me last night.''

''I don't want your thanks.''

''I know, but you're getting it, anyway. You were under no obligation to bring me home. Certainly didn't have to carry me into the building or swab lotion on my cheek. Or…'' She looked away as she pictured her tattered red suit draped across the arm of the love seat.

''Or, what?'' His thumb stroked the pulse point in her wrist. ''What else didn't I have to do?''

''Take off my suit. I know you undressed me to make me comfortable. It worked—I slept like a rock.'' She was talking so fast that the words tumbled over one another. ''I appreciate you taking care of me, Jake. I—''

''I got you settled on top of the bed,'' he explained quietly. ''Then I went next door and knocked on your friend's door. Kathy came over and undressed you.''

''Oh.'' She lifted a hand, placed her palm against his chest. ''Thanks.''

''You need to stop thanking me.'' He put a finger under her chin, nudged upward. ''If I ever take off your clothes, Nicole, I'm going to want you wide-awake when I do it.''

Her heart shot right up to her throat and beat there like a drum. ''Wide-awake would be good.''

When he moved his hand to cup the back of her neck, Jake felt her nerves jitter beneath his palm. He hadn't planned to touch her again. Overnight, he'd convinced himself, very logically, that backing off would be the best thing for both of them. After all, they'd shared only one kiss. A kiss that had knocked him off his feet and onto his butt, but that was as far as they'd gone. It might take him a month of nights burning for her to get her out of his system, but he knew backing off was best.

That was before she'd walked into the kitchen this morning dressed in a cool turquoise blouse and black leggings that hugged legs just short of miraculous. The way she'd piled her golden blond hair on top of her head suggested she'd just gotten out of bed. Since he'd woken her throughout the night he had no problem imagining how she would look lying beneath him, her skin glistening with sweat, all that glorious hair spread like liquid gold across her creamy sheets.

He had never wanted a woman more than he wanted her. Had never feared anything more than this slender, lovely woman with eyes as blue as a summer's day. He wanted her, even though she made him long for things he'd sworn he would never again risk taking.

Now he didn't care about risk. All he wanted to do was take.

He studied her, marveling at how good it felt to have her sitting so close. He had not realized—hadn't let himself realize—how much he missed something so simple as sharing breakfast with a woman he cared about.

Nicole made him remember.

Her lips were full and soft and unpainted; he needed to taste her again just as surely as he needed oxygen to survive. He hadn't chosen to have this avalanche of emotion barrel down on him, but since it had, it was time he did something about it.

His blood pounding, he leaned forward, watching every shift and flicker of emotion in her blue eyes.

"I've got no business touching you, Nicole. No business at all."

She moved her hand up his chest, slid her fingers into his hair. "I've got no business wanting you to touch me. But I have to tell you, Jake, if you don't put your mouth and your hands on me in the next couple of seconds, I'm going to have to get rough with you. I work out, you know. I could probably take you down."

"In that case..." With hunger slicing through him like a silver blade, he lowered his head and plundered.

The kiss was desperate, ravenous, tongues tangling, teeth nipping. The low, humming moan that slid up her throat went straight to his head like a potent drug.

When he tasted the arousal on her trembling breath, he

shoved his fingers into her hair, arched her head back and fed on that lush mouth. Her scent wrapped around him; his head hammered as air tore in and out of his chest.

"I want you." His lips trailed over her jaw to her throat. Her skin was like cream, cool and rich. He could spend hours savoring the taste of her flesh. Just savoring. "I tried not to want you, but I do."

"Jake, I..." Her hands were inside his shirt now, her fingers skimming his flesh, arrowing pleasure and lust into every part of his body. "This is probably a mistake," she murmured as her mouth savaged his throat. "I'm... sure...it...is."

"Me, too." His hand moved up her rib cage, then higher to cup her breast. Her nipple budded hard and tight beneath her silky blouse. "A big mistake."

"I'm glad...we're making it."

"I'm with you."

The pounding in his brain changed in tone, shifted. Suddenly he realized the noise was external, coming from across the room. *The front door.*

Jake jerked his head up just as a key slid into the deadbolt lock. "Anybody else have a key to this place?"

"I..." She blinked, her eyes wide and glazed to a smoky-blue. "Bill. Just Bill."

"Since he's somewhere between here and Cancún, we know it's not him. Stay here."

Jake reached the middle of the living room in three long strides, scooped his Glock off the coffee table without pausing. He jacked a round into the chamber, the harsh ratcheting sound echoing off the high ceiling. He stepped into the entry hall just as the door swung open.

Glock aimed, he moved into view as a tall, dark-haired man strode into the entryway, a key ring dangling from his fingers.

The man froze like a dazzled rabbit, his eyes wide with shock as he stared into the automatic's single dark eye.

"What the hell?"

"Police," Jake said. In one smooth move, he gripped the man's shoulder, spun him around and shoved him against the wall.

Chapter 7

"Wait!"

Nicole's voice squeaked from the other side of the living room as Jake used one shoulder to hold the intruder face-forward against the wall.

Over the past few minutes, his system had throbbed with lust, then veered to alarm. Now, adrenaline had his insides pumping as he conducted a deft, one-handed pat search for weapons.

"Jake!"

Out of the corner of his eye, he glimpsed Nicole rush into the entry hall.

"Stay back!" he ordered.

"I know him." Her eyes were huge, the bruise on her cheek a dark contrast against the pallor of her skin. "This is Cole Champion."

"Your *ex?*"

"Yes."

His body smashed against the wall, Champion inched his

head sideways and gave Nicole a pained grin. "This is some watchdog you got, Nicky. What say you call him off so I can stop polishing your wall with my new suit?"

Biting down on a snarl, Jake took a step back, holding the Glock's barrel aimed toward the floor. "Turn around. Nice and slow."

While Champion complied, Jake's brain cataloged styled jet-black hair, hollowed cheeks and heavy brows above dark, clever eyes. A black suit, crisp white shirt and blood-red tie completed the slickly handsome package. Jake had felt muscles as hard as marble beneath the tailored suit. That kind of strength sent the message Champion could knock anything out of his path without breaking stride. Including a startled woman on a dark front porch.

Jake tightened his hand on the Glock. Despite the sizzling kiss he and Nicole had just shared, he hadn't forgotten he'd spent the night on her couch in case her assailant showed up. Now, he thought with grim satisfaction, Cole Champion had stepped into the web.

Jake turned his head, met Nicole's gaze. "You said Bill's the only other person who has a key to this place."

"That's what I thought." Propping her hands on her hips, she shifted her attention. "Cole, you said you gave me all your keys when you moved out."

"I thought I had." Small lines at the edges of his eyes crinkled as his mouth curved into a smile that revealed perfect teeth. "I swear."

Annoyance flashed in her eyes like lightning as she took a step forward. "Don't bother swearing anything to *me*. Where did you get the key you just used?"

"It's an extra…" Champion's smile faded as she stepped fully beneath the bright overhead light. "Lord, Nicky, what happened to your cheek?"

When he moved toward her, Jake locked a hand on Champion's arm, shoved him back against the wall.

"I told you to turn around. I didn't say you could move."

Champion made a futile attempt to shrug off his grip. "Who the hell are you?"

"Sergeant Jake Ford. I'm the cop who's going to hau you in on breaking and entering."

"You've got it all wrong, pal. I didn't break in. I used key—"

"Which you're not supposed to have," Nicole interjected

"Come on, Nicky, give me a break. It's an extra I forgo about," Champion explained, his expression all innocence "I found it the other day in a box of stuff, so I slipped on my key ring. I planned on giving it to you the next tim I saw you." He swept a hand toward the marble floor wher his key ring had landed when Jake jerked him against th wall. "If your intense cop will let me move, I'll give yo the key."

Jake unclenched his hand from Champion's arm. "Pick up."

Champion scooped up the key ring. "Anyway, Nicky, knocked first." The diamond in the pinkie ring on his rig hand glittered as he nudged a key off the loop. "I knew was too early for you to be at work, so when you didn answer, I let myself in." He gave her the key, along with smile that edged on intimacy. "No big deal, I used to liv here, after all."

The knowledge that Nicole had once belonged to the ma curled a snake of envy in Jake's gut. Realization hit him lik a sledgehammer. Without his realizing it, his feelings for h had pushed right past protective. He now felt possessive an wildly territorial, too. When the hell had *that* happened? h wondered.

"I figured you didn't answer because you were in th shower," Champion continued. "I was going to come up s we could talk."

Nicole's hand snapped closed around the key. "You were going to come up?"

"And wait in your bedroom. I didn't plan on walking in on you while you were in the shower, or anything."

Although he wasn't touching her, Jake could almost feel her spine tense beneath her turquoise blouse.

"Sergeant," she began in a cool voice, "can I borrow your gun? I promise to give it back right after I shoot him."

"There's a tempting request," Jake murmured, deciding he would thoroughly enjoy disliking Cole Champion.

As if reading his mind, Champion slid the key ring into the pocket of his suit coat while his gaze sharpened on Jake. Instantly, Jake was aware of the coolness of the marble floor beneath his bare feet. His hair was uncombed, he needed a shave and his shirt was unbuttoned, its tail hanging out of his jeans. Not the look to convince anyone he was there on business.

A muscle in Champion's cheek jerked. "It's apparent I've come at an inconvenient time."

Damn right, Jake thought. If Champion hadn't shown up, he and Nicole would be upstairs in bed by now...if they'd made it that far before he'd managed to get her naked. The thought had Jake setting his jaw. He knew taking her to bed would have been a monumental mistake. He would only want more of her, and she was a woman he didn't want to risk having...and losing. Logically, he knew all that. Knew, too, that when he got around her, logic no longer came into play. Which was another mistake.

Hell.

He matched Champion's stare. "Why are you here?"

"To talk to my ex-wife," he replied. "Nicky, did you hear about DeSoto? That he died last night?"

She touched a fingertip to her right temple. "I heard."

"No one I've talked to knows any details. I came here to ask you to call Bill. Since your brother and my boss are...*were* friends, the A.D.A. might have some information.''

"Why not call the A.D.A. yourself?" Jake asked.

"Bill and I don't exactly get along. I'm not looking to stir things up with him. I just want some information."

"What sort?" As he spoke, Jake shoved his loose shirttail aside and slid the automatic into the waistband of his jeans.

"I want to know what happened. One minute DeSoto's fine, the next his assistant calls to tell me he died last night. Nobody seems to know why. DeSoto wasn't just my boss, I *liked* the guy. Dammit, I want to know what happened to him."

Champion's curiosity about his boss sounded logical. Still, Jake knew he might be lying through his teeth. He could have murdered Villanova, then planned on using whatever firsthand information Nicole got from Bill to make sure the investigation didn't head in his direction.

Jake glanced at Nicole, saw the reluctant sympathy for Champion's plight in her expressive blue eyes. She had forgiven the guy for breaking his vows and tossing their marriage onto the trash heap. They were now "comfortable friends." Jake doubted it had occurred to her that, if Villanova had been murdered, her ex-husband would land on the suspect list.

Jake let out a slow breath. He needed to interview Champion, give him some rope and see if he threw out a lifeline or hung himself. Because Nicole's presence might have Champion trying to save face at some point, Jake needed to separate them.

Cupping his palm on her elbow, he eased her to face him. "Champion and I need to talk," he said quietly. "I'd appreciate it if you'd download those two match lists you and I talked about."

"Right now?"

"That'd be best."

''Fine.''

''Make yourself comfortable, Champion,'' Jake said, dipping his head toward the living room.

''Sure. I'd appreciate you finding out what happened to DeSoto for me.''

Champion took two steps, then halted in front of Nicole. ''That's a nasty bruise,'' he said quietly. ''You okay, Nicky?''

''I'm fine.'' She stared up at him, her mouth curving at the edges. ''Cole, I don't mind you coming by once in a while. I just want you to call first. And don't think you're free to use any other keys you might have forgotten about. Understand?''

''Clear as crystal.'' He flicked a finger down her nose. ''You always did know how to get a point across.''

She turned to Jake. ''I'll be in my office.''

''Right.''

In silence, Jake studied Champion while the man's gaze tracked his ex-wife across the living room where morning sun slanted through white wooden blinds. Regret, then a far deeper emotion darkened his eyes.

He's still in love with her, Jake realized.

That knowledge shot his thoughts back to Bill and Whitney's reception, to the moment Nicole had smiled coyly up at Villanova as she slid her business card into his coat pocket. The open, smoldering desire in the Latino's eyes had sent a clear message. Granted, Champion hadn't been at the reception, but he might have witnessed a similar exchange between his boss and the woman for whom he still harbored feelings. *Unrequited feelings.* What Nicole considered harmless flirtation might take on a different meaning when viewed by an envious ex. Jake had seen a good number of murders committed because of homicidal jealousy.

Champion's admission that he was not only a co-worker but a friend of Villanova's automatically put him on the suspect list. Still, Jake decided to forgo Mirandizing him. The jury was still out on whether Villanova had been murdered, and there was no tangible reason at this point to think Champion had killed him.

Jake hitched a thumb toward a wing chair upholstered in the same gray-blue as the couch. "Have a seat, Champion."

"Thanks."

"Do you know of anybody who'd want to harm your boss?"

"No." Champion blinked as he settled onto the chair. "Does that mean someone *murdered* DeSoto?"

"I don't have the M.E.'s report yet so I have to cover all bases. Know of any arguments Villanova had with employees? Any dissatisfied customers?"

"No. He was a good guy and a great boss. He didn't have enemies."

"Where were you last night?"

Wariness crept into Champion's eyes. "Out. Why?"

"I like to get a time line so I'll know where everybody was," Jake improvised. "You went out where?"

"You said you were going to give me information."

"We'll get to that." Jake snagged his badge off the coffee table, clipped it onto the waistband of his jeans. "What did you do last night?"

Champion's dark brows slid together. "I had a date."

"Starting when?"

"I left the dealership at nine. Went home and cleaned up. We met at a restaurant around ten."

"It took you an hour to get cleaned up?"

"Yes." The faint tightening around Champion's mouth revealed his growing irritation. "Is that a problem?"

"Not for me." With a slow, grim smile, Jake sat on one arm of the couch. "Did anybody see you last night between the time you left work and met your date?"

"No."

"You ever meet Phillip Ormiston?"

"Yes." Champion's jaw tensed, then relaxed. "Why?"

"When did you meet him?"

"About four months ago." He lifted his fingers to the perfect Windsor knot in his tie. "I met him through DeSoto. They knew each other from working out at a gym called Sebastian's."

Why did everything about this case seem to circle back to the health club? Jake wondered.

"Do you work out there, too?"

"No. I use the gym at my condo complex."

"Have you met the health club's owner, Sebastian Peck?"

"Nicole's mentioned him. We've never met."

Jake thought about Eddie Denson's obituary still folded in the pocket of his sport coat, of the argument about steroids Mel Hall said he'd overheard between Peck and Ormiston. "Do you know a college kid named Eddie Denson?"

"Never heard of him."

"Let's go back to Ormiston. Exactly how did you meet?"

"DeSoto gave him a prime deal on five stretch limos for his funeral home business. When Ormiston came to the dealership to close the deal, DeSoto had me handle the paperwork."

Jake paused, wondering if that purchase had anything to do with the sour investment Ormiston had complained about. "Did the deal for the limos go through?"

"Why wouldn't it?"

"A glitch at the factory? Problems with delivery?"

"It went through without a hitch."

"Did Ormiston mention an investment he'd made where he lost a lot of money?"

"No. Look, I heard Ormiston died on Tuesday night. Did someone kill him?"

"Yes." Jake scowled as if puzzling over a weighty matter. "I'm trying to get this time line in my head, so I appreciate you cooperating the way you are." A case of vague confusion was a tactic Jake used often to nudge a guilty party into cooperating himself into a corner. "Since you knew Ormiston, I have to ask what you did and everywhere you went on Tuesday."

"I worked."

"Did you take a lunch break?"

"Just like I do every day," Champion answered, his voice heating.

"Where did you go?"

"I ran errands."

"Can anyone verify that?"

"Probably not. Every place I went I paid cash." Champion's eyes chilled as he pushed out of the chair. "I don't like your questions, Ford."

Jake let his shoulders lift and fall. "You don't have to like them. You just have to answer them. If it turns out your boss was murdered, you can expect to answer more." *Especially since you have no provable alibi for the time of either man's death.*

"I didn't kill anyone."

Jake rose off the arm of the couch. "Then you've got nothing to worry about."

"You're right, I don't." Champion strode into the entry hall, pulled open the door, then looked over his shoulder. "By the look of things, you and Nicky have something going." A muscle in his jaw jerked. "I can't figure what the hell she sees in you. You're not her type."

Jake gave him a smile that was all insolence. "Like you?"

A faint flush rose from above Champion's knotted tie to his cheeks. "Go to hell, Ford."

Jake's cell phone rang. He grabbed it off the coffee table, checked the display. *The M.E.*

He answered the call just as Champion closed the door behind him with a snap.

Nicole sat at her tidy desk with its long, curved legs, staring unseeingly at the computer's monitor. Behind her, a piece of paper unfurled from the printer sitting on the small credenza that matched the desk.

How had everything spun so out of control? she wondered. Less than an hour ago, Jake Ford—a man she was certain was all wrong for her—had kissed her brainless and melted her bones. With shivering need clawing inside her, she'd been close to dragging him onto the kitchen floor and pillaging. Now Jake was in her living room, presumably interrogating her ex-husband about his boss—*her client*—whose death was probably due to murder.

She pulled her bottom lip between her teeth. Cole couldn't have been the shadowy figure who'd rushed out of DeSoto's house last night and plowed into her. Nor had it been Sebastian, as Jake had implied last night at the hospital.

How could she be certain? she asked herself. How could she know who it *wasn't* when she couldn't even swear the person had been a man? In truth, the only thing she knew for sure was that two of her clients were dead and she'd come close to having sex on her kitchen floor with the cop investigating the case.

A cop who was the type of man she *knew* she should avoid.

Pressing her fingers to her eyes, she attempted to will away the memory of the shuddering jolts of electricity that Jake's kiss had rocketed through her. When that didn't work, she dragged in a deep breath, then another, hoping the breathing exercises Sebastian had taught her would clear her system of Jake's primal male taste and stop her stomach from flipping.

As matters stood, she was grateful Cole had shown up

when he did. His presence had reminded her how, when they'd met, she'd been so blinded by the fire-drenched demands of her own body that she hadn't looked past the outer layer to see the real man. She'd jumped without thought into a swirling tidal wave created by her own hormones and had wound up betrayed and hurt.

Never again. Passion alone was not to be trusted—she knew that better than most. Knew, too, that what she felt for Jake was all passion. Viciously arousing passion.

Sweet holy heaven, had she been aroused!

Murmuring a quiet oath, she reassured herself that her off-the-Richter-scale reaction to Jake's kiss didn't mean she'd lost control of her emotions. After all, she knew with unerring certainty what she wanted, knew the kind of man she belonged with. She had no intention of ever again letting a whirlwind of fiery lust addle her thinking. One day she would step into a man's arms and feel the kind of slow, sweet beginning that promised a lifetime of warm desire and lasting commitment. *He* was out there—the one man, her soul mate. He would walk into her life, and she would *know* him. Until then, all she needed was a little patience.

"Nicole?"

She swiveled in her chair, saw Jake, tall, gorgeous Jake, standing in the center of the doorway. Her heart jolted. She would need patience *and* self-control, she amended as heat licked through her veins and shot into her cheeks. A large dose of self-control would come in handy while she waited for Mr. Right.

He slanted her a curious look. "You okay?"

"Of course." She jammed a loose pin back in her hair. His white shirt was buttoned now, its tail tucked into his jeans. When her palms began to itch with the remembered feel of the sinewed muscles beneath that shirt, she wondered why her overtaxed brain didn't just implode. "Is Cole gone?"

"Yeah. He didn't like my questions and decided not to play anymore."

She hesitated. "Questions about DeSoto?"

"Among other things." As he moved toward her desk, Jake's gaze shifted, taking in the small, tidy bookcases and wood file cabinet that shared space with the matching rose-and-ivory-toned chairs. "The M.E. called," he added, slipping a hip onto the side of the desk.

Nicole wasn't sure if it was his nearness, or the grimness in his eyes—or both—that curled fingers of tension in her stomach. "Was...DeSoto murdered?"

"Same MO as Ormiston. Injected with something that paralyzed his lungs. They're still not sure what that something is. It'll take time to get the toxicology reports back."

She felt tears well up and blinked them away. "Who, Jake? *Why?*"

"I don't know. Yet."

When he reached to touch the hand she'd fisted on the desk, she eased back in her chair, twined her fingers in her lap. It would be so easy, she thought. So easy to accept comfort. So easy to step into his arms again and lose herself in the heat for as long as the fire raged.

He's not what you want, the logical part of her admonished, even as her body and heart yearned.

He said nothing for a moment, his eyes on hers. Finally, he crossed his arms over his chest. "The M.E. is sure enough of the time of death that we can figure whoever it was who knocked you off the porch killed Villanova."

"Good God."

"Is your brother on the outs with Champion because you found him with another woman?"

"Yes. After Bill heard what I walked in on, he wanted to pound Cole into pulp. I had to remind Bill that wasn't the best thing for an assistant D.A. to do."

"It is for an older brother."

"That's what Bill said."

"What does he think about you and Champion still being friends?"

"You don't want to know."

Jake cocked his head. "I need you to tell me more about your ex."

"Because you think Cole might be the killer?" she asked, dread settling in her stomach.

"Because when he walked through your door this morning, he stepped in the middle of a homicide investigation." Jake raked a hand through his hair. "I've got two men murdered. Your ex knew both of them, those are the facts."

"Cole knew Phillip?"

"Yes. That doesn't necessarily mean anything—a lot of people knew both victims. Those are the people I need to look at. You were married to Champion, you lived with him. Who better to tell me what he's like beneath the surface?"

She closed her eyes, opened them. "What do you want to know?"

"You said he's worked for Villanova about half a year. What did he do before?"

"When we met, Cole was a land man for a local oil company."

"That means he researched land ownership records, right?"

"Yes. Then he'd contact landowners to secure acreage leases for drilling, both oil and gas wells. Cole also brokered deals on the side. Of course, he preferred to keep those quiet."

"Why?"

"Because the company he worked for didn't get a slice of that particular pie. I'm not sure the company shouldn't have, but it's a common practice in the industry. A lot of land men broker deals for both their employer and for themselves."

"It's my guess he's pretty good at working deals."

"Very. Cole's a born networker. He seems to know everyone, has a knack for putting the right people together for what needs to be done."

"So, the bottom line is he found people with money to invest in a well that had yet to be drilled. Then he hooked them all up as partners in that well?"

"Right."

"What did Champion get for doing that?"

"A guaranteed percentage of the total money invested."

"What kind of money are we talking about?"

"During the oil boom, a lot. Cole brokered several big deals. In some cases, he also invested in a well he brokered, so he also got a percentage of the profits when the well hit."

"What happens if a well doesn't hit?"

"The investors take a loss."

"Money down the pipeline, so to speak."

"Sometimes a lot of money."

"Suppose Champion didn't invest his own money in a well, just brokered the deal to get the guys with the money lined up. Was the commission he made from brokering the deal safe?"

"Yes."

"He ever have any major losses?"

"A couple that I know of while we were married. That's why Cole stopped putting his own money into a well and worked strictly as a broker."

"Which made his risk minimal. Almost nonexistent."

"When it came to the money, yes." Nicole plucked a pen off the desk, laid it down. "Once in a while an investor who loses gets irate. It's no one's fault if a well doesn't hit, it just happens. That's sometimes hard to remember when your money goes down a dry hole."

"Do you know if Ormiston invested in any wells?"

Jake's question sent a ripple of unease down her spine.

"If Phillip did, he never mentioned it." She rolled her chair back, rose and turned to the credenza. "Did Cole tell you Phillip put money into one of his oil deals?" she asked while she straightened a brass frame that held a family photograph.

"No, Champion didn't tell me that. Is the oil bust the reason he went to work selling Cadillacs for Villanova?"

Turning, Nicole leaned a hip against the credenza. "Yes. Hundreds of people were laid off, Cole included."

"Did he stop brokering?"

"I'm not sure, but I doubt it. He loves the prospect of making money, almost as much as the act itself."

"I'd love it, too, if I could make a profit with no risk to my own bank balance."

The sardonic edge in Jake's voice transformed the unease she felt to dread. "I know you have to consider everyone, but Cole couldn't have killed DeSoto. Or Phillip."

"You're sure about that?"

"Positive. I…" Her voice hitched. "I can't believe this. How can DeSoto and Phillip be dead? *Murdered.*"

"They're dead because someone had reason to want them that way." Jake stood, dipped his head toward the printer. "Is that the list of the women who dated both Villanova and Ormiston?"

"Yes." She turned, retrieved the single piece of paper. When she swiveled around, she bumped right into Jake. She jerked away as if scalded.

"You okay?" he asked quietly.

"Yes." She handed him the paper while avoiding his gaze. "I…two women went out with both Phillip and DeSoto."

Crossing her arms around her waist, Nicole roamed around to the opposite side of the desk. She had to keep distance between them. A lot of distance.

"Rhonda Livingston and Ingrid Nelson," she said.

''Their files were with the ones you had the officer pick up yesterday.''

''If I remember right, Livingston's a Realtor. Nelson's a physical therapist.''

''There's that good memory of yours again.''

''Yeah. Like I said, I've already made appointments for this afternoon to meet with the ten women Ormiston dated.'' Jake checked his watch. ''Now that I know for sure Villanova was murdered, I need to hit up my lieutenant with a new angle on how to work this. If things line up the way I think they will, you may have a new client on your hands.''

''A new client?''

''Me.''

''You,'' Nicole said quietly.

''Two men who dated both of these women are dead. One may be a black widow who mates, then kills. If so, she'll be looking for victim number three. Whether I get matched up with one or both depends on their alibis for the times of the murders.''

A twin mix of emotion assailed Nicole. First, a tug of worry at Jake putting himself in danger. Second, an instinctive, gut-level rejection to his dating other women. She didn't like either prospect.

Nicole moved to the far end of the room, pausing in front of the bookcase she'd filled with leather-bound first editions. ''It makes me sick to think the killer could be a client of Meet Your Match,'' she said, meeting Jake's gaze. ''We run background checks, do personality profiles. *Testing.* How could we have missed someone who kills?''

'' 'Desire to kill' isn't something that gets listed on a person's résumé,'' Jake pointed out. ''You check people out the best you can. That's all you can do.''

When she remained in front of the bookcase, he cocked his head. ''Maybe you'd like it better if I stepped out in the hall while we talk. Would that put enough space between us for you?''

Her throat closed at the hardness in his voice. ''I'm sorry, Jake. It's just that…I think it would be best if we didn't repeat what we did in the kitchen.''

''Eat breakfast?''

''You know what I mean.''

''Yeah, I know.'' He folded the paper she'd given him, jammed it into his shirt pocket. ''That was less than an hour ago. You mind telling me what changed things?''

''Cole. Cole changed things.''

Jake's dark brows slid together. ''You telling me you still have feelings for him?''

''Not that kind.'' She ran her tongue over her dry lips. ''I told you when I met him I lost my head. Big time. I let emotion sweep me off my feet. Jake, that's how it is with you.''

Something dangerous came and went in his gaze. ''Do you think I'm like Champion? The kind of man who'd betray a wife?''

''I don't know what kind of man you are. Not really. And when I'm around you, I don't care. *That's* the problem. I don't think. I just *feel.* That's how it was when I met Cole.''

His mouth thinned to a grim line, Jake skirted the desk, walked slowly toward her. ''Sounds to me like you're comparing us, man to man.''

''I'm comparing the situation.'' Taking a step back, she lodged her spine against the bookcase. ''And it's the same.''

''Is it?'' he asked, pausing a bare inch from her.

''Yes.'' She had to lift her chin to meet his gaze. ''When you're around, I forget, *let* myself forget how dearly I paid at one time because I ignored logic. When Cole showed up this morning, he made me remember. I'm close to doing that same thing with you, Jake. That scares me to death. What happened between us was a physical reaction—''

"Damn right it was."

"—that I don't trust. I learned the hard way the kind of man who suits me. You're not him."

"I seemed to suit you well enough in the kitchen."

"You swept me off my feet, and I let you." She fisted her hands against the memory of the searing kisses they'd shared. Of how far they'd almost taken their attraction. "I don't want that. I *can't* want that," she added for her own benefit.

"You're not the only one with concerns here, lady."

When he leaned forward, she sucked in air against an undeniable longing. If he dipped his head, his mouth would be on hers. Desire shot straight to her stomach, swirled there while she watched anger flash in his eyes.

"Do you think I enjoy knowing I want you more than I've ever wanted any other woman? *Any other woman?*"

"I didn't know," she said almost desperately as her heartbeat echoed in her head.

"Now you do. I've got reasons of my own not to like what's happened between us. *Good reasons.* But, facts are facts and I'm damned if I can help having feelings for you, Nicole. It's too bad you don't want me to have those feelings, because I do. You've got no control over that. What you do have a say about is whether I ever put my hands on you again."

"Jake, it's…"

"I want my hands on you," he continued quietly when her voice faltered. "I want to take you, Nicole. Right here, right now. But as long as you've got a problem with me touching you, I won't."

"That'd…be…best." Her legs were jelly; the only thing that kept her from sagging to the floor was the fact that her spine was jammed against the bookcase.

"Fine, that's how we'll play this." He stepped away. "If

you plan on working here today, I'll have a female officer come over.''

She swallowed hard at his instant transformation into hard-edged cop. He'd given her what she wanted, agreed to the equivalent of dumping ice water on their relationship. So why did she feel as if a big hole had ripped inside her heart?

"It's not necessary to have someone come over,'' she managed to say over her dry-as-dust throat while she tried to untangle her thought processes. ''Don't you think the person who killed DeSoto knows that if I could identify him or her, the police would have shown up on their doorstep by now?''

"That's probably safe to assume. I just don't like making assumptions about anyone's safety.''

"I want to go to the office, Jake. I need to go. Tons of people are around all the time. Mel's right outside my door.''

Jake scowled. "You'll stay with Bill and Whitney at night?''

"Yes. I don't like to be run out of my own home, but there's no sense in taking chances.''

"If Lieutenant Ryan okays it for me to go undercover on dates with Livingston and Nelson, I'll come by your office later today. You'll need to do the standard paperwork, put me in the system just like any other client.''

"Fine.''

"Do you trust Mel to keep quiet about the operation?''

"Absolutely.''

Jake hooked a thumb in the front pocket of his jeans. "Your car is parked in Villanova's driveway. I'll give you a lift there, then follow you to the office. I've got a few phone calls to make while you get ready.''

"I won't be long.''

He nodded, turned, then strode out the door.

Watching him go, Nicole assured herself that everything was fine now. Straightened out. She was no longer in danger of being plundered or plundering. No longer at risk of feeling the breathless thrill one felt when they plunged off the edge of a cliff. Or the shattering pain when one landed. That was what she wanted.

She lifted an unsteady hand to her throbbing cheek. If she'd just gotten what she wanted, why then did she want to race after Jake and fall into his arms? Why did her body ache to be touched by him and only him?

She squeezed her eyes shut as her heart contracted, and wondered if she'd just made the biggest mistake of her life.

Chapter 8

Damned if he would beg, for Nicole or anyone.

Tightening his hands on the steering wheel, Jake whipped the cruiser into the service lane behind a row of trendy businesses to avoid the lunch-hour traffic. No, he wouldn't beg, not even a woman whom he wanted with a fervor that was like a sickness.

After some sort of introspection on her part, Nicole had decided *he* didn't fit her profile. He wasn't the *kind* of man she wanted to drag her to her kitchen floor for manic sex. What the hell did the woman know about the kind of man she wanted?

The absolute idiocy of that last thought brought Jake up short. Easing his death grip on the steering wheel, he flexed his fingers while banking the urge for a cigarette. She'd made one mistake and learned from it. Now she was a romance engineer, for crying out loud. Had probably fixed up hundreds of successful matches. That ought to just about make her an expert when it came to knowing what kind of man she wanted for herself.

That man wasn't him.

"Hell."

Scowling, Jake pulled back out into traffic and immediately changed lanes to pass some cretin going twenty in a cherry-red Beemer. He knew that once he got past the sting of Nicole's rejection and stopped thinking with his glands he would concede she'd done him a favor. After all, he didn't want anything that even resembled a serious relationship, had *sworn* he'd never again involve himself in one. He knew too well the high price a man could pay for loving a woman. A child. Children.

He blew out a breath against the tightness that settled in his chest. It was hard to believe the wife and daughters who were so alive in his heart had been dead two years. Although his wrenching grief had transformed into a dull ache, at times the void Annie and the twins' deaths had left in his life was almost unbearable. As was the knowledge he'd handled his loss by crawling into a bottle and heading toward hell without a thought to the consequences for himself or anyone else. His recklessness had cost one woman her life. His boss had read him his rights, charged him with her murder and seven others, then locked him in a cage. Jake knew he would still be rotting behind bars if it hadn't been for Whitney's dogged belief in his innocence. He hadn't forgotten that his partner had nearly gotten herself killed attempting to clear him of the murders.

Bill Taylor hadn't forgotten, either. Jake had heard the reserve in the A.D.A.'s voice last night when he'd phoned the honeymooning couple in Cancún. Taylor had been understandably upset to hear about the death of his friend, Villanova. When Jake detailed Nicole's injuries, concern had mixed with an undertone of heat in the A.D.A.'s voice. It was when Jake mentioned his plan to bunk on Nicole's couch that he'd sensed Bill Taylor's transformation into a distrustful older brother.

The A.D.A. didn't want his sister hanging around a man who'd screwed up his life so thoroughly. Jake didn't blame the guy. He figured he would feel the same if he had a baby sister.

All things considered, Nicole had been right to cool things, he conceded as he steered the cruiser into the lot bordering the sleek skyscraper that housed Meet Your Match and Sebastian's. He pulled into a parking space, let his gaze slide up to the top floor, then focused on what he knew were the windows of her office. He had enough regrets for one lifetime. Having personal feelings for Nicole—whatever the hell they were—was something he hadn't planned. And was an area he would just have to leave alone.

Along with her.

Which might prove hard to do, he acknowledged. The approval for his going undercover as a single man looking for love was working its way up the chain of command. Jake glanced at his watch. He figured Lieutenant Ryan would get back to him this afternoon with the captain and major's go-ahead for the operation.

While he was waiting for those approvals, Jake planned to drop in on Sebastian Peck. Once it dawned on the Viking god why he was there, Jake doubted he'd be welcome.

Too damn bad.

He opened the cruiser's door and stepped into the noon-day heat. Reaching into his shirt pocket, he retrieved his sunglasses and slid them on.

The forest of blue and purple hydrangeas at the base of the towering structure looked as thick and plush as it had two days ago when he'd first set eyes on the building. The setting might be the same, Jake thought, but he now had information about Sebastian Peck that he hadn't known then. According to Mel Hall, Ormiston had accused the Swede of turning the late Eddie Denson on to steroids. That accusation had allegedly resulted in a heated argument. Less than two weeks later, someone plunged a needle into Ormiston's neck and condemned the man to a torturous death. Mel had also mentioned that Peck didn't bother to conceal a case of white-hot jealousy when DeSoto Villanova hung around Nicole during workouts.

Had that jealousy, along with whatever had resulted during the argument with Ormiston, compelled Peck to do away with both men?

That was a question he hoped to find the answer to during his visit with Peck, Jake thought as he headed toward the building's revolving door.

Five minutes later, Jake strode into Sebastian's. The receptionist with the cotton candy-pink lipstick and matching eye shadow who'd been there the day before gave him a wary look from behind her glass-block desk.

"I need to see your boss."

Her uneasy gaze flicked to her phone. "Uh, Sebastian's in his office. He's on the phone. If you'll have a seat, I'll let him know you're here."

Jake didn't want to give Peck advance warning. "Just point me in his direction. I'll take things from there."

She stabbed a polished pink nail toward a paneled door behind her desk.

When Jake stepped through the doorway, the low strains of a classical concerto filled the air. The soft music was a sharp contrast to the bouncy exercise tune that had blasted in the workout area.

Turning a corner, he found himself in a short corridor painted in soft yellow tones with an open door on either side. Through the door to his right Jake spied the modern-day Adonis sitting behind a mahogany desk as massive as the man himself. Peck leaned back in a black leather chair, a cordless phone wedged between one muscled shoulder and his ear. Except for the desk, the office was all cool black marble and stark white walls. The white carpet resembled sea foam and looked deep enough to wade in.

As if sensing his presence, Peck glanced up. He hesitated, then said, "I'll call you back."

"Sergeant Ford." Peck laid the phone aside and rose. His sleeveless black T-shirt and shorts showed off hulking, well-toned muscles. Beneath brilliant-gray eyes, his mouth curved into a smooth smile. "Is it too much to hope you've decided to get your biorhythms charted?" As he spoke, he glanced at the high-tech sports watch strapped to his wrist. "I can probably also work in that game of racquetball we talked about."

"Some other time."

Jake strode into the office, his scuffed boots sinking into the thick carpet. To his left a small sofa and chairs uphol-stered in white formed a sitting area. On his right a three-foot spray of waxy white flowers speared out of a black marble urn.

"Can I offer you something?" Peck asked, the faint wisp of Swedish sounding in his voice. "We maintain a fully stocked refreshment bar. Juice, high-protein snacks. Maybe some sparkling water with a twist?"

"Just information." Without invitation, Jake sat in one of the visitors' chairs angled in front of the desk. He watched Peck settle into his high-backed leather chair. The man's eyes were calm, his expression easy. Today his blond mane was slicked back into a queue that hung between his shoul-der blades.

"This is a follow-up to yesterday's visit." He reached into the pocket of his sports coat and withdrew a small re-corder. Leaning, he settled the recorder on the front of the desk. "You don't mind if I tape this conversation, do you?"

Peck's eyes flicked to the recorder. "No, that's fine."

"Good." Jake clicked the record button, then eased back

in his chair. "You're entitled to have counsel present, Mr. Peck."

The man clenched his thick fingers, then unclenched them. "Do I need a lawyer?"

"Only you can answer that at this point."

"Why don't you tell me what this is about, then I'll decide if I want to call my lawyer."

"Fine. There are a few things about Phillip Ormiston I'm not clear on. I figure you can help me."

"I told you all I know when you were here yesterday."

"Did you?"

"Yes."

"This goes back to my asking you if Ormiston argued with anyone. You told me no. I have a witness who claims he overhead you and Ormiston have a go at each other."

Wariness slid into Peck's eyes. "We didn't argue. We had an intense discussion."

"Which you failed to mention."

"Nothing came of it. I didn't consider it important."

"Ormiston accused you of illegally distributing steroids to Eddie Denson and you didn't consider it important?"

"The accusation was false, so no. I didn't consider it important."

"*Did* you supply steroids to Denson?"

"No."

"Doesn't sound like Ormiston believed that."

"I can't help what he believed." Peck linked his fingers together on the desk, pulled them apart, linked them again. "He was wrong."

"Did you tell him that?"

"Damn right, I did. He accused me of getting the Denson kid hooked on steroids, of being his supplier. I don't engage in illegal practices, nor do I allow them to go on in my health club."

"Did Eddie Denson use steroids?"

Peck closed his eyes. "Yes."

"He ever discuss them with you?"

"When his family first joined the club. Eddie came in here one night and asked me about steroids, if I'd ever used them."

"Have you?"

Peck nodded. "When I was involved in body-building competitions. That was a long time ago."

"Did you tell Eddie you used them?"

"Yes. I also told him about the risks. He was young. He didn't want to listen. He wanted to bulk up, not hear about side effects associated with steroid use."

"One being violent mood swings. Aggressiveness."

"That's right."

"I read the report on the traffic accident in which Denson died," Jake stated. "Witnesses claim road rage was involved on the kid's part. Suppose his behavior could be linked directly to steroids. Denson's parents might decide to make trouble for the person who supplied steroids to their son. Trouble, as in getting felony charges filed and bringing a civil law suit. Those things could cost someone a lot of money and all his assets. Not to mention his freedom."

Color swept into Peck's face. "I didn't supply steroids to Denson."

"Did Ormiston threaten to go to Denson's parents and tell them you did? Ormiston doing that would have put both you and your business in a world of hurt."

"Ormiston didn't *threaten* anything. Like I said, we had an intense discussion, not an argument. He left here convinced I had nothing to do with Eddie's involvement with steroids."

"Why do you think Ormiston had Denson's obituary in his locker?"

"I have no idea."

"Let's talk about DeSoto Villanova."

"I—Villanova?"

The change in rhythm had thrown Peck off, as Jake had intended. "Do you get along?"

"He's a client." One massive shoulder lifted. "Why wouldn't we get along?"

"A woman," Jake said simply. "I understand you and Villanova have had your eyes on the same woman."

Peck stiffened, hesitated, then relaxed again. "You're referring to Nicole," he said finally.

"Right. I hear you don't like the attention Villanova directs Miss Taylor's way."

Peck's gaze went as hard as granite. "Nicole and I are friends. It's not my place to like or dislike the attention other men give her."

"Maybe so, but you'd like to be more than friends."

"She wouldn't. I respect her feelings. Is there a point to this?"

"I always have a point. Where were you last night?"

"Why do you want to know?"

"Let's start around six," Jake continued. "Give me a rundown on everything you did between then and midnight."

"I worked here at my desk all evening. I didn't leave until around eleven."

"Why so late?"

"I had paperwork to catch up on."

"Did you stay in your office the whole time?"

"Yes."

"Make any phone calls?"

"No."

"Receive any?"

Peck scowled. "No. Why do you ask?"

Jake inclined his head toward the door behind the desk. "That the door you told me about? The one that leads into the hall so you can come and go as you please?"

"Yes."

"Did you use that door yesterday? Slip out, then come back?"

"I used it around eleven when I left for the night. And I didn't 'slip out,' I walked." Peck fisted his hands. "What the hell is this about? Ormiston died two days ago. Why do you care what I did last night?"

"Because the same person who killed Ormiston murdered DeSoto Villanova."

"I... *What?*"

To Jake, the flicker of surprise in Peck's eyes looked genuine. Still, it could have been one hell of a performance on the Swede's part. "I think you heard me."

"Yes. It's just that I don't believe..." He slicked a massive hand across the back of his neck. "You think I killed them both, don't you? I disagreed with Ormiston over steroids. I was jealous of Villanova's attention to Nicole."

Jake smiled. "That sums it up."

"Well, you can just un-sum it." As anger heated Peck's voice, his Swedish accent became more pronounced. "I didn't kill anyone."

"Can you prove that?"

"I don't have to. You have to prove what you're accusing me of. Since I didn't do it, there's no way you can."

Jake cocked his head. "Is that another legal gem from your girlfriend, Monique? The master of *feng shui?*"

"Monique is my *former* girlfriend and my attorney. If you want to talk to me again, she'll be present."

"An attitude like that could give the impression you've got something to hide."

"One like yours could give the impression you live in a world of cynicism and absurdity." Peck studied Jake from across the span of polished mahogany. "If you make it back here for that racquetball game, Sergeant, I suggest you leave time for a herbal detox. You're clearly in need of one."

Feeling totally insulted—and unsure why—Jake rose, retrieved the recorder off the desk and clicked it off. "This investigation is ongoing. I might be back for that racquetball game. Or maybe to arrest you for murder."

"You shouldn't have come in."

As he spoke, Mel Hall slid a silver tray holding a teapot and cups onto the table in front of the love seat where Nicole sat. Today, her assistant wore a cream-colored shirt and pleated slacks that complemented his lean build.

"You need time to recover," he added.

"I'm fine." She forced a weary smile. "Really, I am."

"You don't look fine. You need to let me drive you home and settle you in bed."

He had repeated that same statement at least ten times since she'd walked through the door that morning. "I appreciate you watching out for me, Mel—"

"You're white as a sheet. And that bruise..." He shook his head. "I should have been the one to stay with you last night. I would have taken good care of you."

"You needed to be with your mother. Edna depends on you."

When he joined her on the love seat, Mel's blue eyes sharpened on Nicole's cheek. "There'd be less bruising and swelling today if I'd been there to fix you a compress."

She gave his knee an absent pat. "You took care of me by making sure Sergeant Ford knew to buy the arnica lotion. And ginger ale." She ran a hand over the hip of her gray silk slacks. "Other than being a little stiff from the fall off DeSoto's porch, I'm fine." She didn't add that her head ached like a fresh wound.

Mel sighed. "Well, that's what matters," he conceded, pouring tea into cups with his usual brisk efficiency.

"No, it's not. I..." Her voice hitched against a drag of

grief. "DeSoto and Phillip are both dead. I keep hoping I'll wake up and find it's all been a terrible nightmare."

"What happened isn't your fault, you need to remember that." Mel's mouth curved as he passed her a cup and saucer. "I brewed your favorite, Moroccan mint."

"You're my hero, Mel." Although she felt content sitting on the love seat, sharing a cup of tea with her young assistant, Nicole knew nothing could ease the heavy burden the murders had settled around her heart.

Watching her, Mel retrieved his own cup. "I don't like seeing you upset. I understand how you feel, but there's no way you could have known this would happen."

"You're right." She took a sip of tea, savored its soothing mint taste. "But what if one of the women who went out with both men killed them? If that's the case, then Phillip and DeSoto are dead because of their association with Meet Your Match. We have a duty to make matchmaking safe. It's our job to protect our clients."

"We put Ingrid Nelson and Rhonda Livingston through the same screening as everyone else," Mel commented, referring to the women who'd dated both murder victims. "Neither have any violent tendencies."

"That showed up in testing," Nicole added.

"Which is what we have to depend on." He sampled his tea. "If Sergeant Ford goes undercover, we'll just have to hope he figures out fast who the killer is—Nelson or Livingston."

Nicole stroked a fingertip around the rim of her cup. "If it's either of them. I still can't get over the feeling that it was a *man* who plowed into me last night on DeSoto's front porch."

Mel's forehead furrowed. "What did Sergeant Ford say about that?"

Just talking about Jake had nerves tingling in Nicole's stomach. She hadn't forgotten the hot, drugging kisses they'd shared that morning, or the hardness that settled in Jake's eyes when she'd told him he wasn't the kind of man she wanted. Nor was she likely to forget the cool silence that had hung between them while he drove her to retrieve her Jaguar from DeSoto's driveway.

That cool distance was what she wanted, what she'd *demanded* from Jake, she reminded herself. Whatever her body was telling her, her mind sent a different message. She needed to be smart where Jake was concerned. Sensible. She needed to stay away.

"Nicole?"

Her gaze jerked up to meet Mel's expectant one. "I'm sorry, what did you say?"

"I asked you what Ford said about the possibility of it being a man who hit you last night."

"He—

"—doesn't discount any possibility."

Both their gazes whipped to the doorway where Jake stood. He had changed into a pale yellow dress shirt, jeans and a black sport coat. When Nicole saw he hadn't bothered to shave, her heart did a slow roll as she felt again the phantom stroke of stubble against her jaw.

"Jake…Sergeant." She sat her cup and saucer on the table then skimmed a hand over the neat coil at the base of her neck. "Come in."

"Your receptionist sent me back." He strode in, pausing at the opposite side of the coffee table. His gaze flicked to Mel, then moved back to her. "Is this a good time?"

"Of course." Her already raw nerves jittered. "I take it you're here because your boss approved your going undercover?"

"I've got clearance all the way up the chain of command." His gaze shifted back to Mel. "Nicole's filled you in?"

"Yes. We were just talking about how we'd hate to find

out the murderer is one of our clients. But the bottom line is the killing has to stop.'' Mel rose, swept a hand toward the silver tray. "Can I get you something? We're having Moroccan mint—it's Nicole's favorite. I expect that doesn't appeal to you, so I can bring you some plain coffee.''

Jake hooked a thumb in the pocket of his jeans. "I'll have tea.''

Nicole blinked, as did Mel.

"I'll get an extra cup,'' her assistant said, finding his voice before she did.

"Thanks.''

Nicole rubbed at the ache in her right temple. "Mel, when you come back with the cup, bring a client registration packet. I'll need to fill out the usual forms on Sergeant Ford. When they're done, I'll have you enter his data into the system.''

"Sure thing,'' Mel said, then headed out the door.

She met Jake's gaze. "Do either Rhonda Livingston or Ingrid Nelson have alibis for the time Phillip and DeSoto died?''

"A team of detectives interviewed each woman this morning. Both claim they were home alone when the murders occurred. To a homicide cop's way of thinking, being anywhere alone when a murder happens isn't much of an alibi.''

Edgy with his presence, Nicole rose, picked up her cup and saucer, then moved to her desk. "I expected you'd get your approval to go undercover,'' she said, settling into her leather chair. "So, when I came in this morning, I went over Phillip and DeSoto's files. I've made a list of their similarities so we can work them into your profile.''

"Good.'' She felt the sharp assessment in Jake's whiskey-colored eyes as he slid a hip onto the front of the desk.

"I'll be your counselor of record, but all the other counselors will have access to your data. The two women,

Rhonda and Ingrid, work with different counselors. We can expect both to pull up your data when they see your name has been added to their client's match list.''

''I'd like to meet each woman tomorrow night for a drink. At Encounters,'' he added, referring to the elegant club off the lobby of a nearby high-rise hotel. ''Set up Livingston at seven. Nelson at nine. I can get a feel for each, then take it from there.''

''Take it from there,'' Nicole repeated softly as an unexpected jolt of jealousy turned her stomach into a dozen tight fists. Rhonda Livingston was a gorgeous brunette, Ingrid Nelson a luscious redhead. Pair either woman with Jake, and you'd have a stunning couple.

Picking up her teacup, Nicole drew in a slow breath while irritation scraped at the back of her neck. What was wrong with her? Jake was trying to catch a killer and here she was, dealing with a case of schoolgirl envy.

''Something wrong?'' he asked.

''No, I—''

''Here we go.'' Mel swept back in, carrying a file folder and balancing a china cup and saucer. It barely registered in Nicole's mind that his easy smile faded when he saw Jake had made himself at home on the front of her desk.

''Thank you, Mel,'' she said when he handed her the folder.

Jake wrapped a hand around the cup, leaving the saucer in the assistant's hand. ''Cup's all I need.''

''Fine.'' Mel walked to the table, retrieved the teapot, then retraced his steps to the desk.

''This your uncle's blend?'' Jake asked as Mel filled both cups.

Mel grinned. ''As a matter of fact it is. When it comes to tea, Uncle Zebulon's the best there is.''

Nicole returned her assistant's smile. ''I'll need you to take Sergeant Ford's picture for the file before he leaves.''

"Say the word when you're ready." After returning the pot to the tray, Mel strode out, closing the door behind him.

Nicole shot Jake a look from under her lashes as he sipped from the delicate cup. "I thought coffee was your drink."

He met her gaze over the cup's rim. "Couldn't pass up a chance to sample your favorite tea."

"What's the verdict?"

He set the cup aside. "Moroccan mint lives up to its name."

The tang of soap, mixed with his warm, musky scent drifted across the desk. Struggling to ignore the fluttering in her heart, she forced her mind to business.

"I need to ask you some standard information." She opened the file folder and plucked up a pen.

"Shoot."

"What name will you use?"

"Jake England. That's my mom's maiden name."

"Jake England," Nicole said as she wrote. "Will you use a fictitious address, too?"

"Yeah, a safe house the department maintains," he said, then gave her the information. "We've got surveillance cameras set up there. They'll get everything on tape if the killer shows."

Nicole tightened her grip on the pen. "You know you're putting yourself on a hook and tossing yourself out as bait, don't you?"

"That's my job." His eyes stayed locked with hers. "Thanks for caring, though. Next question?"

"Place of employment?"

"I'm an investor. Self-employed."

"What do you invest in, Mr. England?"

"Jewelry. Stocks. Hog futures. Anything that'll make a profit."

"Hobbies?"

Jake angled his chin. "Did Ormiston and Villanova list any of the same hobbies?"

"Yes, they both played golf."

"Golf it is. I've watched enough tournaments I can talk about the game."

"Do you smoke?"

"Only when I'm set on fire."

Nicole suppressed a smile. "I'll be sure to note you possess a sense of humor." She flipped to a fresh page of the form. "What languages does Jake England, self-employed investor, speak?"

"Other than the slight handle I've got on English?" He rubbed his stubbled chin. "Put me down for courtroom Latin, gutter Spanish, restaurant French and East Side street jive."

As she made the notation, Nicole pulled her bottom lip between her teeth, felt the tenderness from his kiss that lingered there. Was it so wrong to want to be the woman destined to sit in the dim, elegant club with this man? Sharing a drink, a laugh? Maybe more… Oh, God, she wanted.

"What else?"

Looking up, she swallowed around the knot in her throat. "Marital status."

He narrowed his eyes. "Do you take on people who are already married and looking to have an affair?"

"Of course not. We have clients who have never been married, those who are legally separated, divorced, widowed—"

"Widower. I'm a widower."

Nicole thought the abrupt answer was part of Jake England's fictitious cover. Then she looked up and met his gaze. In the space of a heartbeat, his eyes had gone as grim as his voice. "I'm… Jake, I'm sorry, I didn't know."

"No way you could have. Next question."

She dropped her gaze back to the form. "Do you have children? If so, how many?"

"None." He looked away, fisting his hand as it rested on his thigh. "Not anymore."

She reached out, cupped her hand over his fist. "You lost your wife and child?"

He looked back. His face was unreadable now. His cop's face. "My wife and twin daughters." Tugging his hand from beneath hers, he rose, stepped away from the desk. "Hell, I don't know why I told you any of that."

"Jake—"

"I don't talk about it." He shoved a hand through his hair. "Put down that I'm single, never been married. No children...ever." He closed his eyes. "I should have said that in the first place."

A little piece of Nicole's heart weakened and was lost to him. She rose, came around the desk, stopping inches from him. "I'm sorry for your loss."

"I'm sorry, too," he said, his eyes intense, focused on her. "You were right."

"About what?"

"Cooling things between us before they got started." He cupped a hand against her uninjured cheek. "I don't ever want to fall in love again. Hell, I don't think I ever even want to hear the word."

Raising her hand, she curled her fingers around his wrist. She couldn't help reaching out to this man. He'd been hurt, devastated, and try as he might to conceal his feelings, the pain of his loss showed in his eyes.

"Jake, I've been telling myself all day that it was smart to cool things. Sensible." The warm, liquefying pleasure of his touch seeped into her. She decided if she were made of stone, she'd maybe have a shot at sensible. "Now that you're here, it seems that cooling things was the stupidest thing I've ever done."

"It was smart." His fingers moved against her cheek. "I've sworn off women. You've sworn off relationships with men you figure aren't your type. Like me."

"You're not what I want," she said weakly. She knew if he kissed her she would forget all the sensible decisions she'd made. Forget why she'd made them. "It would be a stupid move on both our parts to get involved."

His hand slid to the back of her neck. His eyes had gone as dark as midnight, full of reckless needs. "Then I guess we're both going to be stupid."

"I guess."

His mouth came down on hers, sending a mix of lust and confusion roaring through her. Even as she told herself this was a mistake, a low, greedy moan rose in her throat. Shoving her hands up into his hair, she kissed him with all the need and bafflement that pumped inside her.

"You've got company!"

Mel's bright voice had Nicole and Jake jerking apart, turning in unison toward the door.

Whitney and Bill, tanned and dressed in casual clothes, stood just behind Mel. Nicole noted the grin on her new sister-in-law's face…and the glower on her big brother's. Mel just looked stunned.

Beside her, Jake muttered, "Oh, hell."

Chapter 9

"Well, well," Whitney said half an hour later as she slid into the cruiser's passenger seat. "I go away on my honeymoon, and look at what my partner gets into." She smiled like a cat with a bowl of cream. "With my new sister-in-law. Who'd have thought it?"

"Put a lid on it, Whit."

Jake crammed on his sunglasses, shoved the cruiser into gear and pulled out of the parking lot. Relief coursed through him as they left the sleek building behind. The past thirty minutes in Nicole's office had been absurdly uncomfortable with his partner fighting a grin, Bill Taylor scowling and Mel Hall fumbling teacups and saucers.

All that because they'd walked in on two consenting adults sharing a kiss.

One kiss, Jake thought. One damn kiss and you'd have thought the sky had fallen. Okay, so he and Nicole had been plastered together so tight not even air could pass between them while they kissed each other brainless. Big deal.

Setting his jaw, Jake swerved through the late-afternoon traffic while the voice of a disembodied dispatcher crackled on the police radio. Hell, yes, it was a big deal. He had felt the softening, the heating, the *wanting* inside Nicole while she'd pressed intimately against him. She wasn't the only one who'd felt desire. Even now, Jake wanted her with such intensity that his pulse thudded.

He bit down on a curse. He needed to take a step back and figure out what the hell she was doing to him. If that was possible.

"Don't you think it's time you filled me in?"

He slid Whitney a dark look. "On the investigation?"

She gave him a bright smile, her tan glowing. "That, too."

"We're on the way to Phillip Ormiston's house." Keeping one hand on the wheel, Jake nudged a file from beneath the pile of folders on the seat between them. "He got offed in his foyer Tuesday afternoon or evening."

Jake passed the file to Whitney, noting the crease that had settled between her brows at his firm shift of subject. "Like I said on the phone last night, the killer injected Ormiston in the neck with something that brought on respiratory paralysis. The M.E. confirmed this morning that Villanova died the same way. The puncture wounds on both men's necks are in the same approximate location and about the same depth. Both victims suffocated to death. A tough way to go."

"Yes," Whitney agreed soberly. "It makes it even tougher knowing one victim was my husband's friend."

Jake concentrated on driving while Whitney skimmed the reports and crime scene photos in the file.

"Any idea what the killer injected the victims with?" she asked finally.

"Not yet. The M.E.'s moved the tox tests up in priority now that we've got a second death."

"Was there any sign of forced entry at either victim's house?"

"None, so you've got to figure it one of two ways. Either Ormiston and Villanova knew the person well enough to let him or her get close, or the killer used a ruse—delivery, repair or service con—to get inside."

"What about defense wounds on either victim?"

"The M.E. didn't find any."

"Which means both were taken by surprise." Whitney tilted her head. "Have you checked the repairman angle yet?"

"Gianos and Smith are on it. They're looking at phone records to see if either victim made recent calls for any kind of service. They're also asking associates if either man mentioned that something they owned had gone on the fritz and they'd called someone to make repairs. So far, nothing."

"I take it you've been focusing on the people who knew both victims."

"Yeah." Jake rolled his shoulders in an attempt to ease the knots of tension that had settled there earlier. Despite her inopportune arrival, he was glad to have Whitney back on the job. They'd worked the streets together, risen in the ranks alongside each other. As a team, they operated in seamless harmony, often communicating by looks alone. So far, their clearance rate on homicides was nothing to sneeze at.

"Quite a few people knew both Ormiston and Villanova," Jake continued. "Two being Rhonda Livingston and Ingrid Nelson, the women who showed up on both men's perfect match lists."

"And whom you get to sit and sip drinks with tomorrow night at an elegant club while I huddle in a cramped van, eavesdropping on your conversation."

Jake grinned at the disdain in her voice. "I got the rough part of the assignment, but I live to serve."

"Don't we all," Whitney murmured. "Has anyone made contact with Livingston and Nelson?"

"Gianos and Smith interviewed them this morning. The only thing that remotely looks suspicious is that Nelson's a physical therapist, working out of Mercy Hospital. That could give her access to whatever substance it was the killer injected into Ormiston and Villanova. We can't take that connection any further until the M.E. gets back to us with the tox results."

Whitney nodded. "What about Livingston?"

"She's a Realtor." Jake shrugged. "Not much to go on there, at least until I meet her."

"So the lonely hearts are on hold for now. Who else is on our suspect list?"

"Who isn't?" Jake asked as he steered around a corner. "We've got Sebastian Peck, an Apollo clone who charts biorhythms and can spot a muddy aura from a dozen paces."

"I take it this is Nicole's 'Sebastian'?"

Jake narrowed his eyes. "The same. You ever meet him?"

"No, she's just mentioned he's her personal trainer."

"Who'd like to get a lot more personal where she's concerned. Word is, Peck got a visit from the green-eyed monster whenever Villanova hung out with Nicole at the gym."

"Did you ask Peck about that?"

"Yeah. The bastard didn't deny it."

Whitney arched a dark eyebrow. "Is the sneer I hear in your voice coming from the detached cop or the man who has some personal involvement with a certain witness in this case?"

"Maybe both," Jake shot back. "I caught the Viking health-god in a lie. He turns around and accuses *me* of being cynical and absurd. You show me a homicide cop who brings an attitude of good cheer to the job and I'll show you a cop who has something wrong with him."

"You have a point," Whitney said. "So, jealousy over Nicole is a possible motive for Peck to have killed Villanova. What reason did the Viking have to off Ormiston?"

Jake ran down the argument between Peck and Ormiston over steroids. "So far, it doesn't sound like Ormiston had proof that Peck supplied the late Eddie Denson with steroids," Jake added. "The whole thing's conjecture on Ormiston's part."

"But enough to go to Denson's parents. Witnesses stated road rage was involved in their son's death. That condition could have been brought on by steroids. All Ormiston needed to do was put that bug in the parents' ears and they could have sued Peck for reckless endangerment."

"He could lose everything he owns *and* face jail time."

Whitney tapped a fingernail against the file folder. "So we've got Sebastian Peck with a motive to kill both Ormiston and Villanova. Does he have alibis for the time of both murders?"

"Yeah, and they suck. He claims he was alone in his office. That's convenient since there's a door that gives him access to a hallway two steps from an elevator and a staircase."

"Well, Peck's toward the top of the suspect list. Who else?"

"Nicole's ex, Cole Champion."

Whitney's eyes widened. "Now, there's a man I've heard all about."

"From Nicole?"

"No, Bill. He detests the guy. I don't blame him, considering his baby sister came home and found the creep and some waitress going at it on her own dining room table." Whitney shoved a length of auburn hair behind one shoulder. "How does Champion fit in with this case?"

"He sells Cadillacs at Villanova's dealership. Champion claims he liked his boss and they got along—I haven't been able to shake that yet. All I know is that I bunked on Nicole's couch last night on the chance whoever it was who gave her a concussion showed up to finish her off. Isn't it curious that Champion let himself into her apartment this morning, using a key she didn't know he had?''

As he spoke, Jake tightened his grip on the steering wheel. No way was he going to mention that the guy had broken up an even hotter embrace between Nicole and himself than the one Whitney had walked in on less than an hour ago.

"What reason did Champion give for being there?"

"He said he'd heard his boss had died, but couldn't find out more than that. He wanted Nicole to call Bill and get details."

"Oh, yeah, Bill would have jumped at the chance to do Champion a favor after the way he treated Nicole," Whitney responded dryly. "What's Champion's connection with the other victim, Ormiston?"

"Villanova and Ormiston worked out together at Sebastian's. Ormiston needed to buy some stretch limos for his funeral home operation. Villanova worked him a deal, had Champion do the paperwork." Jake scowled. "I haven't come up with a reason for Champion to have killed Ormiston. So far."

"What about Villanova? What would Champion's motive have been to kill the boss he claimed he liked?"

"Nicole," Jake stated. "I watched Champion while he was at her apartment this morning. The guy's still in love with her."

"He breaks the vows he made to her by bringing some floozy into Nicole's own home, and you think the creep still *loves* her?"

"Doesn't fly with me, either, unless I tie it to what Nicole says about him."

"Which is?"

"Champion's incapable of being faithful to anyone—just

doesn't have it in him. After she figured that out, Nicole forgave him. Now they've got what in her mind is a comfortable friendship."

"But you think it's more than that to Champion?"

"I saw him watching her, Whit. It's a hell of a lot more. He wants her so bad he can taste it. Nicole told me he dropped by her office one day while Villanova was there. If the Latino looked at her the same way he did at your wedding, Champion would have known Villanova was interested. Maybe Champion took offense at that." Jake raised a hand. "Hey, I know the motive's thin, but it can happen. We've worked cases where someone died for the simple reason that somebody else got jealous."

"More than a few cases." Whitney blew out a breath. "Okay, Champion's on the list, a little lower than the Viking, at least until—and if—we come up with a motive for him to have killed Ormiston. Anyone else on the list?"

"Mel Hall."

"Sweet, efficient, *gorgeous* Mel?"

Jake scowled at the description of Nicole's assistant. "Yeah, *gorgeous* Mel the Magnificent."

"What's his motive to kill?"

"Nothing solid, just that he knew both victims." Jake angled his chin. "Ormiston had complained because Nicole hadn't yet found a woman whom he considered his perfect match. He was vocal about it. Mel wouldn't have liked that. He acts like a puppy dog, but if Nicole gets hurt, he'll snap back—I saw that firsthand last night at the hospital."

"Your report said Ormiston changed his mind and called to extend his contract with Meet Your Match. Mel took that call, ordered the basket of muffins to thank him. Mel would have known the guy had changed his tune."

"Good point."

"What about alibis?"

"Mel claims he was at home, taking care of his sick mother when each murder went down."

"Won't she verify that?"

"Mel says she's too sick to do anything. Convenient."

"So, magnificent Mel's toward the bottom of our list."

"Right."

Whitney glanced out the windshield as Jake pulled the cruiser to a halt at the brick guardhouse outside the Stonebridge gated community. "What are we looking for at Ormiston's house?"

"Financial records," Jake said. He rolled down his window, flashed his badge at the guard on duty. Seconds later, Jake inched the cruiser forward while the massive wrought-iron gate drifted open. "Sebastian Peck claims Ormiston was angry over an investment he'd made that went bad."

"Any idea what it was?"

Jake shook his head. "I've asked around, but haven't come up with anything. Even Ormiston's son doesn't have a clue. He gave me the keys to the house so we can check his father's files."

"I shudder to think we might find something here that gives us reason to add *another* person to our suspect list." Whitney laid the file with the others on the seat between them. "We get any more suspects and motives, we'll have to get a secretary to keep track of them all."

"Tell me about it," Jake stated. "I guess it's occurred to you that I'm glad your days of lazing on some Mexican beach are over. I've had my hands full with this and the Quintero case."

"Any luck on tracking down Cárdenas?" Whitney asked.

"Not yet. I'm putting pressure on that worthless snitch, Lira, to get me a lead on Cárdenas's girlfriend. Once I find her and she admits to witnessing the murder, I'll have Cárdenas."

"*We'll* have him, partner," Whitney corrected him as the

cruiser slid along the street lined with massive, elegant houses.

Jake grinned. "Yeah, *we'll.*"

Whitney angled her head. "For the record, whatever's going on between you and Nicole is fine by me."

Jake eased out a breath. He'd known Whitney would detour back to that. Because he loved her like a sister, he let her.

"Maybe it's fine by you, but not your husband."

"Bill might have some reservations about you being with Nicole. He'll get over them."

Jake thought about Bill Taylor's cold stare when he'd walked in on him kissing his sister like a sex-crazed maniac. Jake hadn't seen any questions in the A.D.A.'s eyes—he already knew the answers. And he didn't like them.

"Your husband was there when I got charged with eight counts of murder. Today he sees me with my hands and mouth on his sister. I don't have to tell you what he thinks."

"Jake—"

"Bill doesn't need to worry. Nothing's going on between Nicole and me." Jake tightened his grip on the steering wheel. "Dammit, Whit, neither of us wants anything to go on."

"From what I saw, there's plenty going on between you and Nicole. And both of you appeared willing."

"What you saw doesn't mean anything."

"You and Nicole decided to lock lips just to pass the time? Get real, Ford."

His teeth grinding, Jake whipped the cruiser into the driveway of the house where Phillip Ormiston had died two days ago. Leaving the engine idling and the air conditioner blowing, he shifted in his seat and met his partner's gaze.

"Nicole got burned by Champion. She says she's reacting to me the same way she did to him when they met—going with emotion instead of using her brain. I agree with that

If she was doing any kind of rational thinking, she'd steer clear of me.''

"I disagree."

"Dammit, Whit, you know better than anybody how much I don't want a relationship. I told Nicole that. I don't want to get involved with any woman ever again."

"What I know is that you put up a wall around yourself when Annie and the twins died."

"Do you blame me?"

"No. I also know that you can't live alone for the rest of your life. Some people can do that, but you're not one of them. You need a wife, Jake. Family. It's time to lower that wall."

"Time?" he shot back. Even now he tasted the despair that had engulfed him as he'd stood alone at an empty grave, staring at a granite marker bearing the names of the wife and daughters he loved more than life. "Time to fall in love again and hope this go-around my wife doesn't board a plane carrying a bomb in its belly? Time for another try at fatherhood, while I keep my fingers crossed that my next two kids live to see their first birthdays?"

"Oh, Jake." Eyes filled with compassion, Whitney gripped his hand.

If it had been anybody else but her, he'd have jerked away. Not from Whitney. They'd been through too much together, shared too much.

"No one should have to endure what you did. And it's understandable why you want to hold on to your grief."

"I'm not holding on—"

"Because as long as you do, it's an excuse for not opening your heart to anyone else. Not risking again." She tightened her hand on his. "Grief is like any other emotion, Jake. It eases with time, whether you want it to or not."

He turned his head and stared at the massive brick house in front of them. She was right, he acknowledged. The vicious grief that had ripped at him after he'd lost his family had transformed over time to a dull ache.

"When I was in Nicole's office today, I told her about Annie and the twins," he said, almost to himself. "I didn't mean to. Sure as hell didn't plan to." He met Whitney's solemn gaze. "You and the department's shrink—you're the only ones I talk to about my family. I told Nicole about them and I don't know why."

The corners of Whitney's mouth lifted. "Do you think you're falling in love with her?"

"Hell, no." He realized too late his denial had been too forceful, too instant. "Nicole matters, okay? I don't know how much. Don't want to know."

"You're going to have to figure out how you feel about her. Then you'll have to deal with those feelings."

"The time to do that isn't now." He pulled his hand from beneath Whitney's, gave her a stern look. "Subject's closed, Taylor, so just shove it out of your mind."

"Sure thing." She pursed her lips. "Wanna bet I'll be able to do that a lot easier than you?"

"I only bet when I've got a chance to win," Jake muttered.

Over the next two days, Nicole buried her churning frustration under long hours of work. Always in the past, keeping busy had been the best cure when she found herself unsettled. Right now, she was so unsettled over Jake Ford that she rattled.

The comments she'd gotten from her big brother at his seeing her in a no-holds-barred clench with Jake hadn't helped her nerves. Oh, Bill had been calm when he'd knocked on the door of the guest room he and Whitney had invited her to use until the police snared the killer. Using his best courtroom demeanor, Bill had asked if she was aware the man who'd been devouring her in her own office had recently been charged with not just one count of murder, but *eight?* Granted, Jake had been set up by the real killer, but did Nicole know that the go-to-hell lifestyle he'd been living had directly contributed to one of those deaths? Did she have any idea Jake was seeing the department shrink to deal with the tragic loss of his wife and twin daughters?

Nicole had taken infinite satisfaction at the surprise she'd seen spark in Bill's eyes when she'd advised him Jake *had* told her about his arrest and the loss of his family. It wasn't until she'd stood toe-to-toe with her big brother, poked her finger in his chest and informed him she would kiss whatever man she chose, where and when she chose, that he'd reminded her she'd traveled down the same slippery road with Cole Champion.

Maybe she had forgotten how much her ex-husband had hurt her, but he hadn't, Bill said, cupping his palm to her cheek. Was she sure her getting involved with Jake Ford wouldn't lead to more heartache?

With that question echoing in her brain, Nicole propped her elbows on her desk and dropped her face in her hands.

No, she wasn't sure. Not of anything. Especially of her feelings for Jake. She suspected if she allowed herself to examine them, she would discover she was close to falling in love. Just the thought lodged a hot knot of fear in her throat. How could she trust her own judgment when the one time she'd gone with emotion she'd wound up with a man who'd broken every vow he'd made to her? How could she have taken such care with her heart for so long, then let a tall, handsome cop who didn't want to make promises or expect them sweep away all her good intentions?

She hadn't seen Jake since he and Whitney had left her office two days ago. Reports Nicole had received this morning from two of her firm's counselors attested that Jake had met both Rhonda Livingston and Ingrid Nelson last night for drinks at Encounters. According to both counselors, their clients had oozed excitement over the fictitious Jake England.

Nicole squeezed her eyes shut against the twin images of Jake sharing a drink with the gorgeous redhead, then the slinky brunette. He was doing his job, she told herself. Someone had killed two of her clients; the police were conducting an undercover operation that involved several other clients. With so much going on, it was no wonder she, as owner of Meet Your Match, had tossed and turned the past two nights.

Since the police had things under control, nothing remained for her to do but get a handle on her own emotions. The pounding in her heart and melting in her bones she felt whenever Jake got near were sensations she knew were not to be trusted.

So, she wouldn't trust them. *Couldn't.*

Pulling open her desk's center drawer, she plucked up the business card that Harold Young had slid into her palm a few nights ago. The dinner they'd shared had been a business meeting, Harold being a potential client. Harold Young, Ph.D., Professor of English. Tall and lanky with brown hair and dark, sensitive eyes, Harold was the type of man she'd decided long ago was her soul mate. The exact opposite of Cole.

And Jake.

Harold had yet to sign a contract with Meet Your Match. Inviting him to dinner wouldn't blur her steadfast rule that she didn't date clients. Harold was a safe man, a steady constant in an unsteady world. When she was around him, her brain functioned. She didn't have a problem keeping her perspective, wasn't in danger of tumbling off a cliff.

"Nicole?"

Mel Hall's voice brought her head up. "Yes, what is it?"

Her assistant stood in the wedge of the open door, uncertainty in his eyes. "Are you okay?"

Impatience flared inside her. How could one person ask the same question almost hourly over the past two days?

"I'm fine."

Her clipped tone put an instant hurt in his eyes that tugged on her conscience.

She closed her eyes, ordered her nerves to settle. It wasn't Mel's fault her life was in chaos. He'd asked the question so often because he cared about her. Mel was a dependable presence in her life, he was good for her. She needed to remember that, make a point of telling him more often how indispensable she considered him.

She opened her eyes and forced a smile. "I'm fine, Mel. Just a little edgy, and I'm sorry for that. What can I do for you?"

He inclined his head toward her phone. "Ingrid Nelson's on line one. She says she's already reported to her counselor about her date last night with Jake."

Nicole fingered the counselor's report. "Yes, I read Ingrid's comments." Her *oozing* comments.

"She says she wants to let the boss know personally how pleased she is with Jake."

"How thoughtful of her."

Mel smiled. "I'd say she's more than pleased."

"You would?"

"She called him a genuine eye treat with a top-of-the-line body."

Nicole's blood roared like an ocean in her head. "I see."

Mel's smile faded. "I'm sorry. After the other day it's, well, uh, *apparent* something's going on between you and Jake."

"No." She held up a hand. "I understand why you'd think that, but there's nothing going on. Sergeant Ford and I got carried away, is all." She glanced down at Harold Young's business card. "Nothing like that will happen again."

"To be honest," Mel began slowly, "I think that's good. I hope you don't mind me giving my opinion, but I don't think the cop's your type. Something tells me he's not the best man for you, Nicole."

She tightened her fingers on the business card. She'd been telling herself the same thing since the moment she spotted Jake at Bill and Whitney's wedding. To hear Mel voice the same opinion shouldn't set her teeth on edge, but it did. Which was further confirmation that she needed to get her emotions in line and banish Jake from her thoughts. She would start by inviting the professor to dinner at a nice restaurant that evening.

"You're right, Mel." Squaring her shoulders, she glanced at the blinking light on her phone. She couldn't stop her stomach from roiling at the image of the willowy physical therapist draped over Jake's top-of-the-line body.

"Well…" She cleared her throat against the hitch in her voice. "I'm glad Ms. Nelson's pleased. That's what we want, isn't it? Pleased clients."

"You got it, boss." Mel checked his watch. "It's nearly tea time. What do you want today?"

"Something that soothes the nerves," she replied, then reached for the phone.

Just shy of midnight, Nicole sat at the center island in her brother and sister-in-law's kitchen, a teacup and saucer in front of her. So far, the orange-and-spice herbal tea she'd brewed had done nothing to ease the headache that tap-danced behind her eyes.

She looked up when light wedged through the door; seconds later Bill wandered in. He was dressed in a white T-shirt and gray sweatpants; his blond hair was sleep-rumpled, his face stubbled.

"I didn't know you were up," he said, his bleary gaze taking in her long robe of ivory silk.

"Couldn't sleep," she muttered over the rim of her cup. How could she when she'd just lived through the most tedious, desperately uninteresting evening of her life?

"How was your date with the professor?"

"Going over premiums with an insurance salesman would have been more stimulating."

"Sounds like the guy isn't your type."

Nicole sat her cup onto the saucer with a snap. "I've heard enough about who is and who isn't my type," she fired back. "Everybody's got an opinion. I suppose yours is that I should marry a man who bores me to tears."

Bill blinked, then scrubbed a hand over his face. "I don't recall saying that."

"Well, don't. I'm sick of the subject. I don't want to talk about it."

"Uh, fine." One sandy brow raised, he pulled open the door to the refrigerator, snagged a can of V8, then slid onto the stool beside her. "What do you want to talk about?"

"Nothing." Scowling, she shoved her hair behind her shoulders. "Why aren't you snuggled in bed with your new wife?"

"My wife got called out to work a homicide. It's hard to snuggle when one of the principle parties is at a crime scene."

If Whitney was at a homicide scene, Jake was there, too. Nicole pressed her fingers against her eyes. Why did everything circle back to Jake? Why had she sat during the entire interminable dinner with Harold, thinking about Jake? About his touch. His kiss. About *him.*

Bill settled his hand on hers. "Talk to me, pest."

Despite the pounding in her head, the corners of her mouth twitched at the pet nickname he'd used since junior high.

"Are you ever going to forgive me for getting on the

school's PA system and announcing that Marcia Sue Shannon would be your perfect date for the spring dance?''

"No. I plan to hold that over your head for the rest of our lives." His eyes sobered. "Does the reason you're sitting in my kitchen in the middle of the night have something to do with Jake Ford?''

Nicole started to protest, then sagged back on her stool. "Am I that obvious?''

"I'm tempted to tell you that I zeroed in on your internal struggle using skills of observation honed over years in a courtroom. That would be a lie. Whitney mentioned something.''

"I can't get Jake out of my head. I don't want him there, but that doesn't seem to matter. He just won't leave. I'm not so sure he isn't in my heart, too." She massaged her aching right temple. "I don't know what to do about any of it.''

Bill's hand tightened on hers. "I met Whitney less than six months after Julia broke our engagement. The last thing I wanted or needed was to jump into another relationship, or so I kept telling myself. Whitney had been burned by her ex-husband so her sentiments were the same where I was concerned. In the end, all the logical thinking in the world couldn't keep us apart.''

"You didn't exactly have good things to say the other night about the prospect of my getting involved with Jake.''

"You're my sister. I don't want you hurt. I also don't want to try and run your life." Bill raised a shoulder. "Let's make a deal. You do what you feel is best for you. If some guy turns into a creep, you let me know and I'll beat him to a pulp.''

Nicole pressed a kiss to his stubbled cheek. "Deal.''

Bill grinned. "That offer applies to your ex-husband, you know. I never did get a chance to hammer Champion.''

"You never will. If you get near Cole, he'll run in the opposite direction.''

"He's not as thick as I thought."

The doorbell's chime drifted in from the hallway.

Bill frowned as he rose. "You expecting someone?"

"Not dressed like this," Nicole said, glancing down at her silk robe.

"Maybe Whitney forgot her key," he said before disappearing out the door.

Nicole carried her cup and saucer to the sink. Although her talk with Bill hadn't resolved anything, she felt calmer. More settled than she had in days. Where relationships were concerned, heeding logic wasn't always the right course—Bill and Whitney were proof.

"Nicole."

Bill said her name with such grimness that she jerked around. Her heart gave another jerk when she saw Jake standing in the doorway just behind her brother. He had on jeans, a dress shirt and dark sport coat, his gold badge clipped to its breast pocket. Both men looked as grim as Bill had sounded.

"What's happened?" She took a step forward, peering through the doorway in a futile attempt to spot Whitney. "Is it Whitney?" She fought an ice-pick jab of panic in her stomach. "Has something happened to Whitney?"

"No." Bill stepped forward, put his arm around her shoulders. "Whitney's fine."

"She's on some interviews right now," Jake added as he stepped into the kitchen. "Nicole, I need to ask you about a professor named Harold Young. Is he a client of Meet Your Match?"

"Harold?" she asked weakly. "What happened to Harold?"

The silent look that passed between the men had her jerking from Bill's touch.

"What happened?"

"He's dead," Bill said quietly.

"No… I had dinner with him." She sent the clock on the oven a disbelieving look. "We left the restaurant together three hours ago. *Three hours ago.*"

"Did Young drop you off here after dinner?" Jake asked.

"No, we met there, so we said goodbye in the parking lot." She took a step toward Jake. "You're Homicide. If Harold had died in a car wreck you wouldn't be here. What happened?"

"A neighbor who works an evening shift got home, saw Young lying in his driveway and called 911. We found your business card in the pocket of his suit."

"I gave him the card at dinner." She closed her eyes, opened them. "He asked for my card and I watched him slide it into his pocket."

"So, he's not a client?" Jake asked. "The agency hasn't matched him with either of the women who'd dated both Ormiston and Villanova?"

"No. As far as I know, Harold has never met Ingrid Nelson or Rhonda Livingston." She shook her head. "Do you think one of them killed him?"

"Whitney's interviewing both of them right now, checking alibis if either has one. I couldn't do that since we don't want Nelson or Livingston to know I'm a cop. Not at this point, anyway."

Bill looked at Jake. "Was the killer's MO the same as the first two murders?"

"Looks like it. The M.E.'s on his way in now to do the autopsy. We need to be sure Young didn't keel over in his driveway from a heart attack."

"Do you know yet what the killer's injecting his victims with?" Bill asked.

"No. The M.E.'s using a process of elimination, telling us what the killer didn't use." Jake's brows slid together. "All we know for sure is that the killer has drawn a target on clients of Meet Your Match."

"I told you Harold wasn't a client." Nicole's emotions were rocketing, making it difficult to hold on to any threads of composure. "He'd never been to my office, didn't know Phillip or DeSoto. It's me, isn't it? Harold died because of his connection to me."

"We don't know yet if Young was murdered," Jake said evenly. "But if it turns out he was, then, yes, you're the link. Who knew you were having dinner with Young?"

"No one. I didn't tell anyone."

"Did you write it in your appointment book at work? Jot the time and place on a notepad? Enter it into your computer?"

"No, my getting together with Harold didn't have anything to do with business. It was…a spur-of-the-moment thing. I called him this morning and asked him to meet me at Nikz for dinner."

"Did you get the sense that anyone followed you there?"

"No."

"See anyone you knew, inside or in the parking lot?"

"No."

When the phone on the counter behind her shrilled, Nicole jumped.

"Busy night," Bill murmured as he swept up the receiver.

"Coffee." Remeeting Jake's gaze, she rubbed her hands over her forearms to dispel a chill. "I should offer you coffee."

"Thanks, but I have to meet Whitney back at the station. I'll grab some there."

"Fax it to me now," Bill said, then rambled off the number. "If the warrant's not perfect when you wake that judge up at three in the morning to get his signature, he'll chew you up and spit you out. I'll get back to you after I look over your paperwork." He hung up, then turned. "Looks like I'll be up most of the night, too."

"Perk of being a civil servant," Jake commented.

"One of many." Bill ran a palm down Nicole's hair. "You okay?"

"Yes." Inside, she felt like glass, ready to shatter.

"Sure you are. This isn't your fault, Nicole. None of what's happened is your fault."

"Tell that to Phillip and DeSoto and Harold."

"What I would tell them is that what happened is the fault of the person who jabbed a needle in their necks. That wasn't you." Bill squeezed her arm. "I'll be in my study if you need me."

"He's right," Jake said as Bill disappeared out the door. "None of this is your fault."

Because she could feel hot tears boiling up, ready to erupt, she turned her back on him, pressed a trembling hand to her throat. "It was just dinner. That was all it was. Harold wasn't..." She squeezed her eyes shut as a sob clawed at her throat.

"He wasn't what?" Jake asked quietly from behind her.

When she didn't answer, his hand settled on her shoulder. "What wasn't he, Nicole?"

Her tears blurred the copper pots that hung over the kitchen's center island. "He's dead because of me."

Gripping her shoulders, Jake turned her to face him. "Listen to me. If it winds up Young was murdered, it happened because someone wanted him dead and decided to do something about it. That someone isn't you."

"No, it isn't *me*," she countered. "But if I hadn't been selfish, Harold would be alive right now. I used him tonight, Jake. Do you want to know why?"

His mouth tightened. "I'm listening."

"I wanted to get *you* out of my head." She clenched her fists. "I can't breathe without thinking about you, dammit. I knew Harold would be safe because he's your exact opposite. I thought...if I spent some time with him I would come to my senses. Stop thinking...about you. I—"

She broke, simply broke. Covering her face with her hands, she began to sob.

"It's okay." Jake wrapped his arms around her, drawing her against him. "Just let it out." He stroked her hair while shuddering sobs racked her. "You need to get it all out," he added, his voice a soft sweep against her temple while she wept against his shoulder.

"This isn't helping," she managed to say as pain and shock mixed with her tears.

"It is, if it gets rid of some of the hurt and the misplaced guilt."

When her tears finally eased, she leaned back, staring up into his grim face as she wiped her wet cheeks with her fingertips. "I appreciate the use of your shoulder."

"I'm the guy you don't have to thank, remember?" His eyes were dark as midnight as he studied her. "I'm going to get the killer, Nicole. I'm going to find the slime and cut him or her off at the knees. You have my word."

"I'll hold you to that."

He curled a finger under her chin. "If it's any consolation, I can't get you out of my head, either. Staying away from you for the past two days has been hell. I did it because I figured it was the best thing. For both of us."

"It might be best, but it's not what I want." The admission had her easing out a trembling breath. "Not anymore."

He used his fingertips to brush the hair away from her damp cheeks. "I have to meet Whitney at the station and make reports. Otherwise, I wouldn't walk out of here tonight without you."

"Otherwise, I wouldn't let you."

His hands slid into her hair, his fingers tightening, arching her head back. "Tomorrow night." His mouth grazed hers. "I want to see you, Nicole, *need* to see you. I want you all to myself. Alone."

"Yes."

"I don't know what we'll be dealing with on the case so I don't know for sure what time I'll get loose. Where will you be after work?"

"The gym. I have an aerobics class, then a workout session."

"I'd rather have you there with a lot of people around than alone somewhere. I'll pick you up there." His mouth lowered, his lips skimming over hers, gentle as air, erotic as sin.

A needy moan eased up her throat; her stomach trembled with the warm, rich taste of him. Beneath her silk robe, heat surged through her flesh. She could do no more than breathe his name as her fingers curled on the lapels of his sport coat, holding on as if her legs might give out if she let go.

A minute...or maybe an hour later, he pulled back, pried her hands from his lapels. He kept his eyes on hers as he kissed her fingers one by one. "I'm going to have a hard time thinking about anything else but you until then."

"Me, too," she said, her voice a soft rasp. She touched a hand to his cheek. "A really hard time."

He pressed his lips to her brow, her temples, her cheeks, her mouth until her muscles turned to water. And then he was gone.

Legs trembling, nerves shimmering, Nicole leaned against the nearest counter. She knew she would lie awake the rest of the night, staring at the ceiling, yearning for Jake.

And thinking about a quiet, sensitive man who quite possibly had died because of her.

Chapter 10

The image of ivory silk clinging to the hollows and curves of Nicole's body stayed with Jake throughout the remainder of the night and into the following afternoon. So he sat at his overflowing desk in the Homicide squad room, part of his thoughts focused on murder, the remainder on lush, silk-covered curves.

He knew Nicole had no idea what the sight of her had done to him as she'd stood barefoot in the soft light of her brother's kitchen, her blue eyes shadowed and damp with the remnants of tears, golden hair like a waterfall across her shoulders.

He'd felt desire—hell, yes, he'd felt it! Then something far deeper and stronger than lust. An emotion much more stirring. An emotion that, considering his past and the future he'd mapped out for himself, was more than it should be. Much more.

He'd gone to her brother's house on grim business, yet it hadn't been the task at hand that had him fighting to pull air into his lungs the entire time.

It had been Nicole. Only her. He didn't know how he'd come to care so much for her, so quickly, but he did.

That knowledge scared the hell out of him.

As if beckoned by an elusive phantom, his gaze drifted to the framed photograph leaning on one corner of his desk. Annie, beaming with a mother's love and pride, sat in a porch swing, nuzzling their newborn twin daughters. With Annie, he had felt a quiet kind of rightness, a sweet coming together.

Jake dragged his gaze from the photograph. *Sweet* had nothing to do with what he felt for Nicole. His desire for her, his *need,* was volatile, a fire that raged so hot he couldn't think of anything but her. Nothing but her.

He wasn't in love. He didn't know *what* he felt for her, but he was sure love didn't factor into the equation. He wanted her. Period. She wanted him right back—she'd confirmed that last night. Whatever else was going on inside him, he would deal with it later. Preferably when he could take a breath without thinking of her.

"So, we know for sure the professor was murdered."

Whitney's voice had Jake's thoughts scattering like dust motes in a slat of sunshine.

"What?"

His partner sat on the edge of his desk, her long, denim-clad legs crossed as she scowled down at him. "Excuse me for intruding in your thoughts, Sergeant Ford, but I thought this was a two-sided conversation."

"It is." What the hell had she been saying?

"About our case," she prodded. "We haven't come up with squat. If it's not too taxing for you, we should run through the facts again, try to pick up something we've missed."

Loosening his tie, Jake struggled to clear his brain. "Give me a break, Whit. I didn't log any sack time last night and I spent the morning testifying in court."

"I didn't get any sleep last night, either, but I can at least keep my mind focused." One dark brow rose into a smug arch. "Want to tell me what's on yours?"

"Nope." Running a hand through his hair, Jake glanced around. This late in the afternoon, the Homicide squad room was filled with cops, clerks and the occasional civilian, all going about their business. He judiciously shifted attention to the case at hand.

"Okay." Leaning back in his chair, he steepled his fingers. "We know for sure we've got three men murdered by one killer. Identical MO—all victims have punctures in the side of the neck. All were injected with an as-yet unidentified substance that brings on respiratory paralysis. Whatever the stuff is, it's quick. Like one-two-three-gone."

Whitney nodded. "Let's talk suspects. I checked Rhonda Livingston's alibi. She's covered for all of yesterday evening and last night. She's off the list."

"But not Ingrid Nelson." Jake pictured the redheaded physical therapist wearing a half dress who'd tried to crawl up his chest when they'd met at Encounters. "She claims she was home alone last night when the professor bought it. She's probably left a dozen messages on my voice mail, wanting to set up a second date. She's pushy, persistent, and by the sound of her voice, getting annoyed that I haven't returned her calls. If both Ormiston and Villanova had tried to cool things off, I'm not sure she'd have taken it that well. Nelson stays on the list."

"Agreed." Whitney crossed her arms. "The fact that the professor, our third victim, doesn't seem to have ever had contact with any of our suspects leaves only one link among the victims."

"Nicole," Jake said quietly. "She's the only person we've found who knew all three victims."

"So, why Nicole? Why is *she* the link?"

Jake unearthed a pencil, tapped its eraser on the desk in

time with the thin red second hand of the clock that hung over the unit's assignment board. "Two victims—Ormiston and Villanova—were clients of Meet Your Match. The professor wasn't, so that blows the get-revenge-against-Nicole by-killing-her-clients theory."

"Her relationship with Ormiston and Villanova was a business. Even if the killer perceived it to be personal—and killed them because of that erroneous perception—he wouldn't have known about the professor. According to Nicole, she didn't tell anyone she was meeting Harold Young for dinner."

"Okay, so suppose the killer *didn't* know about the date," Jake said, still tapping the eraser against the desk. "Nicole said she doesn't think anyone followed her to the restaurant but she wasn't watching for a tail, either."

"So, hypothetically, the killer followed her when she left her office yesterday. He waited in the restaurant's parking lot, saw her say goodbye to the professor." Whitney raised a shoulder. "Maybe she gave him a peck on the cheek. That'd be another erroneous perception on the killer's part that she and the professor had a thing going…or were starting something. The killer, seething with jealousy, followed Young home."

"And jabs a needle into his neck before he has a chance to get inside his house."

"Works for me. Jake, we need to put a tail on Nicole." Whitney glanced at the clock. "There's still time to set one up for this evening when she leaves work."

"I've got that covered."

"Oh?"

Jake flicked the pencil onto a stack of file folders. "I'm picking her up. And so no one at your house worries, she'll be with me tonight. All night."

Whitney tilted her head. "Does Nicole know that?"

Jake hitched one side of his mouth. "What, you think

just plan on strolling in, tossing her over my shoulder and carrying her off to my cave without asking if she wants to go?''

"Well, you're a man, aren't you?"

"Sergeant Ford? Excuse me?"

The uncertain male voice had Jake leaning to see around Whitney. His brain cataloged the round face, thinning hair and roly-poly body an instant before the man's name popped into his head.

"Mr. Zucksworth." Jake rose and extended his hand. "This is my partner, Sergeant Taylor." Jake looked at Whitney. "Mr. Zucksworth works for Ormiston Funeral Homes."

"Ma'am." Bradley Zucksworth gave Whitney a polite nod. He wore a black suit with a red rosebud in the lapel and clutched a manila envelope beneath his left arm.

"What can we do for you, Mr. Zucksworth?" Jake asked while Whitney slid off the desk.

"I believe I have some information you'll be interested in," he said, settling into the chair Whitney pulled up. "I can't stay long." He lifted the half glasses that dangled from a gold chain around his neck, slid them on, then peered at his watch. "I'm scheduled to oversee a memorial service at our south-side location. Since the police department is on the way there, I decided to drop this by instead of calling."

"Drop what by?" Jake asked as he lowered into his chair.

"When you were at the funeral home the other night, you asked if I was aware of an investment Phillip made that had gone sour. One in which he lost a lot of money?"

Jake leaned forward, anticipation trickling beneath his skin. "That's right."

Zucksworth worked the metal clip on the envelope, pulled out a folder and handed it to Jake. "I was organizing some of Phillip's files and found this envelope. It had slipped down below the hanging folders and was lying beneath

them. I imagine that's why you missed it when you checke⌐
his office.''

Jake opened the folder, stared at the canceled chec⌐
clipped to the top of a thick stack of paper. Jaw tight, h⌐
tilted the folder Whitney's direction, exchanged a look wit⌐
her before shifting his gaze back to Zucksworth.

"Do you know why your boss wrote a one-hundred
thousand-dollar check to Cole Champion?"

"I had no idea when I saw the check. Actually, I don'⌐
know who Cole Champion is. Being curious, I read the pa⌐
pers in the file. It appears Mr. Champion arranged for ⌐
group of investors to put substantial amounts of money int⌐
the drilling of an oil well in southeastern Oklahoma. A wel⌐
that failed to produce.''

"Looks that way." Jake scanned a letter Ormiston ha⌐
written to the district attorney of the county in which th⌐
well had been drilled.

Whitney leaned in. "Your boss didn't mention the in⌐
vestment to you, Mr. Zucksworth?"

"No, ma'am. Although I manage all the homes in th⌐
Ormiston funeral chain, Phillip and I weren't close. We onl⌐
discussed business. The oil investment was made from hi⌐
personal funds, so there was no reason for him to confide i⌐
me.''

Jake closed the folder, added it to the clutter on his desk⌐
Nicole's ex-husband had denied knowledge of an investmer⌐
in which Ormiston had lost money. Jake looked forward t⌐
squeezing the bastard.

Zucksworth rechecked his watch, slid off his glasses, the⌐
rose. "I hope the information helps find the person wh⌐
murdered Phillip.''

Whitney touched his arm. "It might. Thank you, M⌐
Zucksworth.''

She waited until the short, round man wound his wa⌐

through the maze of city-issue desks, then turned to Jake, who had his head back in the file. "What's the letter say?"

"Ormiston wrote to the Garvin County D.A.—that's the county where the well was drilled. He claims Champion doctored the reports he used to convince investors to put their money in the well. Ormiston doesn't have anything nice to say about Champion."

"Killing Ormiston would have been a way for Champion to make that complaint go away," Whitney pointed out.

"My thoughts," Jake said as he continued thumbing through the file.

"How do you want to play this, Jake?"

"Let's get Champion on our turf. You call him. Be all sweet and nice when you ask him to come in. Tell him I haven't made any progress in the investigation and you have your own ideas about a new direction to go. You take the lead when we get him in interview."

"In other words, I have to be warm as toast to this creep while you get to be surly."

Jake sent her a grim smile. "You got it." They both knew that even during a voluntary statement, the good cop-bad cop routine sometimes helped shake up a suspect. One could never tell ahead of time just what might fall out.

Jake stabbed a finger at the file. "Champion told me he didn't know of any bad investments Ormiston made. If the bastard lies again, he'll have me in his face."

Whitney scowled. "You always get to be the bad cop."

"That's 'cause you're full of sweetness and light," he commented as he reached for the phone. "While you arrange things with Champion, I'll talk to the Garvin County D.A. I want to know what kind of trouble Ormiston could have made for Champion if he hadn't conveniently gotten murdered."

"Like I said on the phone, I told Sergeant Ford everything I know the other morning at my ex-wife's apartment," Cole

Champion said two hours later. "Which isn't much."

"I understand." Whitney gave the man a sympathetic nod across the small table with cigarette burns tattooing its top. "And I do appreciate you coming in so I can confirm a few facts."

Jake slouched in a chair at one end of the table in the cramped interview room with institutional-green walls, bare fluorescent bulbs and a wide expanse of one-way glass. In front of him was a pad on which he made the pretense of jotting an occasional note. The pad was a prop, as was his relaxed posture. He knew Champion would make the automatic assumption that, since Whitney was doing the talking, she was in charge. And that Jake, keeping his mouth shut and taking notes, was the junior partner who presented no real threat.

"So, you liked your boss," Whitney confirmed. "You have no idea who would want to harm Mr. Villanova."

"That's right," Champion answered, directing his full attention and a well-mannered smile toward Whitney. "I have no clue who murdered DeSoto."

Jake could see that his partner's rehashing the information that had come out in his interview with Champion was having the desired effect of lulling their quarry into a false sense of security. Champion looked relaxed in his gray tailored suit, his starched white collar lapping over a crimson silk tie. His raven hair was styled, his dark eyes earnest as if he were eager to assist in finding the person who'd murdered his boss.

Window dressing, Jake knew. On the inside, Champion was a snake—he'd proved that by treating Nicole like garbage when they'd been married. Jake wasn't likely to forget that…or the fact the bastard had lied to him.

Champion glanced at his gold designer watch. "Sergeant

Taylor, could we get this over with fast? I need to get back to the dealership. With the boss dead, we're stretched thin.''

"I can imagine," Whitney murmured, her eyes patient. "Just a couple more questions. You said Mr. Villanova had you handle the paperwork when Phillip Ormiston bought several stretch limos for his funeral home chain?''

Champion adjusted the diamond pinkie ring on his right hand. "Correct.''

"You also told Sergeant Ford the purchase went through without a hitch.''

"It did. I'm not sure what this has to do—''

"And that you're unaware of an investment Mr. Ormiston made in which he lost a substantial amount of money.''

For the first time since they'd settled at the table, Champion's gaze flicked to Jake, lingered.

"Mr. Champion?" Whitney prodded.

"Ormiston's purchase of the limos worked like a well-tuned engine," he replied, shifting his gaze back. "The factory made delivery on the vehicles a few days early.''

Jake slapped his pencil onto the pad. "That oil deal didn't go off quite so well, did it, slick?''

"Oil deal?''

"Don't play dense with me." Jake slid the plastic bag containing Ormiston's canceled check from beneath the notepad, held it up. "You brokered an oil well deal in which Ormiston and six other people paid you one hundred grand each. The well came up dry, which means everybody but you lost money. Lots of money. Ormiston accused you of doctoring production reports of surrounding wells and seismic studies on the potential drill site.''

"I didn't doctor anything.''

"Ormiston thought you did. He went to the Garvin County D.A. and demanded they file fraud charges against you.''

"They didn't. That's because I didn't do anything wrong."

Keeping his expression neutral, Jake shoved out of his chair. The Garvin County D.A. had verified he could find nothing fraudulent about the oil deal Champion had put together. That had gotten the slime off the hook with the law, but not with at least one irate investor.

"Ormiston demanded you repay him one hundred grand." Jake circled the table, purposely halting at Champion's side, invading his space. "He wrote letters to the other investors about joining him in a lawsuit against you. If Ormiston had lived, that dry hole would have cost you some serious money."

When Champion twisted and looked up, Jake saw the sheen of sweat on his forehead. "This was Ormiston's first investment in anything that had to do with the oil business. He didn't understand the risks."

"What he probably didn't understand until later was that *you* had no risk."

"Look, sometimes a drill site looks prime. You've got wells producing in the area. The seismic studies and geology reports tell you the odds are in favor of a well on that site hitting. That doesn't mean it will. In the oil business, you've got no guarantees. That's the case with the well Ormiston invested in. It just didn't hit. I couldn't get the guy to understand that."

"Which caused you one hell of a problem," Jake shot back, his voice a slap in the face. "You had an irate investor claiming you doctored reports. Calling you a fraud. The oil community is tight—you couldn't have kept that quiet. If Ormiston had sued you, it would have cost you big legal fees and a hell of a lot of business down the road."

"Everything was on the up-and-up."

"That why you lied to me about not knowing how Ormiston lost money?"

Color swept into Champion's face. "I didn't tell you because I figured you'd get all bent out of shape. Like now."

Jake leaned, stuck a warning finger in the man's face. "Damn right I'm bent out of shape. I get that way when people lie to me when I'm investigating a murder. Makes me think they've got something to hide."

"Jake, ease off." Playing the soft cop, Whitney waved him back. "Mr. Champion, we know people have all kinds of stresses in their lives. Those stresses sometimes cause them to do things they might regret. We understand that."

"Good for you," Champion spat, then twisted to look up at Jake. "I'm telling you I haven't done anything to regret."

Jake gave him a feral grin. "No surprise there. You don't *regret* anything because you shed your conscience a long time ago. Maybe you never had one. Bet you didn't lose one minute of sleep when you decided to solve your problem by killing Ormiston."

"I didn't kill him!"

"You said Villanova wasn't just your boss, he was your *friend,*" Jake persisted. "Could be you told him about the oil deal with Ormiston. When Ormiston wound up murdered, Villanova started thinking that you'd offed him. Maybe your boss planned on going to his pal, Bill Taylor, just as soon as the A.D.A. got back from his honeymoon. Taylor's got no use for you because you dumped on his sister. He'd have looked at you long and hard for Ormiston's murder. That would have been too close for comfort, so you took care of your boss before he had a chance to put a bug in the A.D.A.'s ear about the first murder."

"You're full of—"

"Mr. Champion…" Whitney laid a hand on the man's wrist. "We can clear up this whole matter if you'd tell us where you were last night."

His furious gaze whipped back to her. "Why last night?"

"Starting around seven," she continued. "We just need a quick rundown of how you spent your evening."

"Dammit, I was supposed to have a date," he ground out, his face red, his voice hoarse.

"Supposed to?"

"The demo I was driving from the dealership broke down on the side of the road. I was halfway between here and Norman. In the boonies."

"What time was that?" Whitney asked.

"Around eight."

"Did you call for a tow?"

"I would have if the battery in my damn cell phone had worked. I spent about an hour and a half working on the car's engine. I finally got it to start."

"Did anyone stop and offer you assistance?"

"Like I said, I was in the boonies."

"Where did you go after you got the car started?" Whitney asked.

"Home. I was covered with grease and dirt and in no mood to go out. The car started this morning, so I drove it to the dealership, directly to the shop."

Jake planted a hand on the Glock holstered at his waist. "I find it interesting you never have a solid alibi when certain things happen. Murder, for instance."

Champion pushed out of his chair. "I've had it with your accusations. If you want to talk to me again, call my lawyer."

"We'll be seeing you," Jake said.

"Go to hell," Champion said, then stalked out the door.

Whitney rose, leaned a hip against the table. "Remember the good old days when people had alibis you could check out? We can call the dealership and find out if Champion brought the car in to the shop this morning, but that's not going to prove it broke down on him last night."

"He covered himself pretty well on the oil deal," Jake

said, biting back on frustration. ''Dammit, Whit, we're getting nowhere on this case. We've got bodies piling up faster than garbage at the county dump, and we don't even know if the killer is a man or a woman.''

''I guess the good news is, we can't fall out of the ditch we're in.''

''A real silver lining,'' he muttered, kneading at the tension just above his eyebrows. ''I'd say the same thing even if this case wasn't close to Nicole. But, dammit, it is. It's too close and I can't get a handle on how the hell to stop it.''

''You're not alone.'' Whitney scooped up the pad and pencil, handed it to him. ''We've both been up all night and day and we need a break. Meanwhile, don't you have a date to pick up?''

''My next stop.'' Jake rubbed at his gritty eyes. ''And here I am, in no mood for company. Not even my own.''

Whitney tilted her head. ''I'll be happy to pick up Nicole, tell her you can't make it.''

He slid his partner a look. ''Not on your life.''

When Jake walked into the workout area at Sebastian's, his mood darkened at seeing the unitard-clad Viking with his hands plastered on Nicole's body.

Jaw set, Jake halted beside a row of StairMasters. The mix of conversation, labored breathing and pulsing music that filled the air dimmed against a hot, searing jealousy he would have sworn he didn't possess. He realized now he'd been wrong about the ivory robe Nicole had worn last night—it hadn't shown *every* curve and hollow of her body the way her eye-popping sapphire leotard did. Darkened with sweat between her breasts, the stretchy material skimmed her incredible body like a second skin.

His blood pumping, Jake drew on logic that told him it was standard operating procedure for a personal trainer to touch a client. How better to demonstrate the right posture for a squat lift but for Sebastian Peck to have one blunt-fingered hand on Nicole's belly, the other pressed against her lower back?

Wiping a hand across the knotted muscles in his neck, Jake turned, caught sight of Mel Hall in a mirror-walled workout pit. Dressed in a T-shirt and gym shorts, Nicole's assistant lay on a slant board, puffing out breaths, his muscles bulging as he performed a set of curls with free weights.

When he snagged Mel's gaze, Jake gave a slight nod. The man's mouth instantly compressed. Mel set the weights aside, mopped his face with a towel and crossed the carpeted surface to stand by Jake.

"Don't tell me you're here because someone else got murdered," Mel said, looping the towel around his neck.

"Not since last night." Jake knew that Whitney had called Hall to find out where he'd been when the professor had bought it in his driveway. As with the two previous murders, Hall claimed he'd been at home, taking care of his ill mother, who'd slept most of the evening.

A line formed between Mel's brows. "Since you're wearing a suit, I get the idea you're not here to work out."

"Nicole and I have plans." Jake glanced back over his shoulder. His stomach muscles unknotted slightly now that she was doing the squat lifts under her own steam while Peck observed.

"Plans?"

"Yeah." Jake looked back at Hall. "Any idea how much longer she'll be tied up with Peck?"

"Their hour's about up." Mel raked a hand through his damp blond hair. "Look, Nicole's had it rough lately. She needs peace and quiet. Time to meditate. No offense, but your hanging around only reminds her of the bad stuff that's happened."

"Maybe you think peering through crystals and drinking herb tea will make all this 'bad stuff' go away?"

Irritation flashed in Hall's eyes, then leveled out. "That's not what I meant."

"Good, because some slime's running around, murdering people. He or she doesn't seem likely to stop on their own. That means I'll be around until this case gets solved."

"What happens after that?"

If Jake hadn't wondered the same thing, he would have told Hall what he could do with his question. Instead, he said, "Who knows."

"Ford?"

Jake turned at the sound of Peck's deep, accented voice. "Yeah?"

"Nicole asked me to tell you she went to get her bag." His eyes intent on Jake's face, Peck pulled a black sweatband away from his blond mane. "I would challenge you again to that game of racquetball, but I don't guess you've got time."

"Not now." Jake knew that Whitney had also checked with Peck for an alibi for last night. Mr. Muscle claimed he'd been driving home alone from a weightlifting demonstration in Tulsa around the time of the murder.

"You have a rain check," Peck said. "I look forward to getting you on the court."

Slaughtering me, Jake thought. "Yeah."

Peck gave Mel a nod before moving off to one of the StairMasters. There, he smiled at a woman who grimaced as if every muscle in her body were weeping.

"You made it," Nicole said from behind him.

Jake turned, noting she'd pulled on a man's oversize white shirt over her leotard. Although the shirt hung open in the front, he figured its loose cut might keep him from ravishing her before they got out of the gym.

His mouth curved as he gazed down at her. "I made it," he repeated softly.

"I'm glad." With her hair swept back in a braid, her blue eyes seemed huge, the bruise on her right cheek a faded shadow. Her skin seemed almost translucent as it glowed from her workout.

Jake knew, in one breath-stealing flash, that he had never wanted another woman the way he wanted her. Reaching out, he curled his hand on hers. "You ready to get out of here?"

"Yes—"

"What about your car, Nicole?" Mel took an eager step forward. "You leaving it here?"

She adjusted the strap of the leather tote she'd slung over one shoulder. "I'll pick it up later tonight."

In the morning, Jake thought, linking his fingers with hers. If she wasn't already clear on the fact that he wanted her to himself all night, she soon would be.

"Okay." Ignoring the towel around his neck, Mel raised a shoulder, blotted his forehead against one arm of his T-shirt. "I'll see you in the morning."

"Remember to give Edna the sugar-free gingersnaps I bought at lunch," Nicole said, giving his arm a squeeze.

Mel beamed. "I won't forget. Those are Mom's favorites." His smile dimmed as he flicked Jake a look, then shifted his gaze back to his boss. "You call me if you need anything. I'm going straight home when I leave here."

"I will."

Jake waited until they'd moved out of earshot, then asked, "Do you get the idea your assistant doesn't approve of our being together?"

"Mel doesn't think you're my type," Nicole said as they skirted rows of exercise equipment. "That you won't be good for me."

Jake didn't choose to analyze why Hall's opinion annoyed

him. It just did. Making no comment, he pressed a hand to the small of her back as they passed through the reception area, then stepped out into the brightly lit hallway. There, he spun her around, nudged her back against the wall and pressed his body against hers.

"I'm more interested in knowing what you think," he murmured.

"I've thought about our being together all day. I think I'm going to go crazy if you don't kiss me."

"Glad to." Responding to a need he could no longer control, he crushed his mouth to hers.

Her lips parted on a quiet moan; instantly, she was clinging to him, her mouth wild and willing. When he pressed closer, her body vibrated against his like a plucked harp string.

His heart pounded in his head while his hands raced over her, exploring the curves and hollows that had tormented him since last night. Every cell inside him burned for her. Every need he'd ever felt was for her.

"I don't care," she murmured when his mouth left hers to ravage the exposed column of her throat. She tugged at the knot of his tie while her breasts rose and fell against his chest. "I just don't care anymore."

A hollow echo had Jake drawing back, turning his head in the direction they'd come. Although he saw no one at the end of the carpeted hallway, he forced himself to remember where they were. He knew if he didn't get Nicole out of the building fast he'd haul her into the nearest janitor's closet and take her there.

"What don't you care about?" he asked, fighting to regain both his breath and his sanity.

"If you're my type. Good for me, or bad. Perfect match, or perfectly awful. It no longer matters." Her skin was flushed, her eyes slumberous as her hand slid up to cup the side of his neck. "I don't understand what's going on around me. I don't know why people are dying. And I don't know why I feel the way I do about you. All I know is that I need you, Jake. All of you.''

Her words touched him, had him framing her face in his palms. ''I should take you out,'' he said softly. ''Buy you dinner. Show you that you mean more to me than just this.''

''Buy me dinner later.'' One of her hands settled over his, her fingers trembling. ''Right now, I want to be alone with you.''

''There's a plan I can't argue with.'' Linking his fingers with hers, he tugged her away from the wall and headed toward the elevator.

Chapter 11

With her head spinning and her vision blurred at the edges, Nicole barely remembered Jake dragging her into the elevator for the swift ride to the building's lobby. Nor could she recall in detail their harried dash to his car. All she knew was that when he slid behind the wheel, he looked at her as though she were a shimmering pool of cool water and he was a man with a desperate thirst.

"My place or yours?" he asked, cramming the key into the ignition.

"Which is closest?"

"Mine."

She nipped the lobe of his right ear between her teeth. "Yours." His warm, musky scent filled her head, made her heart thud. "Does this car have a light and siren so we can get there faster?"

"Trust me, we don't need them."

Later, much later, she would wonder how he managed to handle the car, much less traverse the heavy late-evening traffic without wrapping them around a bridge abutment. Right now, what mattered was getting her unsteady fingers to stop fumbling long enough to get his tie unknotted.

"I want to feel you," she said when she finally managed to work off his tie, undo half the shirt's buttons and shove aside the starched material. A hum of pleasure surged up her throat while her exploring hands slid across his chest, savoring the power of sinew and muscle. She used a light fingertip to trace the swirl of coarse dark hair that circled one nipple, then her mouth replaced her fingertip.

The car lurched; beneath her lips, she felt Jake's heart jolt. "Are you trying to get us killed?" he groaned as the car winked through an amber light.

"Hmm," she murmured, and tugged at his nipple with her teeth.

"You are."

Ten minutes later, the car pulled to a jerky stop. His hands were instantly on her, wrenching her up from his chest, dragging her onto his lap.

His mouth took hers in a dazing, dizzying kiss. Her blood heated like a flash fire beneath her skin, roared in her head. Her fingers plunged into his hair, her body straining against his with urgent need.

He shoved her shirt off her shoulders, down her arms. The buttoned cuffs caught on her wrists, trapping them behind her. For a thrilling moment she felt the heady, arousing sense of being bound, helpless while he tugged her stretchy leotard off one shoulder. Need raged, clawed inside her as his teeth seared a hot path across her exposed flesh.

"I want this off." Wrapping her braid around one hand, he arched her head back to expose her throat to his mouth. "I want you naked."

"You have...to peel off...the whole thing."

On a vicious oath, he shouldered open the door, dragged her out of the car with him.

Nicole had the vague sense of the warm night closing around them, of the car's door gaping open behind them. With a cuff of the white shirt still circling one of her wrists, they staggered together up the driveway, hot, hungry mouths locked. Somehow she wound up facing him, stumbling backward, one arm draped over his shoulder. He swept her up into his arms, taking the porch steps two at a time.

The light beside the front door glowed. When he pulled his mouth from hers and shoved the key in the lock, the heat in his dark eyes seared her. Lust clutched deep in her center.

In one smooth move he shoved open the door, kicked it closed behind him. A weak wash of light coming from somewhere deep inside the house illuminated the small entry hall in silver light and shadow.

When Jake set her on her feet, she discovered that her knees were loose, her head filled with blinding light and colors. If he hadn't shoved her back against the nearest wall and trapped her body with his, she knew she would have crumpled to the floor.

Against her belly, she felt his erection throb.

His breath a harsh rasp through his lips, he caught her face in his hands.

"Tell me." Eyes as black as midnight bored into hers, searching. "Tell me you want this, Nicole. You want us."

"Yes." Her throat was so dry the word was barely audible. "I want us."

His fingers curled into the leotard's neckline, yanking the material down to her waist. With an expert flick of his fingers, he unhooked her cotton sports bra, dragged it off. His hands tight at her waist, he lifted her off her feet to take her breast in his mouth. The air around her thickened; her breath snagged in her lungs as she arched back, her fingers digging into his shoulders.

His mouth fed, suckled, his teeth scraping erotically over her aching, budded nipple. She writhed against the small, exquisite pain, sobbing his name, the wet pulse between her legs pounding.

"Jake... Please, I can't..."

"You can." He lowered her, his mouth coming down on hers, crushing, conquering. His hands ran along her skin, clever, skilled, strong as he stripped off the leotard, the shirt that still clung by one cuff, then her panties.

"You're beautiful." Gazing down at her, he cupped her breasts in his hands, his thumbs performing a slow, erotic massage of her nipples. "Perfect."

The flash of passion, the fury of need that darkened his eyes filled her with a sense of decadent power as she stood before him, naked except for her socks and workout shoes. Time and place became nothing against a hard, driving desire for him. Only him.

"Here." In mindless, liberating pleasure, she shoved her hands beneath his suit coat, forced it off his shoulders. "Right here," she said, frantically tugging his shirttail out of his slacks.

"I've got a bed." His eyes glimmered in the weak light as he fought the suit coat off his arms, flung it aside. "I've got a damn bed."

"Later." Need for him, primitive and overwhelming, surged through her as her greedy hands unhooked his belt, the button of his slacks.

"Here, then." He paused long enough to toe off his shoes and step out of his slacks and briefs before he dragged her down onto the floor with him.

The coolness of the tiles beneath her back registered in her dazed mind as he leaned over her. His mouth began feasting on her flesh, his greedy hands racing over her quivering body in ruthless exploration. Heat pumped through her blood; she felt herself going warm and soft, melting into his touch, becoming one.

Her hot, hungry mouth nipped his neck, his chest. Her

nails dug into the hard ridge of his shoulders. She couldn't get enough of him, of his taste, his touch. He seeped into her, pore by pore.

She gasped when his palm cupped her, molding against her with intimate possession. His fingers moved against her wet heat, relentlessly driving her up, the need for release building, clawing viciously inside her.

"Look at me," he said when her eyes fluttered shut. "I want you to know it's me you're with. Just me."

"Yes." The shadows around them seemed to shift while his fingers stroked. Sensation slid over sensation, building inside her in trembling, shuddering layers, then exploded. Her vision grayed; a half sob tore from her lips.

Strength gone, her hands slipped from his shoulders. She lay motionless, sweat slicking her flesh, air clogging in her lungs, her heartbeat stumbling.

"I could eat you alive," he murmured.

"I could...let you."

He mounted her, crushing his mouth to hers as he thrust himself into her.

A sob of pure, overwhelming pleasure eased up her throat. Her body opened to his, joined with his. Arching, she brought him deeper inside her as if she'd never known a man before. Her hips moved in desperate, greedy time with his, urging him on.

In that fleeting moment before they plunged together into the roaring dark, Nicole understood there would never be room for another man in her mind, in her heart. Jake was the one. The only one.

He'd taken her like a fiend. That was all Jake could think as he lay beside her on the cool tiles while he struggled to clear his fevered brain. Never before had he lost control so totally with a woman. Never before had he been so greedy, so *desperate*.

When his breathing steadied, he found the strength to turn his head. Nicole lay on her side, her eyes closed, her head pillowed against his shoulder, one of her arms flung across his chest. In the dim light, her skin glowed like warm honey.

Reaching out, he stroked a palm down the length of the exquisite curves and hollows that had driven him mad all night and day.

"I attacked you," he said quietly, remorse a hot weight in his belly.

"Hmm." She kept her eyes closed, thick blond lashes fanning her cheeks as she drew in what sounded like a contented breath. "We attacked each other."

Thinking back to the number of times she'd nearly made him wreck the cruiser on the drive there, he had to agree. Still, that didn't excuse the fact he'd treated her with so little care.

"Nicole, I was too rough. Careless. I didn't mean to be, but I was. You have a right to be upset."

Her eyes drifted open, their blue depths studying his face as her hand slid up his chest to cup his jaw. "The only reason I'd be upset was if we hadn't made it into the house before we got naked." She glanced down at the shoes and socks she still wore. "Well, almost naked."

He couldn't help grinning at the thought. "Yeah, the neighbors would have loved that."

She raised her head off his shoulder, one blond brow arched. "So, Sergeant Ford, how many traffic laws did you break getting us here?"

"Including those two red lights I dodged?"

"Including."

He stroked his knuckles along the swell of her breast. "I'd say about thirty, give or take."

"Is that some kind of cop record?"

"For me it is."

A swell of emotion he couldn't name had him sitting up

abruptly, gathering her with him. Somehow, despite all his inner protests and misgivings, he'd made a right move and wound up here with Nicole in his arms.

He used his fingertips to nudge back wispy strands of golden hair that had pulled loose from her long braid. "I'm glad you're here. Glad you're with me."

"Me, too." She caught his lower lip between her teeth. "I like your entry hall," she murmured against his mouth.

Inside him, a deep, dark wanting began to smolder. "Thanks. I've never seen it from this angle before."

"I'd like a tour of your whole house."

He thought about his kitchen with its sink filled with dishes and foam take-out containers overflowing the trash can. "You might want to hold off seeing the kitchen. I'm renting a backhoe next week to shovel it out."

"Okay, the kitchen can wait." She linked her arms around his neck and gave him a wicked smile. "What I'm really interested in is your bedroom. Is it first or last on the tour?"

The weak light coming from the living room cast their separate silhouettes onto the wall. When she leaned and traced the outline of his mouth with her tongue, the two gray shadows molded into one.

One was all he could think as lust slashed through his gut. There, on his entry hall floor, he and Nicole had become one.

"The bedroom's first." He rose, swept her up into his arms. "And the tour starts now."

Nicole woke just after dawn feeling achy and sated...and totally decadent from having spent most of the night being ravished. Stretching like a contented cat, she shoved her tangled hair out of her face. Her mouth curved with the memory of Jake loosening her braid, working a brush through the long, thick strands, then wrapping his fingers through her hair while he eased himself into her wet depths.

Since the moment she'd seen him at Bill and Whitney's wedding, she had told herself Jake Ford wasn't what she wanted. Spent hours trying to convince herself he was far from her perfect match. That might be true, she conceded. Maybe last night she'd taken such a big leap she couldn't possibly land on her feet. She didn't know. All she knew was that she and Jake had shared more than passion during the hours they'd spent together. There were feelings involved, too. Feelings that both of them had tried to ignore. Still, they were there. How deep they went, she wasn't sure. All she knew was that they existed, could no longer be denied.

Turning her head on the pillow, she gazed through the weak dawn light. Jake lay asleep on his side, his face half turned toward her. His jet-black hair was a rumpled mess, lashes as dark as night shadowed cheeks heavy with stubble. His mouth was slightly open, his lips relaxed.

Thoughts of how that mouth had destroyed her control sent a shudder of pure longing through her. Easing out a trembling breath, she had all she could do to keep from reaching out and running her palm over his chest, then lower…

Swallowing past the tightness in her throat, she slid out of bed. She was still groping for answers to how two people who'd been determined to stay apart had wound up together. Answers she knew would only get clouded in the throes of passion. She needed time…and space to do some calm, cool thinking.

At one point during the night, when they'd taken a breather from mauling each other, Jake had gone out to his car and retrieved her leather tote. He'd piled it and the clothes they'd flung around the entry hall onto the top of his bureau. Nicole plucked her hopelessly wrinkled white shirt out of the pile, pulled it on, then padded barefoot down the hallway.

She opened a door that she thought might be to the bathroom, and instantly recognized her mistake. Pale light eased through lacy curtains; two white cribs with pink gingham coverlets edged one wall. A large snowy dresser with crystal knobs stood to her right; on her left were shelves filled with a menagerie of stuffed animals and dolls.

Throat dry, Nicole stood motionless, fingers gripping the doorknob as she breathed in a faint, sweet scent. She could not begin to imagine the grief and sorrow Jake had experienced when he lost his wife and daughters. Couldn't comprehend how a person survived that kind of devastation.

She knew she should step out, pull the door closed. In the end, it was the charming framed prints from fairy tales that pulled her deeper into the room. Sleeping Beauty being kissed by her prince. Snow White surrounded by the adoring dwarfs. Still others from stories Nicole had read as a child, stories she'd dreamed of someday reading to her own children.

When she found herself standing over one of the cribs, she leaned, smoothed a hand across the soft gingham. A fuzzy pink stuffed rabbit sat in one corner of the crib, staring out at her with eyes as blue as a calm sea. She ran a finger down the pink, fuzzy ear that flopped to one side.

"The rabbit was Jeanie's favorite. Jamie took a liking to a black bear."

Jake's voice, coming just inches away, had Nicole jumping. Her heart lodged in her throat, she turned.

"I'm sorry for intruding. I was looking for the bathroom and came in here by mistake."

He'd pulled on a pair of gym shorts, but no shirt. His hair was rumpled as if he'd finger-combed it; his chin looked even more stubbled than it had while he'd slept. It was the hardness in his eyes that told her something more was wrong than him just finding her in this room.

"I told you about the other case I'm on," he said quietly as he stepped to the crib. "The little boy who got killed by a drive-by shooter."

"Yes." She watched him lift the pink rabbit, cup it in his palm as if priceless. "You said he died just because he was standing on a street corner the shooter considered his."

"Right." Jake stared at the rabbit. "When we got to the scene, Enrique Quintero had a bullet in his chest and a toy fire engine clutched in one grimy fist. His mother said Enrique loved that fire engine. I got the idea she took comfort in the fact he'd had it with him when he died."

"Oh, God."

"That homicide happened three weeks ago." Jake replaced the rabbit in its cozy corner, let his hand linger for an extra moment. "Every so often I think I have things under control. Then something like that kid's fire engine jumps up and grabs me by the throat. When I got home that night, I came in here, spent an hour trying to figure out which of the twins' toys Annie had packed for their trip. I needed to make sure my girls had something they loved to hold on to when they died."

"Jake..." Tears welled in Nicole's eyes. Her heart was bleeding for him, she could feel it. She placed a hand on his shoulder. "I'm so sorry."

He shifted minutely so that she had no choice but to drop her hand. "So am I."

"I can't imagine having to go through something like that."

"I don't wish it on anybody." As he slicked his knuckles down her cheek, she watched his face, saw his jaw harden. "And I can't imagine having to go through it twice in one lifetime." He closed his eyes, opened them. "I'm sorry, Nicole. I just now realized I made a big mistake last night."

A chill snaked up her spine. "A mistake…"

"I can't do this again. I thought I could push everything back. Thought I could let myself take a risk. Then I saw you leaning over the crib just like Annie used to. It was like someone stabbed a hot knife in my gut."

She saw the change in his eyes, a subtle but distinct distancing even as he took her hand. "I can't do this again," he repeated softly. "I can't ever do this again."

Panic had her tightening her hand on his. "I understand how you must feel—"

"Do you?" he asked evenly. "Do you know what it's like to lose your whole life in one second? Do you know how it feels to hurt so bad you don't want to take the next breath? How the only way to stop from putting a gun to your head and pulling the trigger is to crawl into the bottom of a bottle?"

"No, I don't know what any of that's like." Her lungs were burning, and the sensation was rapidly moving toward her heart. "You must have good memories of your family, Jake."

"I do." His thumb caressed the inside of her wrist before he eased his hand from hers. "And I took everything for granted. I didn't appreciate the fact that when I got up every morning, Annie had my coffee ready. It was always just there. I assumed I'd spend the rest of my life reaching for her in the night. I believed that, since I saw Jamie and Jeanie each get their first tooth, I'd see the rest come in, too."

He shoved a hand through his hair. "Those are all good memories, Nicole. They're also the ones that eat you alive and send you to the darkest crevices of hell. I dragged myself out of that pit once. I don't have what it takes to do it again."

All the joy that had shimmered in her heart throughout the night turned to ashes, cold and gray. "So, because some terrible thing *could* happen to me in the future, you're telling me you don't want what we might have together, for as long as we might have it. You're turning your back on us.''

"There can't be an *us*. I don't want there to be an us.'' His eyes narrowed. "It'd be best if we both back off. Forget last night happened.''

"Forget?'' She spoke quietly, clinging to the slippery edge of control.

He muttered a ragged oath, yet his eyes remained cool. Passionless. "You told me you learned the hard way what kind of man suits you. That I'm not him.''

Her eyes filled, and she fought back the tears. Her chest ached. There was such a terrible pressure there that she rubbed the heel of her palm against it. Could there have been a worse possible time, she wondered, for her to realize she was in love with him?

"You're right, Jake, from the minute we met I knew you weren't the type of man who suits me.'' Every word she spoke hurt her throat. "But the attraction was so strong. Too strong.'' With an unsteady hand she jabbed her hair away from her cheek. "When I met Cole, I got swept away by emotion, and I paid dearly. Oh, my pain was nowhere near what you've suffered, but I hurt all the same. Even so, I was willing to let you into my life. Willing to risk my heart for you.'' Her voice broke, but she managed to shore it up again. "I just wish you'd told me up front that all you were interested in was a one-night stand.''

He took a quick step forward, locked his hands on her arms. "Dammit, it was a hell of a lot more than that.'' His eyes weren't cool now, but dark and angry as he gave her a shake. "You know that.''

"For me, it was.'' She jerked away, took an unsteady step backward. Then another. Foremost in her mind was the need to get away from him. She clenched her teeth when she remembered they'd left her Jaguar parked at her office building.

"I'll get dressed and call a cab."

"I'm taking you to get your car."

"No."

"Nicole—"

"No!" Her chin angled like a sword when he took a step toward her. "I can't decide how you'll live your life, Jake. I can't tell you that you can trust me to stay with you by promising nothing terrible will ever happen to me. You've chosen not to take that risk."

Hands fisted, she dragged in a ragged breath. "I *choose* to leave here in a cab. You want me to back off, get out of your life. Forget. Fine, that's what I'll do."

Hands trembling, Nicole paid the cab driver, unlocked the Jaguar and slid behind the wheel. Her breath was shallow and hot, the pain sweeping through her vicious. Jake had been determined to push her away and she'd been powerless to stop him. She had the clawing, agonizing feeling that she would spend the rest of her life wondering what they had lost in that pink-and-white bedroom.

Still, she had her pride. He'd rejected her. If it burned a hole in her, she would fill the empty, throbbing space in her heart. She had her work. Her family. She didn't need Jake Ford.

The ringing of her cell phone had her closing her eyes. She didn't think he would dare call. Not after he'd just broken her heart. A heart that still loved him in spite of it.

Swallowing around what felt like shards of glass in her throat, she grabbed the phone from her tote, clicked it on.

"Hello?"

"Nicole? I...my dear God."

"Mel?" The shaky panic in her assistant's voice had her fingers tightening on the phone. "What's wrong, Mel?"

"It's Mother."

"Has Edna taken a turn for the worse?"

"She's dead, Nicole." His voice broke on a sob. "I woke up this morning and...found her dead."

Chapter 12

"Enjoy your cell, scum sucker."

Amid a flurry of curses, Jake shoved Ramon Cárdenas into the hands of a burly jailer. It had taken two nights of intense tracking, but Jake's snitch had finally come through with the whereabouts of Cárdenas's girlfriend. After dealing herself out of a murder charge, she'd sung like a diva about how she'd witnessed her boyfriend gun down little Enrique Quintero.

Case closed, Jake thought as he walked out of the jail. He passed a small, dim alcove where a receptionist's desk sat empty. Rays of morning sunlight threaded through the window behind the desk.

A scowl settled over his face as he turned down the hallway that led to the Homicide office. At this point, he should be feeling the rush, the lift that always came at the end of a hunt. Even bringing down Cárdenas didn't ease his frustration. Work had always been a salve, a way to keep his mind focused, push away unwanted thoughts. That wasn't the case this time, which he'd proved after spending the past days and nights brooding over Nicole.

She'd given him exactly what he'd asked for. She'd backed off. Walked out of his life. Hell, she'd probably already forgotten about the night they'd spent together. According to Whitney, Nicole hadn't been sitting around brooding. Mel Hall's mother had died from complications of the diabetes that had rendered her a near invalid. Nicole had handled funeral arrangements for her distraught assistant, stayed almost continuously at his side. With all that on her plate, Jake figured he'd spent a lot more time thinking about her than she had about him.

That last thought irritating him enormously, he swung past the report clerk's office where several night shift typists wearing earpieces entered data into computers. Had he really thought he could shove the woman he'd been close to falling in love with out of his life and not think about her? Not wonder if he'd made a huge mistake that he'd pay for until the day he died?

Blowing out a breath, he assured himself that questioning what he'd done was normal. Expected. Putting the brakes on a relationship that had nowhere to go had been the best thing for both of them. As his brisk footsteps echoed off the hallway tiles, he refused to hear the mocking voice inside his head that called him a liar—and a coward.

He needed sleep, he told himself, swiping a hand over his gritty eyes. Everything around him seemed a half beat out of sync because he'd snagged only minimal sack time over the past seventy-two hours. He planned to go home and crawl into bed after he finished the follow-up reports on Cárdenas's arrest, but that was a couple of hours down the road. Until then, he would rely on caffeine to keep him going. As he turned a corner, Jake glanced at his watch, saw it was nearly eight. If his luck held, one of the day crew would have already hit the office and brewed a fresh pot of coffee.

Minutes later, he strode into Homicide where Grant Pierce and his new partner, Elizabeth Scott, were already at work at their desks. Jake caught the heady scent of fresh coffee, and blessed them both. His lightened mood veered to one of caution when he spotted Whitney. Shooting out waves of irritation, she lobbed her purse onto her desk then jerked off her blazer. He recognized the fire in her eyes, knew why it was there.

"What the hell kind of partnership do you think we have, Ford?" she asked when she caught sight of him. "You get a tip on Cárdenas's girlfriend's whereabouts and don't call me?"

"The tip came at 1:00 a.m.," Jake said after reaching their desks that butted against each other. "I brought her in for an interview. I didn't pick up Cárdenas until an hour ago."

"What difference does the time make?"

"You're still on your honeymoon. I figured I'd give you a break and let you stay in bed with your husband."

"I ought to shoot you in the kneecap just for saying that."

Out of the corner of his eye, Jake saw that Pierce and Scott were both leaning back in their chairs, watching the show.

"Things worked out without my needing to call you in. I used some uniforms as backup, so the arrest was no big deal. I thought I was doing you a favor by giving you a couple more hours at home. You'll just have to get over not being in on this one." He ran a hand through his hair. "I really need coffee—"

"Get over it." Jamming her hands at her waist, Whitney took a lethal step forward. "You've been in a surly mood for days. I put up with it, figured you'd get around to telling me what put the burr under your butt, so I didn't press. Five minutes ago I walk in here and find out that my *partner* took

down one of our suspects—*our* suspects—without bothering
to let me in on it.''

"Chill out, Whit, would you? I was just trying to give
you more time with your husband.''

"Bull!'' A finger stab to his chest accompanied the word.
"This new stupidity of yours has nothing to do with my
status as a newlywed, and everything to do with my sister-
in-law.''

When Pierce sent up a wolf whistle, Jake's vision blurred
to red. "That tears it!''

Locking a hand on Whitney's arm, he towed her toward
the back of the office and into the small storage room where
file cabinets lined the wall.

"Nicole's got nothing to do with my mood,'' he countered when the door swung shut behind them.

"Oh, really?''

"Really.''

Jerking from his touch, Whitney moved to the small table
that sat in the room's center, propped a hip against one edge.
"Nicole hasn't spent a lot of time at the house lately, but
when she was there, she was quiet, withdrawn. At first I
figured that was because of Mel's mother—I know Nicole
was fond of the woman.''

"Yeah.''

"I went to the funeral yesterday afternoon. I stopped by
Mel's house afterward to pay my respects and to see Nicole.''

Jake ran a palm over the knotted muscles in his neck.
He'd wondered repeatedly how Nicole was handling the
woman's death. "How is she?''

"Near exhaustion. Mel's badly shaken, so she's trying to
give him both support and comfort. Plus, the house was
filled with friends and relatives. Nicole was on her feet the
whole time, making sure there was plenty of food on the
table, that everyone had something to drink.'' Whitney's

dark brows furrowed. "She looked so pale I thought she might faint. I filled a plate of food for her, found us a quiet corner and insisted she take a break. She put up a good front, but she finally broke and told me what happened between the two of you. Jake, how in holy heaven could you be so dense?"

He set his teeth. "I did what I had to do."

"You *had* to toss away a chance for happiness by forcing a wonderful, sensitive, *gorgeous* woman out of your life?"

He opened his mouth, shut it. Put that way, he sounded like an idiot. "It's best."

"For whom?"

"For both of us." He crammed two fingers inside his shirt pocket. When he found it empty, he wished fervently he'd never given up smoking. "Breaking things off was best for both of us."

"You panicked, Jake," Whitney said, her eyes softening. "You walked in and found Nicole in the twins' bedroom, and you got scared that history would repeat itself."

"Yeah, I got scared," he shot back. "All I could think about was having Nicole, then losing her, like Annie."

"So, instead of waiting for fate to deliver a blow that might never come, you did it yourself."

"That's right." He thought about the miserable nights he'd lain awake, reminding himself how heady it could be to find a woman whom it felt so right to be with. How seductive. And how devastating when she was gone.

Standing there, in the small, dim room that smelled faintly of aged paper, the helplessness of his need for Nicole swamped him, severed the tight leash he'd kept on his thoughts. It hit him then—he hadn't *been* falling in love with her when he broke things off. He'd already stopped falling and had hit the ground full force. He just hadn't realized it.

He had thought loss was the most painful thing of all, but

now he knew there was something much worse. Regret.
Dammit, he didn't want to regret Nicole.

He muttered a curse. "What have I done?"

"You've been human," Whitney answered quietly. "For
most people, it's more comfortable to sit back, not take a
risk. It can also be lonely. You deserve to spend the rest of
your life with a woman you love and who loves you. You've
got a second shot at happiness, Jake. Not everyone gets that.
You'd be a fool to throw it away."

"I'm a fool, all right," he said, letting the misery of the
past days flow over him. He saw again the image of how
Nicole's face had paled, how her eyes had gone huge and
hollow with hurt. He eased out a breath against the vicious
guilt. "I hurt her, Whit. Bad. I ruined everything."

"So, go fix it."

"Like Nicole will even give me a chance."

"She's as unhappy as you."

"She'll kick me. Then she'll send me packing."

"Not if you say the right words." Whitney's mouth
curved. "Crawling on your hands and knees while you're
saying them would be good. I'd plan on doing major grov-
eling."

"Yeah."

A light tap on the door brought both of their heads around
had them saying a simultaneous "Come in."

Elizabeth Scott poked her head through the open door.
"Either of you kill the other yet?"

Whitney shook her head. "We decided that'd be too much
trouble."

"One less homicide to work," Elizabeth said cheerfully.
"The M.E.'s on line one, asking to talk to either of you. He
said he has the tox reports back and he knows what it is that
killed your victims."

"About time." Jake walked to the table while Whitney
stabbed the intercom button on the phone beside her.

"Dr. McClandess," Whitney said. "It's Sergeants Taylor and Ford. We understand you have the tox results?"

"Yes. The testing took longer than usual because the substance the killer used is so rare. You're looking for someone who has gotten his or her hands on pure curare."

"Curare?" Jake frowned. "Isn't that the poison some natives put on the tips of hunting spears?"

"Exactly. Curare is also used medicinally as a muscle relaxant."

Whitney pursed her lips. "How is that possible, Dr. McClandess? How can a poison be used as a medicine?"

"Curare is not harmful if swallowed. Surgeons often use a derivative of curare as a preoperative relaxant. The natives who harvest the substance often brew a drink of herbs and curare to relax muscles before setting fractures. It's when curare is injected into the bloodstream that it can kill. A fatal dose brings on immediate respiratory paralysis."

"Which is the cause of death of our victims," Jake stated. "Yes."

Jake nodded. "How rare a poison, Doc? How could the killer get his or her hands on a vial of the stuff?"

"That's a good question. Curare is extracted from several varieties of trees that grow only in South America."

Jake caught a flash in Whitney's eyes as she leaned closer to the phone. "*Only* South America, Doctor?"

"That is correct."

Whitney looked at Jake, mouthed a word that he missed, then she looked back at the phone. "What did the killer use to inject the poison? Just a regular needle and syringe?"

"That's another thing. We just finished the comparison of the puncture wounds on all three victims. We knew the wounds were all similar in depth. Our toxicologic studies on the tissue sections of the injection sites show the depth of all punctures are exactly the same. That means the same amount of pressure was used to inject all three men. It's unlikely someone jabbing a needle into a person's neck could manage that.''

Jake kept his eyes on Whitney while he bit back an urgent need to hear what she had snapped to. They had to finish their conversation with the M.E. ''How did the killer pull off three same-depth injections?'' he asked.

''My guess is by using a spring-loaded Syrette,'' Mc-Clandess replied. ''Its needle would penetrate the flesh the same depth every time. Numerous Syrettes are sold containing premeasured doses of drugs for people allergic to bee stings and other ailments. Another option would be a lancet a spring-loaded instrument used to stab a finger to get blood.''

Jake narrowed his eyes. ''Like diabetics use?''

''Yes.''

After a few more questions, the call ended. Punching the disconnect button, Jake met Whitney's gaze. ''What have you got, besides the fact that Mel's mother was diabetic, so he'd know how to use a lancet?''

''Yesterday, when I was at Mel's house, Nicole introduced me to his uncle Zebulon. While the uncle and I were chatting, he mentioned he distributes exotic woods for a living.''

Jake pulled from his memory what Nicole had mentioned about the man. ''He cultivates fresh herbs as a hobby. What about the exotic woods?''

''They all come from South America. Zebulon Hall told me he makes monthly business trips there. Jake, that's how Mel could get his hands on curare.'' She frowned. ''But why? Why kill all those people? What would he think it could gain him?''

''Let's go ask him and his uncle.''

''Zebulon Hall's leaving on a nine-thirty flight. One of Mel's neighbors is taking him to the airport.'' She glanced at her watch. ''That doesn't give us much time to get him.''

"You know what he looks like, so you'd better cover the airport."

"I'll radio ahead to the airport police, give them Hall's description so they can start narrowing the field."

Jake reached for the phone. "I'll call Nicole, tell her to lock the door of her office until I get there. I want her the hell away from Mel."

"Oh, God."

"What?"

"They're not working today." Whitney shoved her auburn hair behind her shoulders. "I saw Nicole in the kitchen this morning on my way out. She was putting together a basket of pastries to take to Mel's house. Said she didn't want him to be alone so soon after his mother's death."

"She's alone with him." Fear for Nicole rolled through Jake in a wave that left every nerve raw, every sense alert. "I'll try her cell phone. Maybe she's not there yet," he said, punching in the number. Seconds later, he cursed, slammed down the receiver. "Her phone's not on." He fought for calm and logic. "Give me Mel's address."

Whitney rattled it off as they dashed out the door. "Jake, get there fast. I've got this sick feeling that Mel has some sort of plan that involves Nicole."

"His plan is about to get changed."

Nicole pulled her Jaguar into the driveway of the tidy, two-story house, its white shutters glowing beneath the bright morning sun. She knew Mel was expecting her, knew he was alone with his grief and she should go in right away. Instead, she rested her head against the back of the seat and closed her eyes while fatigue pressed down on her like a lead weight.

She was so punchy with exhaustion she shouldn't even be able to think, yet that was all she'd been doing. Thinking of Jake. She would survive his absence in her life, she knew that. Still, the grief and loss she felt were so fresh it was hard to imagine a future when she wouldn't hurt.

Yet, that was what she had to focus on, she reminded herself, rubbing the heel of her hand over her aching heart. Had to concentrate on getting over Jake.

With the warm sun angling through the windshield, she felt herself drifting. Her mind had slid into a half sleep when a sharp tap on the window next to her ear jolted her.

Swiveling her head, she stared through the window at Mel's concerned face. "Are you okay?" he mouthed.

Feeling a stab of guilt at having caused him to worry, she hit the lock's release button.

"I saw you out here," he said as he pulled open the door. "You were so still that I thought something was wrong."

She plucked up her purse and the basket of pastries off the seat beside her, then slid out of the car. "I'm sorry, Mel, you shouldn't have had to come out here."

"You're okay?"

"Of course." Forcing a smile, she skimmed a hand down the boxy aqua silk blouse that matched her slacks. "Just resting my eyes. How are you doing?"

"Fine, now that you're here. Losing Mom still seems like a bad dream."

"I know, Mel. I'm sorry."

He smiled gratefully when Nicole handed him the basket. "You brought my favorite."

"Blueberry muffins, at your service. I thought we'd have them with some tea, then we can tackle the paperwork you need to fill out."

"Thanks. I don't know what I'd do without you."

As they walked up the driveway, she studied him out of the corner of her eye. He wore a pullover shirt and khaki pants; his blond hair gleamed beneath the sun. His eyes were clear blue and unshadowed. She was glad Mel had at least gotten some sleep last night.

They walked through the front door, down the hallway and into the paneled living room that always brought cozy winter evenings and log fires to Nicole's mind. The kitchen itself was homey, its soft yellow paint setting off deep blue counters.

"I take it your uncle Zebulon caught his plane?"

"The neighbor who works at the airport picked Uncle Zeb up in plenty of time," Mel said, settling the basket on the nearest counter. "I feel guilty saying this, but I'm glad he's gone. I'm glad everyone's gone and it's just the two of us."

Nicole gave a distracted smile across her shoulder while she pulled teacups and saucers out of a cabinet. "It's not easy to lose someone you love, then have to put on a strong face for so many people." She retrieved the big kettle off the stove, then walked to the sink and turned on the water. "I'm not going to stay all day, Mel. I know you need time to yourself."

"I need time with you."

His voice, coming from just behind her, had her fumbling the nearly full kettle; it dropped into the sink with a clatter. The instant she turned, he clamped his hands on either side of the counter, trapping her.

"The first time I saw you, I couldn't get my breath."

"Wh-what?" she stammered.

"I could smell your soap and your skin. You smiled at me and my mind clouded." His gaze slid down her body. "I thought about us together. A million times I've thought about us."

"Mel—"

"I love you, Nicole. I know you love me."

With the water gushing in the sink behind her, she stood stunned, her heart hammering, her breathing shallow while she stared up into eyes that seared into hers.

"Like a friend," she said carefully. "I love you like a friend."

"That will change."

"Mel, I don't know what to—"

The sentence ended against his mouth. He hauled her against him and captured her lips in a hard, greedy kiss before she could take one full breath.

"Stop it!" Shoving him back, she jerked from his grip, staggered sideways. She had to be calm, she told herself as she turned to face him. Until this instant, she'd had no idea he had a crush on her, but that was clearly the case. He was young, she reminded herself. She needed to take care with his ego.

"I know you're upset about your mother."

"Yes, but it's going to be all right. Because you're here with me."

"Yes, I'm here to help. You're not alone. You have a lot of *friends* like me to help you."

"We're more than friends. I cherish you, Nicole."

Struggling for calm, she took a deep breath. "I wish you had told me before how you felt. We could have talked about this. I could have explained—"

"I couldn't tell you, not as long as Mother was alive. I'm an only child, she was my responsibility. It wouldn't have been fair to ask you to burden yourself with caring for an invalid. The doctor kept telling me it was a matter of time until Mother passed on." His eyes darkened. "I knew we could be together then, so I waited. But that didn't stop me from protecting you. I've been protecting you all along."

Her scalp prickled. "What do you mean, 'all along'?"

"Ormiston, Villanova, the professor." He smiled. "For you. I did it for you."

"Oh, God. Oh, God." She heard the whimpering panic in her own voice and bit down fiercely on her lip. Mel was standing between her and the kitchen door. Behind her was a utility room that led to the garage. She knew from taking out a bag of trash the day before that the door to the garage was kept locked, the dead bolt requiring a key that hung on a peg beside the dryer. If she ran that way, she wouldn't have time to grab the key and deal with the lock before Mel grabbed her.

She pressed her lips together to stop them from trembling. She had to think. Had to buy herself time until she figured out how to get away. "You killed them all?"

"That's right. I'll always protect you."

The earnestness in his face made her stomach roll. "What were you protecting me from?"

"Ormiston was in a rage that you hadn't found him his perfect match. He called, bad-mouthing you and the company. He threatened to sue. He insisted on talking to you, but I wouldn't let him because his language was so vile. I tried to calm him down. He wouldn't listen to reason."

"But you said he changed his mind." Growing fear had her voice shaking. "He wanted to extend his contract."

"He didn't. I told you he did so you wouldn't be upset over what he was saying about you. I drove to his house— followed another car in through the gate while the guard was gone. I rang the bell and told Ormiston all he had to do was sign a form and we'd refund his retainer. He invited me in."

"You...killed him for that?"

"He wanted to hurt you!" Mel's fist slammed against the counter hard enough to rattle the teacups she'd placed there. "Villanova just wanted you. He would have used you, then tossed you away."

"DeSoto..." Nausea swirled in her stomach, up her throat. "He *flirted* with me. There was nothing between us."

"I saw the way he looked at you at your brother's wedding." Mel's eyes narrowed. "That last time he was at your office, he stopped by my desk. He told me you wouldn't date him anymore so he'd signed a contract to have a reason to see you a lot. He said that way he'd have a chance to change your mind about him. I told him he was wasting his time, that you would never have anything more to do with him. He didn't like hearing that."

The coolness in Mel's smile had the blood draining from her face. She remembered Jake saying DeSoto had been angry when he'd seen him at the elevator. *Jake*. God, she needed Jake.

"I wanted Villanova home that night so I left messages for both him and the woman he had a date with. I told them both the other had to cancel. I went to his house and told him I was sorry for what I'd said. When I told him I could help persuade you to see him again, he asked me in."

"And you killed him." This couldn't be real, Nicole thought. It *couldn't* be.

"I'm sorry I hit you and knocked you off the porch," Mel said, his eyes filled with remorse. "I didn't know anyone was there, didn't know it was *you* I hit. I never would have left you alone and hurt in the dark, you have to believe me." He wiped a hand across his face. "I ran the opposite way from where you'd parked your car, so I didn't see it. I didn't know it was you I'd hit until Kathy called and said you needed me at the hospital. When I saw the bruise on your cheek, knowing I'd put it there, I wanted to die."

"Harold?" Nicole asked through trembling lips. "Why him?"

"You called him, invited him to dinner. He wouldn't have been good for you."

"It was just dinner, Mel. Just dinner."

"He would have made you unhappy. I know."

"How...did you find out I'd asked him out?"

"I listened in on your phone call. I listen to all your calls. I read your mail. Talk to your friends. I know you so well, Nicole. Everything you're thinking, I know."

When he took a step toward her, she skittered back. "Stay away from me."

Hurt slid into his eyes. "I'd never hurt you, Nicole."

"You've hurt a lot of people."

"I've protected you. That hasn't stopped you from hurting me."

She dragged in a breath, fighting back panic. "How did I hurt you, Mel? How did I ever hurt you?"

"That night, when you left Sebastian's with the cop. I stood there, knowing what he was going to do to you. What you were going to *let* him do. I followed you out in the hall, saw you kissing him." As he spoke, Mel's lips tightened, his hands curved into fists. "I was going to kill him, too. Then Mother died and you came to me. You stayed with me. I knew you'd see how perfect we are together."

"Jake" was all she could say as a dawning horror drained her blood.

"I don't have to kill him now. When your sister-in-law was here, I overheard you tell her you're not seeing him anymore. If you don't see him, he can't hurt you."

"That's right, he can't hurt me. You don't have to do anything to Jake." Her vision blurred at the thought of Mel plunging a needle into Jake's neck.

"I took really good care of Mother. I tried to protect her from the disease." As he spoke, his eyes welled with tears. "I couldn't save her, the doctors said I did all I could. But I can take care of you, Nicole. You'll see. Nobody's going to hurt you as long as I'm around."

"I...need...to turn off the water." Biting down on terror, she forced her numbed legs to work. Her fingers were shaking so badly, she could barely turn off the tap. Fighting back hysteria, she put her hand to her throat as she stared down at the kettle sitting in the sink. Full of water. Heavy.

Away was all she could think as she clenched her fingers around the kettle's thick handle. She had to get away.

"You'll see I'm right, Nicole. You'll see."

"The hell I will." She whirled on him, swinging the kettle. The blow caught him on the side of his face. Water spurted from the kettle, sprayed across the floor. Mel landed sideways against the counter, his arms flailing. He hit the floor in a shower of china and muffins.

She dashed past him. His hand shot out. His fingers grabbed her ankle. With a jerk he brought her down hard onto her hands and knees. Screaming, she fought like a madwoman against his hold.

"I love you." His hand tightened, dragging her toward him. "I'll never hurt you."

Struggling, she scrambled for a handhold. Water from the kettle had turned the floor's ceramic tiles as slick as ice. Fear bubbled in her brain as he dragged her deeper into the kitchen. "Let go!"

Somewhere in the distance she heard wood splinter, then the slap of shoes against wood.

"Nicole—"

"No!" Twisting, she kicked out with her free foot. Through a morass of terror her brain registered the solid blow she'd landed to Mel's ribs.

"Let her go, you bastard!"

At first she thought she'd imagined Jake's voice, that the shadowy figure leaning over Mel was only a vision. But the gun pressed against Mel's head was viciously real. Deadly.

"Jake." She gulped lungfuls of air. "Jake…"

"Nicole, stay still." With his eyes fixed on Mel, Jake leaned in. "I said, let her go."

Mel sobbed, then his hand loosened its grip on her ankle. She scrambled up, her heart pounding like a piston. A dizzy wave of faintness drenched her body with sweat. She teetered when she discovered her legs would barely support her.

"Nicole, move back," Jake ordered. He waited until she'd complied, then he said, "Okay, Hall, get up. Slow. You even breathe fast, I'll shoot you."

Mel rose, his hands raised. His shirt was wet on the front.

Blood trickled from his cheek, which was already purple with bruising. When his gaze locked with Nicole's, she saw the tears in his eyes. "I did it for you. I love you."

Her whole body shaking, she looked at Jake. His eyes were hard, his mouth set as he held the gun on Mel with a rock-steady hand. "He killed them...all three. He's ill. He needs help."

"He gets a cell first."

"I need you, Nicole." Mel's tears intensified. "I want to give you everything. I can't live without you."

"I'll see you get help." She felt physically, almost uncontrollably sick. "That's all I can do."

"That's not enough. Not near enough."

"It has to be."

Late that night, Jake rang the doorbell of Nicole's apartment. All day he'd analyzed the scene at Mel Hall's house, thinking about the panic that had hammered through him when he raced onto the front porch and heard Nicole scream. And the mix of fury and fear that gripped him when he saw her struggling on the floor with a killer.

Jake knew those images ought to be the ones that stayed with him. Instead, foremost in his mind was what had happened after the uniforms had led Hall away and he'd walked back through the house and into the living room.

Nicole had stood facing him, her arms wrapped against her waist, hands clamped tight on her forearms. She'd been sheet pale. Trembling. His need to touch her, to comfort, had been overwhelming, so he'd reached out. She'd jerked back, her chin snapping up, her eyes desperate and proud. If he lived to be one hundred, Jake knew he would never forget that gesture or the look on her face. Or the pain that had stabbed into his heart.

He had pushed her away—what the hell else had he expected from her?

He'd planned to wait until morning to see her. Give her time to recover some from the trauma, then plead his case.

If he had to wait another minute, he'd go crazy.

He jabbed the bell again. She had refused to spend another night at Bill and Whitney's and insisted on coming home. Despite the fact Nicole hadn't answered the phone when he'd called, he knew she was inside.

He was studying the lock, wondering how badly she would maim him if he picked it when the door opened.

She looked like a dream, standing in the same ivory robe she'd worn what seemed a lifetime ago. Her hair was loose, tumbling down her shoulders, looking like spun honey in the soft light.

His stomach clutched when she stared at him without expression.

"I'm tired, Jake. I don't feel like company."

When she started to close the door, he slapped his palm against it. "I need to talk to you. Tonight."

"Jake—"

"Please. Nicole, please."

She eased out a breath. "I suppose it's best to get it over with."

"Get what over with?" he asked when he stepped inside.

"I planned on calling you tomorrow. I didn't thank you for saving my life today. That was rude of me—"

"*Rude?* A killer had you in his clutches and you're worried about your manners?"

"I just want you to know I'm grateful. Thank you."

His teeth clenched against the coolness in her voice. "You keep forgetting, I'm the guy you don't have to thank."

She turned, walked into the living room. "I also wanted to talk to you about Mel."

The last thing Jake wanted to talk about was Mel Hall. "What about him?"

"How could he have been so obsessed, and me not

know?'' As she spoke, she lowered herself onto the arm of a wing chair. "How could I work with him day after day and not see how he felt?''

"He didn't let you see.''

"But we were so close.'' She squeezed her eyes shut, opened them. "If only I had seen, I could have done something. Stopped all those people from dying.''

"Something like that always seems possible when you're working it out backward.'' Jake walked to where she sat, looked down into her shadowed eyes. He wanted to touch her so badly he ached. "I'm a cop, and all I saw was what might be a case of puppy love on Mel's part. I didn't see what was really going on inside him, either.''

"What about Mel's uncle Zebulon? Whitney said he gave Mel the curare. Do you think Zebulon knew what Mel was doing?''

"Whitney and I don't think so. The uncle admitted to giving Mel the curare to brew in tea to help ease his mother's pain. So far, we think that's the truth.'' He took a step closer. "Mel's going away for a long time. He can't hurt anyone else.''

"He's so sick.'' She pressed her fingers to her lips. "I'm going to make sure he gets help. I *need* to help him.''

"Then that's what you should do.''

She rose slowly, as if the weight of the world lay on her shoulders. "I guess that's all. Goodbye, Jake.''

His throat raw and his palms sweating, he took a step toward her, blocking her path to the door. "You think that ends it?''

She blinked. "No, Jake, *you* ended it days ago.''

"I thought I could push you away and go on with my life. I thought doing that now would be smarter than losing you somewhere down the line.''

"You did what you thought was best for you. I don't want to rehash—''

"I didn't want to face the fact that I wouldn't let go of losing my family because to do that was to accept it." He scrubbed a hand across his face. "Annie and the girls are gone. Dead. I didn't die along with them, although for a long time I felt like I had."

Nicole's lips trembled. "I don't know why you're telling me—"

"You were right when you said I have good memories of my family. I do. But it's all memories. I want to start living in the now, instead of back then. I've probably been ready to do that for a while, but I didn't know it until you stepped into my arms at Whitney's wedding. You made me feel alive again."

"It…was just a dance."

"It was everything. I just didn't know how to handle how you made me feel. I do now." Desperate she might send him away, he reached for her. When she didn't resist, he gathered her to him. "I need you, Nicole." He buried his face in her hair, breathed in her soft, warm scent. "I love you."

He felt her body jerk, then go still. "What did you say?"

He leaned his head back and gazed down into her shocked face. He could read the nerves in her eyes as clearly as he could see their color. "I need you."

"The other thing."

He ran his hands up and down her robe's silky sleeves. "I love you. I'm asking you to give us another chance. And to marry me."

She flinched back, one hand pressed to her heart. Wariness clouded her eyes. "I, no. I…don't know."

He frowned. "What don't you know?"

"What to think." She put a hand to her temple. "From the moment we met, I've been on this emotional roller coaster. For a while, all I did was tell myself that you didn't fit the bill, that you were all wrong for me."

"Well, now you can tell yourself—"

"Then, that morning in the twins' bedroom, even as you were pushing me away, I realized I'd fallen in love with you."

The fist around his heart eased. "Thank God." He reached for her, but she stepped back, held up a hand to stop him.

"No, I need to work this out, Jake."

"We love each other. I have to believe everything else will work itself out."

Wrapping her arms around her waist, she matched his gaze. "Maybe you think what you've said to me tonight is true."

"It is true."

"What if you're wrong? What if you suddenly realize you're not sure you can let yourself risk again? How do I know you won't wake up some morning, knowing you've made another mistake? That you can't let me into your life? That we should just forget what's happened between us?"

A current of self-directed anger swept through him, burning brighter at the knowledge he'd caused her so much pain.

"I'm sorry I hurt you. I never wanted just one night with you." He shook his head. "As for my being sure, do you think I would tell you that I need you, *love* you, then ask you to spend the rest of your life with me if I wasn't sure?"

"I told you, I don't know what to think. That scares me."

He, too, was scared. Afraid he'd screwed up so bad that he'd lost her. "I'm asking for a second chance, Nicole. I'll do whatever it takes. Tell me what it takes."

She looked up at him, her eyes unreadable. "Twice in my life, I've been hurt by men."

"I'm not proud knowing I'm one of them."

"You hurt me, Jake. But it's mostly my fault."

"How could it be your fault?"

"I knew better, is how. I learned with Cole what could

happen by jumping into a relationship and going solely with emotion. I knew, yet I did the same thing with you. I'm not going to do that again, Jake. Never again.''

Just the thought that he'd lost her stopped his heart. ''Nicole—''

She angled her chin. ''I want us to date.''

''Date?'' He wouldn't have been more surprised if she'd picked up the coffee table and smashed it over his head.

''Dating is my business, after all.''

''Look, I'm not going to register with your agency and go out with a bunch of lonely hearts while you're making up your mind about me. Dammit, I'm in love with *you*. I'm not available.''

''You're already registered with my agency.''

''For an undercover operation under a fake name.''

''Which is a nice loophole since I don't date my clients.''

His eyes narrowed as hope flared inside him. ''Maybe you'd better explain exactly what you've got in mind.''

''I don't know you, Jake. I'm in love with you, but I don't *know* you. I don't have a clue what your favorite color is. I don't know if you have hobbies, what you do on your days off, what type of movies you like. Your favorite foods.'' Stepping toward him, she cupped her palm against his cheek. ''I want to get to know the man I've fallen in love with. I *need* to get to know you. I'm asking you to give me time, as long as it takes, for my head to catch up with my heart.''

''By dating. You want us to date.''

''Yes.''

''Exclusively?''

''Yes.''

He let out the air clogging his lungs. He hadn't lost her. ''Just date?''

''For now.''

''And while we're dating, I'm supposed to keep my hands off of you?''

"Do, and you're a dead man." Her mouth curving, she rose on tiptoe, her lips skimming his. "Some people sleep together on the first date, you know."

"Good point." He pulled her to him, slid his arms around her waist, his mouth taking hers in a long, slow kiss. When he felt her sway against him, he shifted his lips to her throat. "It's red," he whispered, nuzzling her soft flesh.

"What's red?" she murmured.

"My favorite color."

She tilted her head back and looked up at him, her lips parted, her eyes smoky with desire. "Red. That's a good start."

"I thought it might be."

Her hands slid up his arms, his shoulders, then twined behind his neck. "We could go up to bed and you can tell me all about your hobbies."

"I've got a lot of hobbies."

"You do?"

"Yeah." Grinning, Jake swept her into his arms. "This could take all night."

* * * * *

SPECIAL REPORT:
Peril and passion over Texas skies

WHISKEY SPRINGS, Texas (AP)—In December 2000, authors Maggie Price, Merline Lovelace and Debra Cowan bring their pulse-pounding, heart-stopping three-in-one volume SPECIAL REPORT to Silhouette Intimate Moments. In this dramatic collection the hijacking of a federal prisoner transport plane puts three couples' lives—and their love—to the test....

For an exclusive of Maggie Price's story "Midnight Seduction," just turn the page....

Chapter 1

Christine Logan's throat tightened when she saw the storm had shattered every window in the airport concourse. Ragged pieces of glass glinted from walls, planters, and the padded seats that had toppled throughout the passenger boarding gates. Gleaming shards hung like stalactites from the ceiling.

Outside, rain fell in a torrent. Damp gusts blew through the open panes, chilling the air. Christine's flesh prickled beneath the coat Quinn Buchanan had draped over her shoulders.

"Does the terminal still have its entire roof?" she asked.

The maintenance manager nodded. "Damnedest thing I've ever seen, especially when you consider we've got fencing, oil well rigs, baggage carts, roofs off a couple of hangars and other debris scattered across the airfield. We found the upper cab of the control tower sitting in the middle of runway Three Five Right."

Christine shook her head. "Did all the controllers make it out on time?"

"Yes, lucky for them."

Christine slid a look toward Quinn when he stepped away to respond to his police dispatcher's call on his radio. After years of shimmering hurt that had slowly transformed into dragging regret—and a final knowledge that she'd gotten over him—how could his presence still make a direct assault on her nervous system? *How?*

Reaching up, she fingered the gold hoop in her right ear. From the moment Jeff Buchanan introduced her to his kid brother, the chemistry between her and Quinn had sizzled. Even now, that clearly hadn't changed. She scowled. So, fine, he was still pulse-stopping handsome, and she was still physically aware. All she had to do was ignore her hormones and get over it.

Pulling her gaze from Quinn, she studied the destruction around her. As perverse as it seemed, she was glad of the more immediate problems that faced her. They would keep her thoughts off Quinn until she got that treacherous awareness under control.

She turned back to confer with the maintenance manager. "Pete, I want to inspect the airfield before I hold a staff briefing. Can you get away to take me?"

"You're the airport director," Pete stated. "You say go, we go."

Just then, Quinn rejoined them, his mouth set in a grim line. "One or more prisoners have taken control of Marshal's Flight 407."

Christine's mouth went dry. "Is anyone hurt?"

"That's unknown. There's an alarm in the cockpit that sends an emergency signal. The pilot managed to hit the button and radio to the transfer center that a prisoner had a gun. After that, all communication from the plane ceased. The FBI's sending in a negotiator and hostage rescue team by helicopter. The weather's playing havoc with their ETA." Dipping his head, Quinn met Christine's gaze. "Until they get this hijacking resolved, your airport essentially belongs to the feds.''

She lifted her chin. ''We'll cooperate fully with law enforcement, Captain, but Whiskey Springs is *my* airport.''

He flashed a grin. ''That's what I expected you to say.''

Quinn's grin had always done devastating things to her. It still did, she discovered when her heart jammed against her ribs.

Swallowing hard, she looked at Pete. ''I need to find some rain gear before we go out on the field.''

''What we've got down in the maintenance office isn't fashionable, but it'll keep you dry.''

''That's all I ask.'' Shrugging off Quinn's suit coat, she handed it to him, felt the glide of his fingertips across hers. A frisson of heat shot up the back of her neck. Her gaze rose slowly to meet eyes as blue as a cool, calm ocean.

The tornado, she assured herself when her clenching stomach sent panic skittering through her system. This was the second day of her new job and she had just survived a tornado that had devastated the airport. She had a hijacked plane filled with federal prisoners parked on one of her taxiways. *Those* were the reasons her emotions teetered on a wild pendulum. *Those* were the reasons the air around her was so thick she couldn't seem to drag enough oxygen into her lungs. Quinn's presence had nothing to do with it. Couldn't have anything to do with it. He had loved her, then walked away. She had put him behind her long ago and gotten on with her life. She was a professional, she could work with him. That was all that was required of her. Nothing more.

She would do nothing more.

So why did her conviction feel like a lie?